Réveil

by Zee Lacson

The Woolgathering Series

Book 1: Reverie
Book 2: Revenant
Book 3: Réveil

John
Introducing me to a life
beyond the best my dreams can offer.

Cale
Being the hope I have for humanity.
You are confirmation that I did right in this world.

Caden
Embracing the world's potential without fear.
And teaching me to do the same.

Hunter
2012 – 2023
All the fur and all the love.
The goodest doggo our family could hope for.

The difference between a dream and a nightmare is light.

Nightmares are always such an intense, deep kind of black. Hues of blue and purple. A perpetual type of nighttime. And always so cold.

At least I'm not standing in the snow. Instead, the hardwood floor is covered with a long thick runner. The light directly above me is off. I can just make out the smooth silhouette of the naked bulb. Heavy drapery covers the windows—as if it isn't already dark enough inside. I can't see anything through the small opening between the curtains, so it might not matter.

Only the faint yellow glow at one end of the hallway casts any luminosity on the scene. A scene ripe with ghoulish possibilities. The weak moans emanating from the room are almost requisite at this point.

Speaking of bad decisions …

It wouldn't be the first time I've walked toward certain danger instead of away from it. It's a surprise I've made it seventeen years without being killed as a result of my decision-making.

I remind myself to breathe but to do so quietly lest the moaning monster waiting on the other side hears me. I wipe my clammy hands on the side of my jeans and psych myself up.

With stealth mastered over years of sneaking into the kitchen for cookies in the middle of the night, I make my way to the lit room. The worn carpet helps muffle my Chucks. But the close walls, adorned with old patterned wallpaper, and a low painted ceiling trigger a claustrophobia I didn't realize I have. I clench my jaw to stop my teeth from chattering; it isn't cold enough to warrant this.

I catch a whiff of something unpleasant as I get closer to the open door. Not the sourness of spoiled milk but the foulness of decay. Burning and rotten. Like bad eggs on fire. Maybe it's the source of the eerie glow. A bad choice of breakfast food.

I make it to the doorway without being discovered. There is no plan, of course, for what I will do when I get there.

It's a child … or a goblin. I don't have the best angle from my vantage point by the door jamb, but the dresser mirror on one side of the room reflects a macabre sight. Illuminated by the glow of a stained-glass nightlight, the figure is squatting on the chest of a sleeping man. The man's dark hair is matted with sweat. He isn't trying to get away, but the visible veins on his neck suggest an internal struggle. He seems to shrink from the weight. With every exhale, a translucent wisp of glittering smoke trails from the man's open mouth.

This is where the sound is coming from. A whispered final breath.

Until this point, I hadn't appreciated the gravity of my situation. It can't possibly be real.

I close my eyes, hoping that when I open them again, I won't see a dying man. But closing them only means I can hear the soughs of expiration more clearly. It means the stink of death is more pungent. It means every one of my other senses immerse me more fully in this nightmare. I already know before I open my eyes again that the scene has not changed. That the impossibility has been made real. The terror I'm feeling certainly is.

Tears in my eyes blur the horror. Silent tears are the only way I can scream.

There is movement in the shadows; it occurs to me that I have been so involved with what is happening in the light that I have neglected the darkness. I try not to move, thinking I can remain undiscovered.

Even in limited visibility, I recognize familiar golden-green eyes. They belong to a boy who very much does not belong in this scene. We recognize each other almost at the same time, but we both stay in place. The open doorway between us threatens exposure. And neither one of us is willing to attract any unwanted attention.

I open my mouth but don't dare make a sound. He doesn't say anything, either. It is only after something changes inside the room that he makes a sound—somewhere between a warning and a gasp of surprise.

The goblin child has abandoned the sleeping man. It has slowly turned its head in our direction. Its eyes are large, endless pools of liquid black. The longer I look into them, the larger they seem … until it is all I can see. It is encompassing, and I find I am unable to move.

Everything dark about a nightmare is in those eyes. I can't see past the black. It leaks into the rest of the room, engulfing everything into oblivion. I have tunnel vision, compelled to stare deeper into the vacancy. The nothingness.

I should be able to close my eyes. I should be able to break free. But my mind is betraying me, telling me I don't want to. I lose my will along with any sense of time. It is both one second and several hours. I could stay in it until I died and would not care.

Something comes between me and the darkness. An ever-changing mix of green and gold.

Ethan.

New Year

I woke up.

I wasn't dead. I wasn't swallowed into the loch of hellish darkness. It wasn't even the middle of the night. It was almost noon on New Year's Day.

At least that's what the display on my phone read when I found it by my bed and brought it up to my face.

Then I promptly dropped it *on* my face when it suddenly rang.

The phone tumbled off my bed, still ringing. I wrinkled my nose and rubbed it. Thankful there was no one else in the room to witness my humiliation, I felt for the misbehaving phone.

It was on the sixth round of the familiar melodic tone that I was able to tap the green button to accept the video call. I gave up on my face and ran my fingers through my hair as a makeshift brush. The call connected before I could do much else.

"London! Are you OK? What was that? *Where* was that? Did *you* do that? Were you *skipping*? On purpose?"

Ethan.

He was stringing the sentences together so fast that it sounded like one big question. I watched his hazel eyes, that mix of green and gold from my dream, dart around. He was trying to take in whatever visual information he could get before I could even open my mouth. I was holding the phone so close to my face there wasn't much else he could see. I could have been in a cave, or I could have been sitting on the toilet. The only clue he would have had was that wherever I was, it was pretty dark.

"What?" That was my eloquent response. I answered with a question; I couldn't process everything and needed to stall until I could form coherent thoughts.

He lifted his eyebrows but didn't respond. I rubbed sleep out of my eyes. Then halfway to running my hand up my forehead, I realized how I looked in the tiny square on the corner of the screen.

Even with just the light from the video call, I could see that I had only been able to flatten most of one side of my chin-length hair. The other half was still wildly dreaming and defying gravity. I had a deep line running up my cheek from the crease on my pillow that I had apparently spent most of my REM sleep on. At least I got the crust out of my eyes.

This was not exactly the vision I wanted to be when my long-distance boyfriend of just over two months called.

Aces, London. Way to kill the attraction.

I pulled back a little, hoping I could hide in the shadows. He didn't seem to notice my disheveled state. He was more annoyed by my lack of response than by what I looked like.

He waited, but his impatience manifested itself in the way he was able to set his mouth in an impossibly straight line. The summer sun of New Zealand overexposed one side of his face and left the other in a slight shadow, making his expression seem more severe. He also looked much more alert than I felt.

"What happened?" I asked. He tightened his jaw, and I could see the effort involved as he restrained from rolling his eyes.

"Yes," he agreed. "What happened?" Keeping it one question at a time was probably the best way to sort things out. I couldn't really answer him when I had the same questions.

"Were you sleeping too?" I continued to prod.

He gave one curt nod. The very first real answer to all the questions and one worth noting.

"What did you see?" I needed to know if we were talking about the same thing before I could make sense of anything that had happened. He gave me a look that was equal parts restlessness and frustration, but he obliged anyway.

"Creepy house? Little demon bugger choking a bloke in his own bed? Any of this ring a bell?" Sometimes his accent made it difficult for me to understand him. Especially with a somewhat unreliable internet connection and so soon after being jolted awake. But I got the gist of what he was saying, and it seemed on point. I didn't know yet if that made things any better.

"Yeah, ditto," I observed. We must have been sharing the same dream. Or nightmare, anyway. Another thing worth noting. "So, I didn't skip to you?"

Skipping was the term I had grudgingly accepted for my recent ability to dream myself somewhere else. I felt uncomfortable saying it and always hesitated a fraction when I used it. But we understood very little of these unstable occurrences and couldn't think of a better word.

The first time I skipped, I met Ethan in one of New Zealand's woodlands. Halfway around the world. I had thought he was a figment of my imagination. Or someone from an alternate universe. Except that he found me in California, proving to me that we both lived in the same world. Then shortly after that, I met my dead mother somewhere in Chicago. Or a version of her. We haven't figured that out yet, either.

It's been a weird past six months.

He looked at me with righteous indignation for a second before saying anything. "It's nine a.m. on my island," he finally yelled, swinging the phone around to demonstrate his point. Lens flare filled the camera. "Not smack in the middle of witching hour!"

His face filled the screen as he brought it even closer to himself so that I could see him articulate his words. "Does it *look* like I'm trapped in Dracula's mansion with a misplaced *Maero-imp-golem* hybrid monster?!"

His very animated and colorful response caught me off guard, and I surprised even myself by laughing aloud. I threw one hand over my mouth, almost in apology. One corner of his lips curled up in response to my reaction. It was a triumphant grin of sorts. The tension that was knotting his eyebrows together eased. Seeing him relax made me happy, which made it easier to laugh some more. We were caught in a moment of release.

"So no," he confirmed when my laughter settled into a smile. "You, for certain, did not skip to me. That was somewhere else entirely. Somewhere colder."

I shivered once, involuntarily, remembering how it felt to be in that room. "I *pulled* you into a dream with me?"

That had never happened before. Not that we had much experience, but still.

"I don't know," he admitted. "Looks that way." The crease between his eyebrows was back. Our moment of levity went as quickly as it had come. "What does that mean?"

I shrugged. I didn't have an answer to that. "Could you touch things? Did it feel real to you?"

He didn't answer right away. He paused to consider the experience. He was very deliberate that way. It was just another thing I loved about him. Everything he said had more substance because he was never frivolous with his words.

When he answered, it was with confidence. "Yes. The walls were textured. They were covered with some kind of fabric, not paper."

I nodded. I remembered that as well.

"And I could smell things," he continued. "It was an old house. It had that old house smell." He wrinkled his nose a little as if that would trigger his memory. It was adorable. "It smelled like mothballs and cedar or something of the sort?"

"Haunted house smell?" I offered with a knowing nod.

"One hundred percent haunted house smell." He grinned. The very edges of his eyes crinkled when he did, and I forgot that we were talking about something horrible.

Taking my phone with me, I got out of bed. I tugged at the blackout curtains. I didn't realize how much apprehension was still dammed up inside me until it all rushed out as the afternoon California winter sun rushed in. Not quite as obnoxious as summer but significantly sunnier than what I was used to in the Midwest, where I had grown up.

"Why were you still sleeping anyway?" I asked, remembering the time difference that separated us. "Don't you have to wake up, like before dawn or something when you're in boot camp?"

"I'm still on medical leave," he reminded me. "Bullet holes, yeah?"

It wasn't as if I could forget. I was there when those bullets made those holes he so casually mentioned. He made it sound less traumatic than the worst moment of my life. "I mean, I thought medical leave stopped today," I clarified.

"No, this bugger and all the fun dressing comes off today." He lifted his shoulder to show off the cast he had around his right arm, a souvenir from being on the receiving end of an automatic weapon. It was a serious injury, but the alternative would have been much more permanent. We were both very lucky. "I have to go through rounds of physical therapy before I can be certified for regular duty. But come Monday, I can attend classes again."

Few people in the world would know that the eagerness in his voice to attend class was more of a supernatural occurrence than him having survived gunshot wounds. "Was it a bad idea for me to sleep in today?" he asked.

"Who knows? If you didn't, maybe I wouldn't have been able to pull you in." I shrugged. "But then again, if I didn't pull you in, I might have been dinner for that goblin child." It was easier to joke about a nightmare when I was standing in the sun. "Thanks for saving my life, by the way."

"Don't make it a habit," he warned. There was an edge to his voice that betrayed how seriously he meant that.

"It's not like I do it on purpose."

"Oh, it's just a knack, is it?"

"You play with knives and dodge bullets ... well, you dodge *most* bullets," I amended, laughing a little. "Sometimes, you catch them with your body for medals."

He wasn't amused. Which made it funnier to me. "I physically manifest myself in scary places when I dream." I shrugged like it wasn't a big deal. "We all have skills."

Best Friends

A message popped up on the screen, mercifully concealing Ethan's expression. It was from one of my best friends, Brieann, letting me know she was at the door.

Knock. Knock.

I swiped up to clear the message and returned to the call. "Bree is here. Can I call you back?"

Ethan looked past the camera to something. His lips twitched a little as he ran through his responsibilities in his head. "Maybe. If I don't answer, I'll try calling you again before you go to bed."

That had become our routine since Ethan flew back home a few weeks ago. A call in the morning and a call before bed. Being in a long-distance relationship required adjustment. I missed him terribly during the time in between, but I tried to remember that I always had something to look forward to. Some days were harder than others.

"I love you," he said, ending the call before I could respond.

"I love you too," I said to the blank screen, suddenly lonely.

I stared at the screen a beat longer than what was probably normal. As if I was waiting to welcome that mucky feeling I knew would follow every time I ended a call with him. A barometer of my discontent.

But I didn't wallow in it. Instead, I texted Brieann back so she knew that I'd gotten her message. If I waited too long to answer her texts, she would become impatient and would resort to actually calling. She responded with a thumbs-up. I tossed the phone on my bed so I could get dressed.

Jeans always fit better when they've been worn a few times after being out of the wash. I found the pair of jeans I had discarded on the floor the night before. I changed out of the top I used as jammies and put on a T-shirt. Then I grabbed my favorite soft blue hoodie.

I retrieved my phone from the bedcovers and was deleting notifications when I tripped over a box by my door. It was a harsh reminder that I wasn't very adept at multitasking. The instant regret I felt for that split second when I almost went face-first into the door had me silently swearing into the universe.

I was prepared to toss the innocent package in the face of whoever left it there for me to trip on until I remembered it was me. A new pair of Converse sneakers tumbled out of the open box. I had laid the box by the door because I had every intention of wearing them today.

My irritation was short-lived. I was already smiling when I bent down to pick up the gold metallic high tops. They were a surprise gift from Ethan. A surprise for me because I didn't expect them and a surprise for him because they took longer than he'd anticipated to arrive.

A pair of sneakers was not a common present to receive from one's boyfriend over the Christmas season, but he knew that Chuck Taylors were the only things I wore, and these ones were particularly hard to find. The All-Stars were a combination of silver, gold, and bronze. This was practically jewelry for me.

I was inclined to wait for a special occasion to wear them, but I figured today was a good first run. I pulled them on without bothering to tighten the laces. I loved them. Not only did they look amazing, but I also felt an extra connection to Ethan when I wore them. I held on to every physical thing that connected us. After thinking he was just a figment of my imagination for so long, it was comforting to have these reminders that he really existed. It helped me feel a little less lonely, and I was in a lighter mood when I finally made it to the front door.

Brieann was sitting on the front steps, her back to me. She was leaning against the shoulder of a reddish-haired boy, her boyfriend, and my other bestie, Drew.

The two of them had been dating just shy of a month. I was told they bonded over their mutual worry about me. Before that, they operated in such different social circles that the idea of them getting together could not have been predicted. Not so much because they were polar opposites but just because it didn't seem like it would work.

At first glance, kids would say that Brieann was out of Drew's league. Not that Drew wasn't good-looking in his own right. He just wouldn't seem to be Brieann's type. She was the blonde-haired, blue-eyed cheerleading captain straight out of an '80s cult classic. He would have been in the same movie but as a background extra. Good enough for Hollywood but not interesting enough to have speaking lines. He also often smelled of paint.

She loved him anyway. And he deserved it. Drew was far more mature than most guys we knew. And he managed it with the confidence of someone comfortable with who they were. As far as I was concerned, he was solid leading man material.

I may be a self-proclaimed introvert, but I'd found that I didn't make the same boundaries for them as I would the rest of the world. Not that they would concern themselves with any boundaries I'd put up anyway. They would just assume that it didn't apply to them. They'd be right.

They both turned at the sound of the door opening. Brieann's high ponytail hit Drew right in the face. Drew's expression told me this wasn't the first time it had happened, and it wasn't worth talking about. I laughed. She had no idea.

"You do know that we have a working doorbell?" I pointed at the yellowing button protruding from the outside wall.

Drew got up and held out a hand for Brieann. She took it and pulled herself up with the grace of a natural dancer. "The last time I rang your doorbell on a weekend, you yelled at me."

That was true. I did.

"She didn't yell at *me*," Drew said. He winked before Brieann could turn to him. His posture of exaggerated innocence made her narrow her eyes in suspicion.

"You offered to feed me," I said, interrupting her process.

"Food is always the best deterrent," he agreed wisely.

"Speaking of food, did you guys want breakfast?" I offered, opening the door wider to let them in. I walked toward the kitchen, and they followed.

"It's lunchtime, London," Brieann said at the same time Drew responded with enthusiastic affirmation. She looked at him in disbelief.

"I'm not going to say no to French toast." Drew shrugged, unapologetic. He sat on one side of the counter. I opened the refrigerator door, hoping for some kind of culinary inspiration. Random containers of takeout leftovers had been shoved in almost every available space. I knew I would have to clean it all out later, and the thought of it was already giving me a headache.

"Did you just wake up?" Brieann asked. I didn't even know why that would surprise her. She stood behind Drew and wrapped her arms around him, snuggling as if for warmth.

"Yeah," I responded, closing the refrigerator door a tad more aggressively than necessary. Organizing that disaster would have to be a Future-London problem. Present-London had problems of her own. Present-London needed to eat.

"We stayed up well after midnight. I don't think the boys even slept; they were still packing when I called it quits. I swear the sun was coming up."

The boys referred to my three older brothers, Liam, Chase, and Locke. None of them actually lived with me and my dad anymore, but they had been visiting for the holidays. It had felt really good to all be under the same roof, but it also meant I didn't have a lot of privacy. There was always at least one brother around whenever Ethan called. I didn't think it was a coincidence.

I eyed the plate of leftover Christmas cookies on the end of the counter. Eggs were used to make those cookies. That was practically breakfast, right?

I turned my attention to the pantry. It was even less promising. There were five cans of SPAM and roughly eight cans of beans, but nothing particularly appealing or easily accessible. My brothers had cleaned out all the chips. They had left half a bag of sliced bread, though. I poked it half-heartedly. I was seriously starting to find a reasonable excuse to have those Christmas cookies for breakfast.

"Where is everyone?" Brieann asked.

I looked at the clock on the wall more out of habit than any real need to check the time. Dad's favorite retro chrome timepiece confirmed what I already knew. "Probably at the airport? I vaguely remember something about an early flight."

"Do you just want to grab grub at Caden's?" Drew offered, possibly sensing my frustration. He was always sensitive to that sort of thing.

"I notice you've been frequenting Caden's more often now that your mural is immortalized on the outside wall," I said. "I'm sure that has absolutely nothing to do with it, right?"

"I assure you, that is a mere coincidence." His grin confirmed that it was, in fact, *not* a mere coincidence. "I am not at all averse to free food, but I hear that the ambiance at Caden's is simply unparalleled."

I'd always liked Caden's. Even before Drew's mural was installed last Thanksgiving. It was where Ethan and I had our first real date. That fact alone was enough, but it didn't hurt that they actually had good food and great service. They can open all the fancy restaurants and fruit bars down the college strip they want, but as far as I was concerned, nothing would ever reach the level that Caden's was on.

"Can't beat the ambiance," I echoed. But what really convinced me was the fact that it meant food that I didn't have to cook myself or a kitchen I didn't have to clean up after. "Solid plan. Let's go." I shut the pantry door behind me with a sense of satisfaction. As if I had won some war against the kitchen when, in fact, I was conceding the battle. Either way, I had no regrets.

Nachtmahr

"I'm sorry, what?" Drew asked around a mouthful of meatloaf sandwich.

I was twirling my Phad Thai with my fork. Caden's served a hodgepodge of culinary dishes, which was a big part of their charm for me. They had everything from buttermilk chocolate chip pancakes to chilaquiles to fish fry Friday. Sometimes, you could even ask for something that wasn't on the menu. It was glorious. If having a spirit restaurant was a thing, Caden's would be mine.

"Another nightmare?" Brieann asked, her tone layered with worry. She had her fork poised over a healthy protein bowl but stopped before she even started.

"Although"–Drew pointed, fry in hand; he had opted to order french fries instead of French toast–"the last time you had nightmares, they weren't *really* nightmares. And something good actually came out of it."

He was right. The last time I'd had nightmares, or at least what I thought were nightmares, they were actually some kind of latent semi-corporeal, magical psychic messages from my own departed mother. It wasn't something anyone could anticipate, so it had been a harrowing experience at the beginning.

"I think the big difference is that in this one, someone was actually dying." I took a bite off my fork and realized that, despite the unappetizing topic of conversation, I was very hungry.

Brieann put a hand over her mouth, and Drew grimaced.

"I almost don't want to know, but I feel like it's important," Drew said slowly. "Who was dying?"

I shrugged. "Some guy my brother's age, I think?"

"Which brother? You have three."

"Same, same," I insisted, disregarding the inaccuracy. There were eight years between Liam, the eldest, and Locke, the youngest, but it didn't mean much. They were all old. "Somewhere in his late twenties, maybe? I don't think I know him."

"Who was killing him? Was it a psycho clown? I bet it was a clown. Clowns are evil." Drew pointed his french fry at me again with a little more vengeance than before, causing a bit of the salt to fly off the end. He nodded vehemently at his own suggestion.

"It wasn't *It*, Drew."

"Clowns are still evil," he insisted. This was some kind of phobia of his that needed to be further explored at another time. Or exploited. I shook my head.

"More shadows?" Brieann suggested. "Was it a spirit? A ghost?"

"This was more like a goblin of sorts." I was struggling. "It was small. Like a toddler or young child."

"I think I've seen this movie," Drew said. "Was the kid ghost white with black eyes?"

"Well, it wasn't really a kid," I admitted. "Just kid-sized. Like a jacked-up toddler. Like if a professional wrestler and a … a …" I couldn't think of a good example. "… a *boulder* had a kid."

They stared at me without expression for a second before suddenly both bursting into laughter. The heaviness in the air made room for a different emotion.

"A boulder?" Brieann repeated incredulously.

"I hate to be the one to tell you, London, but that's not how baby-making works," Drew added unhelpfully. That just made Brieann laugh harder.

"A boulder!" she said again, a little louder.

"He was the strong, silent type." Drew took on the deep tone of a movie trailer voice-over. "Sure, he was dusty but still super attractive." Brieann was laughing so hard that she was leaning against him.

I crossed my arms in front of me, torn between being annoyed that I was the butt of their jokes and glad to have interrupted the tension. "Shut up! You know what I meant!"

"I don't know if *you* know what you meant." Drew practically howled. Brieann might have had tears in her eyes at that point. I stuck my tongue out but let it go on until they calmed down. I waited until the laughter subsided enough for them to start eating again.

"It did have black eyes, though," I continued. Remembering that paralyzing sensation made bile come up my throat. I swallowed it back down. They must have picked up on my distress because they shared a look that I didn't know how to interpret.

"Were you really skipping?" Brieann asked a little more seriously.

I nodded. "Ethan was with me, so he confirmed."

Forks were dropped. Drew and Brieann both stared at me with slightly slackened jaws. I liked being able to shock them like that. The tables had turned, and I felt like the one laughing.

Drew rubbed his eyes with one hand. "Hold up," he said, holding up his other hand for emphasis. "Ethan was with you? How?" He dropped both hands and just looked at me, completely flabbergasted. "Just … *what*?"

It was comical. I took another bite of my food.

"I think you need to start from the beginning," Brieann said reasonably. Drew agreed.

Drew and Brieann were the only other people in the world, outside of Ethan and my father, whom I spoke to about my ability. I used to be afraid that they would think I was crazy. How could I expect them to understand when I didn't understand it myself?

They surprised me with an acceptance that I didn't think existed and restored my faith in humanity. Drew was able to make sense of things on an emotional level, making me feel normal and giving me the courage to talk about it. Brieann tried to make sense of the magic. Neither of them were ever judgmental and often helped me sort through what it could mean and how to control it. We were all learning about it together.

"I remember being in a straight-up *Addams Family* type house." That wasn't very accurate. "Well, it was way smaller."

"So, like an *Addams Family* type apartment?" Drew suggested.

I grinned. He had a talent for normalizing the weird. It was a superpower he wielded well.

"No, bigger than an apartment. There were stairs. It just felt tighter? More closed in than a mansion." I made motions with my hands to try to describe the right size in relation to our suggestions.

"*Addams Family* in a single-family home somewhere in the city," Brieann declared in a tone that meant I should move the narrative forward. Her mother was a realtor. She didn't care about the venue. "Ethan was with you?" she asked again, reminding me to stay on topic.

"I didn't see Ethan right away, so I don't know if we got there at the same time or if he arrived later. But I really couldn't see very much either way," I explained. "It was dark, so I knew it was nighttime. There really wasn't a lot of light. Except in one of the rooms."

"So, of course," Drew surmised sarcastically, "that's where you went."

I didn't know how annoyed I should be that he guessed that.

"Always go toward the light, right?" I offered by way of explanation for my actions. Drew shook his head but didn't respond. "I saw Ethan for sure when I got to the doorway. He was there too. Not inside the room but in the hallway outside with me."

"The suspense is killing me. What was inside the room?" Drew asked.

Brieann spoke over him with questions of her own. "Were you in New Zealand? Did you skip to him, or was he dreaming too? Was he surprised? What did he say?"

I looked between the two of them, trying to decide who to answer first. "Ethan didn't say anything because what we both saw in the room was horrifying. There was a guy lying on his back in the bed with the … the goblin thing just sitting right on his chest. Like a demon cat wanting breakfast."

Brieann wrinkled her nose. It didn't seem to affect Drew's appetite. He took another bite and nodded sagely. "Cats are evil too. Right up there with clowns. They work together." I was beginning to wonder at this point what things he *didn't* think were evil.

"It wasn't a cat. It was a goblin monster thing acting like a cat. And the guy was dying. He was making the worst sounds. He was obviously having a hard time breathing. Like the monster was just super heavy sitting on his chest like that."

Something I said made Drew stop mid-chew. Anything that made Drew stop eating was significant. His expression became thoughtful.

"What?" I asked, slightly alarmed by the change in his demeanor.

He swallowed. "Put a pin in it," he said. "It reminded me of something, but I can't think of it right now." He looked annoyed with himself and retreated into his head. He was only half participating until he could figure this out himself.

"Did you see the man die?" Brieann asked in a loud whisper that was meant to be respectful but also unmistakably morbid. I shook my head.

"I don't know. The monster left him and turned to us. Bree, he had the creepiest eyes!" I remembered the emptiness of them and how it kept me in place. "I couldn't look away. It was like he didn't have eyes … like the sockets were just black voids."

She shivered at the description, and this time, I did too. The nightmare had faded somewhat in the light of day, but the impression it made was still strong. It might have been less than a fraction of a second, but there was a moment when I thought I was really going to die. "Ethan stepped between us, and that broke the connection."

I looked down at the delicate silver chain wrapped around my wrist. It was a vintage child's ID bracelet with Ethan's name on it, a gift he had given to me in person. It was the only physical link he had to a past that he couldn't remember. I didn't think it was something he should be giving away, but he said it was to remind me that I was loved. It was a physical link to him that I never took off. Except when I was dreaming. I shook my wrist a little so that it would shift. It was lightweight and almost unnoticeable, but the feel of the metal on my skin was comforting. It felt real.

"That was when I woke up."

Brieann slumped back in her chair, emotionally exhausted from my story. She was such an empathetic person. It was one of the things that made her so likable and easy to get along with.

"Henry!" Drew blurted out so loudly that Brieann sat up again. He looked delighted with himself.

"Henry," he said again, as if he had solved all the mysteries. Brieann and I looked first at each other, then back at him with equally blank expressions. He looked a little less enthusiastic by our lack of response.

"Henry?" This time he said it as a question.

"Your boyfriend is broken," I told Brieann.

"Henry Fuseli?" he asked, but he clearly already knew it was hopeless. I shook my head. The name meant nothing to me.

"You know the dead guy?" Brieann asked him, almost gently, like he was broken.

"I don't actually know if he's dead," I corrected.

"What? No. That's not who I'm talking about anyway," Drew interrupted. He was impatient. "Henry Fuseli is a Swiss painter from, I dunno, the 1800s, I think."

I shrugged. His name wasn't at all familiar. Brieann shook her head, also at a loss.

"You guys suck," he declared, seemingly disappointed in our lack of culture.

"We can't all be art prodigies, Mr. National-Art-Honor-Society. That's why we keep you around," I said brightly, baiting him.

"What's so important about Henry Fuseli?" Brieann asked before Drew could retaliate. She was forever the diplomat. Her redirection worked.

"He painted *The Nightmare*."

"Is that the one with the screaming, melting ghost?" Brieann asked.

"No," I said before Drew could answer. "I think you're talking about *The Scream* by Munch." I winked at Drew. "See? I know *some* things." He didn't seem impressed.

"London is right about Munch," he conceded. "Totally different movements even. Munch is an expressionist. Fuseli's work is Romanticism."

"Now you're just showing off," I accused. He grinned and didn't deny it.

"The particular painting I'm talking about, *The Nightmare* or *Der Natchmahr*, is a painting of some kind of monster sitting on a sleeping woman," he continued. "It's like an incubus or something. Whatever the mythical evil spirit is that suffocates sleepers." He wiped his hand on his jeans and fished for his phone. "Here, easier to show you."

He found the painting in question with a quick internet image search. He triumphantly dropped his phone in the middle of the table as he took the last bite of his sandwich.

The haunting painting was that of a woman on a bed lying dramatically in a position that no real person ever slept in. The incubus Drew was talking about was sitting on her chest but not looking at her. Its head was turned like an owl giving the impression that its eyes followed you when you moved. In the shadows, it looked like there was a horse's head.

"Yikes," Brieann said.

"Did you say Romanticism? That doesn't seem very romantic at all," I observed. "Also, no horse in my dream. At least I don't think so."

"But did the monster look like that?" Brieann asked.

I didn't really want to, but I took a closer look at the artist's rendition. The incubus in the painting was roughly the size of the one I had seen, but this one looked more like a hairy ape and not as terrifying. "Not really." But I knew that I didn't sound very sure of myself. "Definitely not the same eyes. The one in the painting looks more like a troll you'd read about in fairy tales. The one I dreamed about just seemed more … evil."

Brieann was reading the description of the painting. "It says that it's supposed to represent the sleeper's experience of sleep paralysis or a heavy weight on the chest. The sleepers die because of it."

"That sounds accurate," I admitted. The presence of this painting didn't sit well with me. It wasn't exactly the same thing, but it seemed too much of a coincidence.

"Well," Drew concluded, "this is proof that at least you're not the only one to have ever witnessed a dream killing."

Homebase

"Get some rest," Brieann instructed when we pulled up to my driveway.

Drew parked the car but didn't shut off his engine. Instead, he got out so he could move his seat forward for me. His two-door 1979 BMW wasn't the most convenient means of transportation. It didn't always start right away, and the passenger's side door was inoperable from the inside, permanently child-locking anyone that rode with him. But the candy-red exterior was unblemished, albeit worn, and he kept the interior cleaner than he did his locker at school.

Things don't have to be perfect in order to be loved.

"You know that you can't control it when you're tired," Brieann added as I pushed at Drew's unyielding chair. He found the sweet spot that effortlessly slid the chair forward, causing me to face-plant into the back of his headrest.

His expression sat firmly between apology and amusement. "I can't control it no matter what," I complained to Brieann as I glared at Drew.

Brieann, oblivious to the silent war between me and her boyfriend, was giving me a look of impatience that I've often seen on mothers with young children. "That's not entirely true, and you know it."

I had been able to visit Ethan deliberately through meditation a couple of times since he left. It had been Brieann's suggestion, and it had worked, however erratically. Ethan didn't think it was a good idea for me to keep trying, but he was also the one that insisted it was important to try to control it. Some control was better than none. What Brieann said was true. I was just too sulky to concede with grace. "Yes, Mother," I grumbled.

Obviously, being the more mature one, she took the high road. "Namaste!"

Drew pushed his chair back again and rooted himself into the driver's seat. He winked at me. "Remember to balance your Prada." The statement was more for Brieann than for me. He was intentionally provoking her.

"It's *prana*!" she corrected right away. "How is she supposed to balance Prada? By holding a designer bag in each hand? That doesn't even make any sense." If she was on to his obvious tactics to trigger her, she didn't let on.

"Balance your *prana*," she clarified, turning her attention back to me.

Drew shrugged, not bothering to suppress his grin. It was as if he set a daily personal goal to antagonize us purely for his amusement. Did that make him sadistic or masochistic?

I shook my head and smiled at them both. Whatever his intentions, I felt better for it. "See you Monday." I waved at them as Drew drove them away.

Dad's X5 wasn't in the driveway, so I knew he wasn't home yet. I wasn't too concerned. It wasn't unusual for him.

When I got inside, I actually sat down to remove my new shoes instead of kicking them like I normally would. I set them by the stairs. I was not known to keep pristine-looking shoes. It was one of the reasons I loved wearing Chucks. The shabbiness looked intentional. But then, I had never received a pair from Ethan before. These needed to be protected.

I sat on the couch in my socks and stared at the fake Christmas tree that took up too much space. The heaviness of real-world responsibilities, temporarily deferred by discussions of supernatural monsters in art history, weighed on me. The tree had to come down.

I groaned aloud, complaining to the universe at large since I didn't have a captured audience. With eyes half closed, I spotted the last of the red and green foil-wrapped chocolates sitting in the coffee table candy dish.

I popped each one in my mouth as quickly as I could unwrap them. Not because I was hungry but because I needed the emotional sugar fix. I texted Dad a house emoji and a question mark.

He responded by calling me. Sometimes he did that when he was too impatient to translate.

"Hey, sweetheart." He sounded distracted. "I'm at work. Traffic wasn't ideal, so I just decided to go straight after the airport."

"I figured." Though honestly, I hadn't given it much thought. "Did you have lunch?"

"There were sandwiches in the faculty lounge."

"Were they fresh?" Dad's meal choices were often questionable. "Or had they been sitting there since before winter break?" I braced myself. The slight pause that followed didn't instill a sense of confidence.

"I'm sure they were fine," he assured me in a voice that told me he wasn't very sure at all. He couldn't see me rolling my eyes, but I hoped he could pick up on it somehow.

"What time will you be home?"

"Probably by dinner. There are some papers I want to finish grading."

"Uh-huh," I replied, unconvinced. "You're just avoiding coming home so you don't have to take down the Christmas decorations."

"Of course not, sweetheart," he responded with too much innocence to be sincere. "But since you mentioned it, you probably should get started on that since school starts on Monday and all." I could hear the smile in his voice.

"Diabolical," I accused.

"Parenting privilege," he countered. "Someday, you'll have that too. Just not anytime soon. Make sure you tell your boyfriend that."

"And on *that* cringeworthy note, goodbye, Dad."

He was laughing when I hung up.

I didn't get far dismantling the Christmas tree because Ethan called. Other than this morning's alarming video call, it had been a week since I'd been able to have a private conversation with him. A week of Locke's juvenile rendition of *Ethan-and-London-sitting-in-a-tree* …

So when Ethan called, I abandoned the tree lights. And this time, at least my hair was brushed.

"Hi," I answered, almost shyly. The mix of unanswered questions and doomsday impressions that had unsettled me so much earlier had time to settle, making way for the happy little flutters I got whenever I saw him.

He was walking while on the call. The video was shaky and a little choppy, but the connection was clear. Beautiful blue skies of summer were behind him. He broke into a large smile when he saw me, holding the phone away from him and lifting his right arm so that I could see. "No strings on me!"

His smile was contagious, and I found myself near laughing in delight. "Bravo!" I said because I couldn't clap my hands and hold on to the phone at the same time. "How did it go?"

"It was actually pretty dodgy," he said, dropping his arm and bringing the phone closer to his face. "Those wrappings were ripe! Be glad you can't smell it from there."

I laughed. "How does it feel to be free, stinky man?"

"I'm a cadet," he quipped. "There's no freedom here." But he didn't mean it. The distance between us notwithstanding, I knew he was also happy to be back. Being a part of the Defence Force meant something bigger to him. It was the family he'd never had. His sense of belonging.

"It's stiff, and it aches," he complained. "I didn't think it was possible, but it itches now more than it did before. The air is filled with invisible buggers."

"Don't scratch it!" I warned.

"Yeah, yeah, she'll be 'right. I won't." He fixed me with a reassuring smile. "I'm off to the dunny to wash off the stench." The smile became a pensive line. "I wanted to check in with you."

Our easy dialogue transitioned to a more solemn discussion. I knew he didn't have a whole lot of time, so I gave him the bullet points of what had become a post-incident analysis over lunch with Brieann and Drew. His expression became more serious when I brought up the not-so-romantic artwork of Henry Fuseli, visionary of dramatic maidens, goblins, and horse heads.

The existence of a two-hundred-year-old painting that was so similar to what we had witnessed heralded the disconcerting sentiments of dread. Although not a perfect account of what we saw, the scene had all the troubling elements that made it unmistakably similar.

Minus the horse.

Expectedly, he agreed with Brieann that I should rest before I exhausted myself and risked skipping again.

"You know I love being with you," he assured me. "I'd just much rather it not be with monsters or ghosts or death or whatever danger you attract when you skip."

"I attracted *you* the first time I skipped." I pouted. Skipping to him *was* dangerous. And at one point, it had involved death. I could tell from his expression that he was also thinking about those circumstances. I yielded.

This was not a new argument. We had been on opposing sides of this debate from the beginning. I'd had more persuasive assertions in the past but could not find it in myself to bring them up. Perhaps because I couldn't shake the feeling that something was after me. Hunting me. Wanting to consume me. I wasn't all that eager to make it real.

"I'm sorry." I apologized immediately. I picked up the candy wrappers I had strewn on the table earlier. I crumpled them with one hand, looking at them instead of looking at Ethan. The foil crimped between my fingers, the sharper corners folding into themselves until they formed little chocolate-scented balls of tin. "You're right. Brieann is right." I looked back at him.

His eyes softened, pacified by my retreat. "We can talk more about this later, yeah?"

I nodded, making an effort not to be difficult. I flicked the tight foil bead between my fingers to the empty candy dish. It arched perfectly to the center of the bowl, made contact with the surface, and bounced right out. I sighed.

"If I could be sure I could keep you safe, I'd selfishly always want you in my arms," he added, mistaking my reaction as a response. "Let's just play it safe for now."

The call ended when he got to his barracks. I put the phone facedown on the couch and stared at the offending foil ball that had rolled to the edge of the coffee table. The temporary energy I siphoned from the holiday-themed confectionery was exhausted, whether from the phone call or all the things that went unsaid. I was suddenly too tired to stay awake.

I pushed my phone further away from me and curled up into a ball myself. Then I took a nap.

Bonjour

I wasn't scared.

I hadn't intended on skipping. I was actively trying to avoid it. The power nap I took after Ethan's call helped me feel refreshed. I woke up with more energy, and although I didn't get back to taking down the infamous fake tree that took up a third of our living room, I was able to clear out the refrigerator and make sense of what leftovers were worth keeping and what should have been dumped out three days ago. I may have gone through six Tootsie Pops in the process, but it got done.

Dad was home in time for dinner, and we even got to conference call my brothers over dessert. And because I didn't have to share, I got double the ice cream scoops. For all intents and purposes, one would call it a quiet, low-key evening.

Ethan couldn't call, but he texted me before I went to bed. I made sure I went to bed early. The first time I ever skipped, I was in the hospital. It wasn't too long after that I realized skipping happened when I was sick or tired, which made it that much more difficult to control. I made sure that I was under the best of conditions, and there was no reason I should worry about unwanted skipping.

But I skipped anyway.

I was wearing the exact same clothes I had on the last time. Jeans, check. Tank top, check. Hoodie, check. Old pair of Chucks, check. It was like the uniform of my dreams. Except for that one unfathomable time when I was wearing an actual dress when I skipped to Ethan. I still do not know why that happened, but I am glad it only happened once.

Of course, I had skipped to the place of nightmares. It wasn't the middle of the night anymore, though. The heavy window drapes that had concealed tall windows were pulled back this time, letting in the early morning light. It was a soft light. The kind caught in old paintings or romance movies. The kind you imagine falls gently on the skin of fairytale princesses to wake them. Dreamlike.

The windows themselves were shut, filtering the light into a diffuse glow. There was a draft, but it felt refreshing rather than forbidding.

It's amazing the difference light can make. That and the very welcoming smell of coffee. There was also something else I couldn't recognize but already knew it had to be delicious. Like freshly baked bread with an added hint of vanilla.

I looked down the hall where we had seen the man attacked. The door was open, but there were no ominous sounds this time. It was a good type of quiet. It was the quiet of libraries. Not the quiet of cemeteries.

Had it not been for everything else being exactly the same, I would have thought I was in a completely different place. Feeling much more confident in my safety than I had been before, I cautiously looked over the banister.

It had been too dark to see anything before, but in the daytime, the light was enchanting the beauty of the small space, caressing the threads on the wall covering and the curve of carved wood. There was character in the details. It was the respectable endurance of age rather than the sinister facade of something that would not die.

In the middle of the room, out of place among the semi-ornate collection of generational treasures, were modern moving boxes. They were strewn about in the disarrayed fashion of someone who has never experienced moving or lacked the organization for it. One box had already been taped shut, but the rest were all half filled. Some with folded clothes, others with items that were not sufficiently wrapped for any kind of safe transport.

The last time I was here, there seemed to be a very clear path to follow. Now I felt like I had too many options. Should I investigate the murder room? Should I try to get out of the house?

I decided that it would be better, in the interests of self-preservation, to try to create distance between anything murderous and myself … no matter how non-threatening things seemed. I couldn't see the front door from where I stood, but it would be safe to assume that I'd find it downstairs.

Of course it's never easy.

I was caught between the haste to get out and the need to do so quietly. I assessed my surroundings. The stairs didn't have the same thick carpeting as the second floor. Instead, it had a runner over the hardwood held down by brass rods. Carpet helped muffle the sound. The runner ended at the foot of the stairs, but the hardwood continued as far as I could see.

I held my breath almost as hard as I held on to the banister for support. My steps were noiseless, but I couldn't do anything about the pounding of my heart that was echoing in my ears.

I could see the front door. It was made of the same dark wood as the banister, with a small hatch on the upper half that must be used to check for visitors.

Almost there, London. You've got this.

I was two steps away from the ground floor when it occurred to me that I didn't know what was waiting for me outside. What if it was worse than an empty room?

I hesitated. Caught up in my indecision, I didn't notice someone had entered the room.

I couldn't miss the sound of a dish hitting the hardwood floor. I straightened up and jumped the remaining two steps. I spun around, backing up as I did, hoping that I could get enough distance between myself and this new complication.

It was the man that Ethan and I had seen on the bed. The one that was dying.

Except he wasn't dead.

He was standing on the other side of the room, holding a fork. What looked like a Danish of sorts was upside down on the floor in front of him, next to the upside-down plate. His expression mirrored what I was feeling. Panic.

"T'es qui ?!"

La Rêvasseuse

I glanced over my shoulder to see how far I was away from the door, but the man had crossed over his felled pastry and was closing the distance between us. He'd got over his shock a lot faster than I did.

It was only after a few more phrases that I realized he was speaking French and not some alien language from netherworlds. Regular, everyday French. He was just speaking it really, really fast. And loudly.

"Um …" I stuttered, closing my eyes and willing my brain to work. I needed a phrase, and I didn't think *oú est la bibliotéque* ? could help me at that moment. Although *oú sont les toilettes* ? might work because I felt like I was going to be sick.

"Um … um …" I wasn't able to form a sentence fast enough,

but he stopped anyway. The pause gave me a chance to get my words out.

"*Je ne comprends pas le français* !" I was able to stammer out, opening my eyes wide. I had two and a half years of public school French classes under my belt. It wasn't even French Honors. Just French. And I took it only because it was a prerequisite for graduation. My accent was terrible and garbled. It would have certainly garnered me a failing grade had I been in class. I repeated it over and over again. Each rendition was slightly better than the last until it looked like he finally understood me.

He blinked at me. "English?" he asked, his voice clipped with impatience.

I swallowed and nodded, not trusting myself to speak.

He considered me in silence for a few breaths. He was probably judging me. I was likely less of an intruder and more of a dumb tourist to him. His dark eyes were bloodshot, perhaps from lack of sleep, but they remained alert regardless. Underneath his wrinkled shirt, his muscles tensed. "Who are you?" he asked, his voice heavy with a French accent. "What are you doing here?" Fortunately, his English was much better than my French.

"My name is London," I said, wondering if giving him my real name was a bad idea.

"London? Like the city?"

Every. Single. Time.

I nodded. "And I don't know where here is," I admitted. This felt very familiar. Except I wasn't in the *wop wops* of New Zealand this time. And it wasn't Ethan that had found me.

"You are in Grenelle," he said, much less suspicious of me than Ethan had been. I looked at him blankly. It must have been evident that the information meant nothing to me. He sighed heavily. "You are in Paris," he amended.

Paris?!

"Like the city?" I mumbled before I could stop myself.

He relaxed a little. "Yes." His smile was that of tired irony. "You are in the city of Paris. This is my home. I am called Laurent."

He pinched the bridge of his nose like I do when I'm fighting a migraine. He turned his back to me to pick his breakfast off the floor. He muttered something in French, perhaps disappointment over his wasted meal. "You should not be here," he added, his back still to me.

"I'm sorry," I said automatically. "I don't know how I got here."

"I know how," he said with a casualness that felt completely out of place. He was tired. I heard it in his voice. He picked up a checkered kitchen towel that was thrown into one of the moving boxes and knelt on the floor to wipe the last of the sticky residue. He started to walk back to where he'd come from, which I assumed was the kitchen.

I followed.

"You do?"

The hardwood stopped at the entranceway, where it met the patterned tile that ran throughout the entirety of the small room. The proportions were all wrong. It was the kind of kitchen one might find in an apartment, not a house. A small window over the single sink faced the wall of an apartment building. It wasn't a great view, but it was enough to let light into the room. Enough for the small potted plant sitting on the sill to look healthy.

He tossed the squandered tart into an overflowing can, almost hidden under the disproportionately small sink. Then he faced me, wiping his hands on a fresh kitchen towel.

"*Oui, je sais.*" He alternated between French and English without a change in tone. It made it that much more difficult to decipher. He hung the towel on the handle of a small stove.

"You are, of course, a *Rêvasseuse*," he said like that explained everything.

"I'm sorry," I said again, not understanding. "What is that? What does that mean?"

He paused, confused by my reaction. His eyes narrowed in suspicion, but whatever he was looking for on my face, he did not find. He chewed on his lip, thinking. "It is … ah … how do you say?" The term was eluding him, and I couldn't help. He snapped his fingers, looking around the room as if the word he was looking for would materialize in front of him.

He was the same man Ethan and I had seen. I was sure of it. Unless he had a twin. This man who was firing rapid *Franglais* at me seemed as different from the dying man in the room as this whole house was from the nightmare. He seemed younger than I had initially thought. His dark hair, no longer matted on his forehead with sweat, was styled. He had the disposition of a gamer who had been online a straight forty-eight hours but could still drag himself to class if he absolutely needed to.

"Ah, *oui* !" he exclaimed, snapping me out of my musings. He pointed at me for emphasis.

"You are a Woolgatherer."

The Companion

"I'm a *what*?"

All of a sudden, this felt more unreal than any dream I'd ever had. It was already a lot to process the fact that I was in a Paris kitchen for no reason. I was speaking to a guy that was no longer surprised to have found a strange teenager in the middle of his living room. And instead of having to explain myself, he was explaining me … to me.

"A Woolgatherer," he repeated, slowly articulating each syllable. He pouted a little, his lips pushing together almost like a kiss. He was chewing the inside of his cheek. "Of course you must be. You dream, *oui* ? Then you are in your dream?"

I nodded; there wasn't much else I could contribute.

"*Voilà* !" he said, waving a hand in my direction. When I didn't respond, he looked at me as puzzled as he was frustrated. "You don't know this? This is not your first, *non* ?"

I shook my head, answering both questions at once.

"*Je n'ai pas le temps pour ces conneries*," he mumbled more to himself than to me. I may not have been able to understand his words, but he conveyed his impatience without difficulty. "How? How do you not know?"

"How do *you* know?" I finally asked.

The only difference between my confusion and his was that he understood English more than I understood French. That and the fast-rising exasperation weaved into each new sentence. He was waiting for me to retract my question, and when I didn't, his response was guarded. "My mother was a Woolgatherer. *Alors*, I am one as well."

I shook my head, feeling a little lightheaded. "So you skip too?" His eyebrows crumpled together like colliding fuzzy caterpillars. Of course he wouldn't know what I meant. We made up that term because we didn't know any better. "I mean, you go into your dreams?"

The caterpillars lifted apart in a moment of clarity but quickly fell back together in greater confusion. "*Non, non*." He pushed the heels of his palms into his eyes.

He dropped his hands. Our combined aggravation was reaching critical mass. "Only daughters are able to dream that way, *oui* ? Sons do not. We are only Woolgatherers by blood." His eyebrows arched in a way that meant he was looking for confirmation from me as well.

He knew significantly more than I did, so there was no way I could offer anything useful. "I don't know," I admitted.

He threw his hands up in the air again, yelled something in French, then stormed out of the room, kitchen towel whipping in his hand. I could hear him muttering more to himself. I had clearly interrupted more than just his breakfast.

I was reeling with all this new information. *Woolgatherer*. There was a name for people like me. There were *more* people like me. Laurent had answers. I stepped toward the entry to follow him.

"London?"

There were many reasons I was surprised to hear my name spoken in Ethan's voice. Not just because I wasn't expecting him but because he wasn't there a second before.

I spun around so fast that I lost my balance. That wasn't surprising. I lose my balance often. Everything else was just contributing factors.

Ethan caught me when I stumbled into his arms. He held me tightly to him so I could balance on my own. And even then, he didn't let go.

I was wrapped up in the sensation of being so close to him. The extra seconds slowed enough that I went from surprise to joy and, finally, to selfish indulgence.

His plain military-issued undershirt wasn't as soft on my cheek as my bedsheets, but it smelled of New Zealand summer air and my Ethan. That made it better than the silkiest Egyptian cotton, in my opinion. I looked up at him, momentarily forgetting that I was in the middle of an existential crisis, and allowed myself to smile. Except he wasn't smiling back at me.

"What are you doing?" he admonished in a low voice. "Why are you skipping?"

A little annoyed that he didn't share my misplaced bliss, I pulled away from him to straighten up. "It's not like I was planning to skip," I argued. "Yet here we are." I threw my hands up in the air. There was no control here. It felt like nothing was ever consistent when it came to my abilities. Our theories were all just theories, and they seemed to all be wrong.

He clenched his jaw the way he does whenever he's faced with something he doesn't approve of. I knew that it wasn't directed toward me but to all the questions that didn't have satisfactory answers. I took offense anyway.

"Can we figure that out later?" I asked, impatient. "No one is dying right now, so it seems relatively safe. More importantly, I think there's someone here who seems to know all about skipping!"

I was energized by his presence. What had been overwhelming before his arrival was now exciting. It didn't look like he shared my optimism, but that was something I expected. In fact, it was something I depended on. He was my anchor, keeping me on steady ground whenever I was floundering.

I turned to lead the way out of the kitchen.

At that moment, Laurent returned, presumably to yell at me in French some more. Ethan pulled me back behind him; I guessed he intended to get between me and what he perceived as a new danger.

Laurent dropped the plate he was carrying back to the sink. It fell to the floor for the second time. He held the fork still in his hand. It was a reaction so similar to the one he had when he saw me just a few minutes earlier. It would have been comical, but at that moment, it went unrealized.

The plate fell on its side, rolling across the floor in a lazy circle before falling face down and sliding to Ethan's feet. It didn't shatter, but its collision with the sturdy kitchen tile left it chipped. Laurent didn't appear to notice. He didn't even look at it. Neither did Ethan.

"Laurent …" I meant to introduce Ethan, but I didn't have a chance to say more. Laurent's surprise had escalated. It was closer to fear rather than the grouchy impatience he had with me. He backed up, hitting the frame of the entrance in his haste.

He stopped a little past the threshold, his knees bent, looking ready to sprint, and one hand still on the frame. His grip on the fork tightened. *"Impossible,"* he muttered. His eyes were wide and frantic, possibly how mine were earlier when I had first encountered him.

I tried to step around Ethan, but he held me back. The atmosphere was charged with fearful anticipation. Laurent's eyes darted from Ethan to me to the fork in his hand. Ethan slowly took a step back, pushing me even further behind him. His street brawling experience and the beginnings of military training allowed him to calculate things that I couldn't factor. He flexed his right arm slightly. An imperceptible motion that I only noticed because I knew that he still didn't have full use of it.

Laurent's breathing quickened.

Ethan exhaled slowly.

I should have paid attention. I should have been alert. There was an obvious fight brewing that should have commanded all my senses. Instead, I found myself staring at the smooth, creamy surface of the damaged plate that had landed by Ethan's feet. As I stared at it, my perception shifted. The plate seemed to be increasing in size but also increasing in distance. It was like a camera trick.

The room muted, and before the lights began to throb, I shut my eyes.

When I opened them again, I was five thousand miles away. Back in the safety of my bed. Ethan was not with me.

Bridging the Distance

It had been a lousy night.

It was just after one a.m. when I woke up, wondering if I had left Ethan with Laurent when I skipped away. He responded to my text immediately, which meant that he'd made a safe exit.

That was the good news.

The bad news was that it took another hour before he could actually call. Staring up at my darkened ceiling didn't make the time go any faster. It wasn't his fault. Sometimes it just took that long for him to be able to sneak out and find an isolated enough place where he wouldn't be caught. I waited for him, of course. And when he was finally able to call, we argued in strained whispers.

I was eager to talk about what Laurent had said. I'd learned more about myself in that short visit than in our endless guessing and theorizing. It wasn't a lot, but it was a start.

Ethan acted as if I had skipped on purpose. He wouldn't move past it. That was totally unfair, and I felt that his attitude was completely uncalled for.

Sure, after I had calmed down the next morning, I was able to see that his anger was misplaced fear brought about by genuine concern for my well-being. But that wasn't the case when we were having the conversation.

There were so many more important things to talk about, and I didn't appreciate being on the receiving end of what I perceived were unjust accusations on his part. It was the middle of the night. My sleep had been interrupted. I was cranky. And scared. And confused. And thrilled by the prospect of someone out there who might understand me.

He, on the other hand, was just being a … a … poop head.

I hung up on him. He tried calling back, but I put my phone on silent and shoved it under my pillow. What I really wanted to do was yell into it before I threw it against the wall so the last thing he'd see would be the wall coming at him. The fact that the wall was painted the same color as his eyes would have made it more gratifying.

But I needed my phone. So I had to satisfy myself by screaming into my pillow until I fell back into a troubled, restless sleep.

I hated it. I hated arguing. I hated being at odds with him. I hated being apart.

Long-distance relationships suck.

I carried the emotional turmoil with me well into the day, where I decided to take it out on the blameless holiday decorations that needed to come down. It was a task I was tackling all by myself. Yet more evidence of the unfairness in the world and the tragedy that was my life.

I may have been swearing at ornaments when Dad found me.

"We're angry at glitter now?" he asked in a tone that was perfectly balanced between mocking and concern.

"I never liked glitter," I growled. "Glitter. Is. The. Herpes. Of. The. Art. World." I punctuated each word by putting the manufacturer's shatterproof claim to the test, throwing one offending ornament into the box with excessive force. I missed the box completely, and the bauble, coated in red glitter, bounced a few times on the hardwood. It scattered even more glitter on the floor before rolling under a chair.

I threw myself backward on the couch, swearing loudly as I went. Not caring that Dad was in the same room. Or maybe because he was in the room.

"Whoa, there, sweetheart." There was no anger in his voice. It was more just to get my attention. He made room on the cluttered coffee table for his coffee. Then he sat down on the couch next to me. "What's going on?"

When I turned to look at him, I was already crying.

I let him put his arms around me while I cried on his shoulder like I was six years old again. I braced myself for the interrogation that was sure to come, but he didn't say anything. He let me cry. He was fully present for me without pressure or lecture. I didn't know what modern-day parenting manual he got that move from, but that pure acceptance made me cry even more.

Dad was a patient man. It could have been a byproduct of raising three boys and one girl all by himself. He had always given us our freedom, encouraging us to ask questions and take risks. He called it "freedom with expectations."

He didn't set many rules. Far less than any other parents we knew. We never had a bedtime. We never had a curfew. We could attend parties. We could throw parties. As long as we were responsible and kept him in the loop, he let us do our own thing.

Either he'd discovered the secret to perfect parenting, or we were just abnormally amazing children. I liked to believe it was the latter. He liked to take the credit. It was probably just luck.

"I'm sorry." I hiccuped, trying to get my emotions under control. I was apologizing for swearing. I was apologizing for making a mess. I was apologizing for *being* a mess. I sat up and wiped my face with my shirt. Classy.

"Fighting with the boy?" he guessed. It was a gentle question filled with sympathy. It was almost enough to get me started again. I held my breath and stared at my hands. "You know," he added with a wan smile, "it's not really whispering if you're whispering really, really loudly."

I groaned, burying my face in my hands. "Let's go ahead and add mortification to the list."

He chuckled a little and put a hand on my back to let me know it wasn't as bad as I imagined it was. "Stealth Ninja, you are not."

I took a little offense in that, but it wasn't a battle I wanted to fight. I sighed and dropped my hands. "Why is it so hard, Dad?" I turned to look at him and saw his tender look of understanding. "Things were so much easier when we were together. I don't understand why it's so different now."

I was new to being in a relationship. Ethan was my first boyfriend, so maybe my expectations were unrealistic. But our relationship wasn't typical to begin with. We connected through magic. The world had conspired to bring us together against all odds. Against reality.

From our very first encounter, there was an unmistakable pull toward each other. It was the gravity of our fate. It was our shared destiny. Surely, that meant something.

Whenever we were together, I felt the absoluteness of it. We were so strongly united. So assuredly meant for each other. That certainty had been put to the test since he'd left. Things had been different. There was a disconnect. Doubt replaced belief. I questioned everything.

Dad didn't answer right away. When he finally spoke, it was ladened with underlying wisdom. "Did you ever notice that when the two of you fight, you raise your voice?"

The question in itself sounded like a reproach, but the manner in which he asked it was one that preceded a teaching moment. It was his way. He was part parent, part college professor. I felt the heat on my face. I couldn't help that. It was embarrassing regardless of the intent. I nodded.

"But whenever you're alone together, you talk in hushed tones." He lowered his voice in demonstration. Just above a whisper.

"And sometimes," he continued with a little glint of knowing mischief in his eyes, "you don't even speak at all?"

This was getting worse. If Dad's intent was to shame me into submission, it was working. The heat on my cheeks intensified. I closed my eyes. "Yes," I admitted in a strangled voice. "Enough. I get it. Stop yelling at each other. I know."

He chuckled. "Oh, I don't think you do. That wasn't my point."

"What, then?" I didn't know how much more of this I could handle.

"When your hearts are close together, sometimes you don't even need words."

I opened my eyes and saw that behind his own were years of experience and unspoken moments.

"You yell when you're angry," he continued. He made fists with each hand and stretched his arms wide. "Because your hearts are further apart, and you're trying to bridge that distance. When the physical distance changes, you need to find other ways to keep your hearts together." He brought his fists back together until they were touching. Then he clasped his hands. "You can't continue in the same way that you have and expect things to stay the same. These are different circumstances and unless you change to adapt to them, things will fall apart."

There it was. The revelation that eluded me. It sounded so obvious now that he said it. It was ridiculous to assume that the same routines would work for a completely different situation. It almost never did.

"Realize this, sweetheart," he added, "when the two of you are already physically distant, don't say things that push your hearts further away."

The tears I had were different now. I understood what he was saying. We didn't need to yell to hear each other over a bad connection. We had to adjust our position for a stronger signal. It wouldn't be easy. But it was simple. And it would be worth it.

I was crying because I had hope again. I had faith. I had the wisdom of both my parents. I knew that whatever the challenges, we could handle them.

I threw my arms around him. "Thank you, Dad." My voice was gruff from both the hug and all my emotions. "You really are the best."

"Again"–he laughed–"this is what I'm saying."

Woolgatherer

Ethan and I were able to share a video call later that evening. I apologized for being rude. He apologized for not being receptive to what I was saying. I made an effort not to raise my voice. I made an effort to use words that were intended to connect us. Two minutes into our conversation, my heart ached from missing him so much, but I also felt that we were closer together than we had been the past few weeks.

"What did he call you?" Ethan asked when we got around to talking about Laurent.

"A Woolgatherer, I think. I mean, he said something in French, but I don't remember."

Ethan grinned. He knew my dislike for learning a foreign language landed just below my dislike for learning history. It wasn't because I had anything against foreign languages. Or anything against learning. They were just subjects that weren't very kind to me or my GPA.

"I looked it up," I continued before he could tease me about it. "It means 'daydreamer.' "

"I've never heard that before," he admitted.

"Neither have I. But he didn't make it up. I mean, it exists in the dictionary and everything. I just don't know what it means to me, you know?"

"Maybe the French word would reveal more. I mean"—he shrugged, that maddening grin back in place—"if you could only remember it …"

I stuck my tongue out at him, but I was smiling. This all felt so much better than resentment and anger.

"He said that only daughters skip," I mused.

"He said skip?" He was rightfully surprised.

"No, no … he didn't know what I meant right away. Which means"—I pointed out with a tiny bit of triumph—"it wasn't the right word!" We had debated over the correct terminology, and it was Ethan that suggested skipping. I couldn't come up with a better suggestion.

"What term did he use then?" Ethan challenged.

I thought back to the exchange. "I don't think he mentioned a term. Unless it was another French word that I missed."

"OK, so what you're saying is that my suggestion is still the best option." That smile of his wasn't wavering. Although it was partially at my expense, I loved seeing it. It was contagious.

I rolled my eyes. "He said his mother was a Woolgatherer, and so he was one too. That means my mother must have been a Woolgatherer."

"A Woolgatherer that *skipped*." His smile was getting wider. He was really enjoying this. And I found that I was too.

"Interesting you should point that out," I said. "Because he said that daughters do but *sons* don't. Sons are only Woolgatherers by blood."

"That means you can skip because your mother did but your brothers can't?"

I shrugged. "It sounded like that."

"Like what? A recessive gene?" His face scrunched together in deeper confusion.

"I don't think that's how that works, but I got a C in Biology. Your guess is probably better than mine."

He didn't look satisfied with my response.

"My dad did say that my mom was waiting for me. That I was special." I recalled that very difficult conversation I'd had with Dad. It was the night I found out the truth about my mother. About how she died. "Maybe this is what he meant."

"Have you not spoken to him yet about all this?"

I hadn't. I should have, but the argument with Ethan had consumed me and pushed everything else aside.

"We talked about other things," I admitted without wanting to admit anything. "But I'll ask him tomorrow."

I went to bed feeling good. I hadn't realized how much underlying stress I was struggling with. Skipping wasn't the root cause of my anxiety. Being apart from Ethan was. Skipping just complicated things.

I felt our connection had been re-established. Along with the confidence that the signal would only get stronger. I was filled with nothing but promise; there was no room for troubling dreams.

Patroness

I was pleased with myself.

It took the entire weekend, but I was successfully able to take all the holiday decorations down by Sunday afternoon. All by myself. Dad was merely a spectator. It didn't bother me at all. Glitter notwithstanding. What had been contributing to my tragic life the day before was now just another notch in my belt of achievements. My outlook had changed, and what a difference that made.

I celebrated by finishing up that plate of leftover Christmas cookies in the kitchen.

"This needs to go into storage," I told my unhelpful audience of one. I patted the top of a stacked bin to get his attention.

Dad looked unimpressed. He was slouched comfortably on the couch. He held his tablet with one hand and picked up his half-empty coffee mug with the other. "I believe you're a capable young teen with equally healthy and strapping friends." This was the disadvantage of not having my brothers around. Manual labor.

"Fine. I'll see if they'll come over after school tomorrow." I started to push the bins closer to the walls. Just so that we would have a little more room. The plastic containers slid easily on the hardwood.

"Watch the floor," Dad admonished without looking up.

I left the bins where they were.

I sat next to Dad, but instead of reaching for the TV remote, I played with an old Polaroid. It was a photo of me as a baby, roughly eight months old. And while I was clearly an adorable subject, that was not what made this photo special. What made it exceptional was that my mother was the one holding baby me on her lap. This was a photo of her.

Dad looked at me sideways and noticed what was in my hand. He put down the tablet but not the coffee. "What?" he asked, knowing that there was at least one unasked question in the air.

I hesitated. Not because it was a difficult topic for me but because I knew it was painful for him. In the past few months, he'd had to navigate as much uncharted territory as I had. Except his path was hampered by extra emotional explosives. He was a man that had relocated for a new job. A father that had cared for his daughter in the hospital. A husband that had lost his wife. Twice.

It was a testament to his character that he wasn't an alcoholic, chain-smoking, chronic gambler with a drug problem. Even more so that despite everything, he continued to be an incredible role model and parent. I didn't want to add to his burden.

"Why did she drive all the way to downtown Chicago?" I blurted out, still staring at the photo.

He sighed, knowing what I was referring to and perhaps knowing that the question would come. Seventeen years ago, when we lived in the northern suburbs of Chicago, my mother left my brothers in the care of a neighbor and traveled over fifty miles to the city. With baby me. In the middle of a snowstorm. It was unsafe. It was irresponsible. It didn't make any sense.

She died that night. Kept me safe and warm but at the ultimate expense. We were left with so many unknowns.

"I wish I knew," he replied to the question I'm sure he'd asked himself more times than I had. Long before I even knew to ask.

I had expected him to drop the subject. He had never liked talking about things before, and this was that much more uncomfortable. But when I looked at him, I found him studying me. Like he was weighing something in his head.

"What?" I asked. It was my turn to recognize that there were unsaid things waiting to be spoken.

"Nora lived in Chicago." He said it like a confession. There was a catch in his tone that suggested there was something more. A suspicion he didn't want to voice.

"Nora?" The name was familiar but also out of context. He waited for me to come to the expected conclusion by myself. "Like, my godmother, Nora?"

Nora was my mom's best friend. They had known each other for about as long as she had known Dad. Liam, the eldest of my brothers, was the only other person that remembered her. I'd heard stories about how close they had been, but that was all I knew. Stories. She never once came to see me when I was growing up. I didn't even know what she really looked like.

"You think Mom went to see her? What did Nora say?" I assumed that when Dad said he'd called her friends, Nora would have been first on his list.

Dad spun his coffee cup slowly between his fingers. The liquid was no longer hot, but he treated it like it was, cupping his hands around it gingerly. He sighed again, looking weary and uncertain. "Couldn't reach her." His shoulders slumped, and he swallowed hard. "When they … when they found you …" He faltered. What he meant to really say was, *When they found your mom's body in a frozen car half buried in the snow*, but that was a hard thing to articulate. "I thought for sure Nora had some kind of emergency. Something that made it necessary for your mother to make the trip."

"An emergency?" I repeated incredulously.

He rubbed his forehead. He was caught between wanting to shelter me and wanting to share. I met his gaze with what I hoped was one of maturity. I wanted to know more. I wanted all the information that had been kept from me for so many years.

"Nora was pregnant. Not very far along, but I thought maybe something went wrong." I could tell that his reasoning was flimsy. And that was why he was reluctant to share it. He was throwing possibility darts in the dark, hoping one would land on a reasonable explanation.

I was throwing my own right next to him.

"If something was wrong, then she'd need Mom to drive through a deadly blizzard for what? Moral support?"

He shrugged again but didn't dispute it. I was certain that was what he was thinking, and he must have known it sounded weak, but it was his best guess. And he had been guessing for years.

I had good friends of my own. Whenever I needed them, Brieann and Drew were there for me. There were no blizzards in California, but I didn't think that would stop them anyway. "I can see that … I guess."

Dad looked at me. There was a strange sense of relief in his eyes. He wasn't my father. He was just a grief-stricken person hoping to find validation. Part of me was alarmed to see him so vulnerable, but another part of me was grateful to be able to give him a fraction of the comfort he'd selflessly provided all my life. "I can't say I wouldn't have done the same if Brieann or Drew needed me," I admitted.

He smiled a small and tired smile. "But I never heard from Nora. She didn't even come to the funeral. She just disappeared." I could hear the abandonment in his voice. He had thought of Nora as a friend too. But she wasn't there when he needed her the most. And that was a twist of a knife already deeply buried in his heart.

"I suppose it was just as difficult for her. They were so close. And in her condition, maybe she just couldn't make it." He was making excuses for her. And maybe for himself so that he wouldn't resent her.

I felt anger for him. I didn't have anything invested in Nora. I knew of her, but I didn't know her. She meant nothing to me. And although I knew Dad didn't mean for me to feel this way, this made me dislike her. Of course, we didn't know what really happened, but until I had evidence otherwise, this was the new truth.

She was the reason Dad didn't have a wife. She was the reason I didn't have a mother. She was the reason our family was incomplete.

Until that moment, I hadn't realized that I was looking for someone to blame. That was Nora. And I hated her.

Sarramauca

I was in Laurent's kitchen. I instantly recognized the window without a view and the colorful patterned tile. Faint music was coming from another room. The kitchen looked different. The disarray of the main hall had reached this one. One cabinet had been left ajar, revealing almost empty shelves. Some dishes had been wrapped in paper but left on the counter. The can was overflowing even more.

"Toi encore ?"

Laurent's exasperated French was surprisingly familiar. I turned to face him, smiled awkwardly and gave him a small, apologetic wave. *"Bonjour,"* I said with an accent that made it obvious why I was not in French Honors.

Laurent was massaging his temples with long fingers. It didn't look like he had showered since I saw him last, but he had on a different shirt, albeit with the same wrinkles. The skin under his eyes drooped and sagged like they carried the weight of all his sleepless nights.

He swore.

It was in French, but it sounded like a swear word. I didn't ask him to elaborate.

"Your companion?" he asked with what sounded like angry resignation.

I looked around as well, wondering the same. "I don't know," I admitted. "Maybe? It's still early." California was twenty hours behind New Zealand. I always went to bed before he did.

Laurent did not look like he appreciated the possibility of Ethan showing up.

"Ethan is my boyfriend," I told him. It still sounded strange saying it aloud. It felt both real and made up. Having a long-distance boyfriend was sometimes too reminiscent of a time when I thought he wasn't even real. "He's harmless."

That wasn't true. Ethan was far from harmless. At seventeen, he was already the recipient of a Victoria Cross, the most prestigious award for valor in the presence of an enemy. He had been shot at and survived. Before he joined the military, he had already demonstrated crazy knife-handling skills with the butterfly knife he carried with him everywhere. Between early training and strategy classes that he was already mastering, he was just at the beginning of realizing his potential. He was capable and dangerous.

But these were things I didn't think Laurent needed to know. Or wanted to know.

Laurent narrowed his eyes. He didn't believe me. "It's impossible, you know."

Was he implying it was impossible that I had a boyfriend or that this very possible boyfriend was impossibly harmless? "What's impossible?"

"Your boyfriend."

That didn't help.

"What *about him* is impossible?"

"That he dreams with you." He said it like it was the most obvious thing. "You, *oui*, you are a Woolgatherer's daughter. Him, *non*. It is impossible." He sighed. "But then, what is impossible anymore these days?" He turned his back on me and walked out of the kitchen. This time, I was able to follow.

I glanced behind me before leaving the kitchen, just in case Ethan *did* show up. He didn't.

We walked back into the room with all the boxes where he had first discovered me trying to sneak out of his house. There were even more boxes now, but a greater percentage of them had been taped up. Laurent knelt in front of one and started taping. "I don't have time for you." The sound of the tape gun punctuated his irritability.

I couldn't blame the poor man. He was visibly stressed, and my presence was adding to his burden. "Ethan isn't a Woolgatherer," I said, confident that I knew the difference now. "I think I take him with me."

He didn't look up. "I do not care." He finished one box and turned his attention to another, not slowing down. "Go away."

"I can't control this. I don't know why I'm here."

"Not my problem." The tape gun was loudly at work. "First, a *Sarramauca*; now, an Idiot *Rêvasseuse*."

"Is that the thing that was attacking you?" I was trying to make sense of his sentences through context clues.

He stopped with his arms outstretched and a length of clear packing tape between them. He glared at me at first. Then one of his hands faltered, causing the tape to crumple and stick together. "*C'était toi* ! You were there."

"Hey, you saw us? Great. I mean, not that something horrible was trying to kill you is great, of course not. That's not what I meant. I mean, like, I didn't think you did." He just continued to stare. I realized that I had just made his near-death experience all about me.

"I mean, I don't expect you to, like, right away recognize me. You were pretty busy at the time. There was a lot going on." I jammed my hands into the pockets of my jeans, feeling like the most inconsiderate douche dweller. "The whole thing was grisly," I finished lamely and bit my bottom lip to stop myself from making things worse. I grimaced.

He looked at the mess of tangled tape between his hands and dropped the tape gun. Then he sat on the floor, legs stretched out in front of him. "I am alive because of you. You and your impossible boyfriend." His eyes lost focus; although he was looking right at me, he was seeing past me.

I felt that his realization should have been laced with a little less incredulity and maybe a little bit more gratitude, but at least he had stopped glowering at me. I took that as an improvement.

"So, yeah, what was that anyway?" I asked, trying to erase how badly I'd summarized his near-death experience. I shuffled my feet.

"*Sarramauca*," he mumbled, not moving from where he sat.

"What's a … *Saramawkha*?" I butchered the word.

"A *Sarramauca*," he corrected, devoid of emotion. He had reached his emotional capacity and was now operating mechanically. "It is the ghost that takes dream souls."

"It's a *ghost*?"

He shook his head, and his eyes refocused on me. "Sorry. *Non*. Not so much. Ah … how do you say? Bad spirit? It is what causes the *cauchemar*. It feasts on your soul."

That didn't sound any better.

"You're telling me," I clarified, "that there is a genuine *monster* eating our souls? Like a legit monster?"

He nodded slowly. "Monster. That is a good word." The word itself was the least important thing, in my opinion.

"How is that even real?"

He shrugged, a man resigned to his fate. "It is the world."

I wasn't ready to embrace monsters as fact. Certainly not soul-sucking dream monsters. Why couldn't it have been rainbow unicorns? Or good fairies that grant wishes? Why did it have to be so awful?

"Where does it come from?"

He picked up his tape gun and exhaled heavily. Pulling himself up to a kneeling position, he ripped off the tangled tape. He crumpled it and threw it to the side. Then he pulled out a new strip and resumed his task. "No one knows. It is older than old. It began as an Occitan legend." Even the sound of pulling tape had lost its anger. "They say that the beast comes as a woman."

"That was most certainly *not* a woman we saw trying to kill you."

His laugh was bitter. "*Non*, not a woman," he agreed. "The Sarramauca can change its form."

"A shape-shifter?" Of course it was a shape-shifter. It wasn't horrible enough as just a monster; it should also have the ability to deceive and manipulate you too. Of course.

Laurent nodded. "It can come as a woman. It can come as a man. It can come as a beast. No one knows its true form. We only know it for its hunger. For the way it squeezes your life. For the way it kills." The tape gun in his hand was shaking. He dropped it. It lay unmoving on the box. His hand continued to shake. He made a tight fist.

I could see the torment reflected in his tears. His breathing had become haggard. He must have been reliving the trauma of the other night. He closed his eyes. It kept the tears at bay. He dropped his head, his whole body shaking in little tremors. There was no way for me to know the hell raging in his mind, too fresh to forget.

I had been in the room for only a few minutes, and it was a nightmare that I couldn't wash away quickly enough. His nightmare was so much worse. So much more personal. So much more horrible.

"The Sarramauca hunts *Rêvasseuse*." His voice was just above a strangled whisper. He took a shaky breath and exhaled long and slow. He opened his eyes again, but the tears were still there. "When one is found, there is no escape."

"You escaped," I pointed out, hoping that it would comfort him.

"*Oui*, only because of you."

Asabikeshiinh

"How do you stop it?"

Laurent's brisk irritation had drained away, leaving behind a tired shell. "There is no stopping a Sarramauca. You look, and you are frozen. It touches you, and in time, you are dead for certain. Your only hope is to run and hope it doesn't find you."

I looked back at the mess of packing boxes. "Is that what you're doing? You're going to run?" It seemed like a very drastic course of action. Although what was the appropriate action when the discussion revolved around a mythical monster that wanted to use your soul as a chew toy before dinner?

"This was my parents' home." He was wistful as he was tired. I could almost see the thousands of memories playing in his mind's eye as he looked around the emptying house, flickering like a movie montage overlayed around him.

I knew because that was how it was for me when we left Illinois for California. That last walk-through was a culmination of all the memories collected within the walls. Laurent looked at his house the same way. The difference was that Illinois never truly felt like home for me, and I had wanted to leave.

"I grew up here," he continued, laying a hand on the hardwood floor that had echoed many growing steps. "They left it to me." His shoulders slumped. "But the Sarramauca will return, and I cannot be here when it does."

"How come it hasn't come back yet?"

"*D'abord*, it is temporarily … how do you say … not hungry." He got to his feet with a groan, brushed the seat of his jeans in a manner that seemed more out of habit than any real need to clean up, and gestured for me to follow. "It hunts when it is hungry. It stops when it is not. I have a little time, I think? But I do not know for how long." He led the way up the stairs and to the room at the end of the hall.

It was the room Ethan and I had peeked into the first time we skipped together. This time, the drapes were pulled open, letting the light fend away the nightmares. The room must have been the first one packed because all surfaces were cleared of most items, leaving dark shapes where a light layer of dust could not reach. There was an open suitcase on the floor, overflowing with clothes. A corner of the room had a couple of filled boxes waiting to be taped.

The emptiness of a room stripped of belongings spoke more of what had been removed. I was sad for him. He was going to abandon everything. This was all the home that Laurent knew, and he didn't want to leave.

I followed his gaze to an item hanging over his bed. It had been intentionally left behind. It was a small misshapen hoop hung from one end. The frame was wrapped in leather, and within it was a woven net made of what looked like thick tan-colored cord. Despite the lopsided shape of the frame, the netting inside was perfectly symmetrical. Like a web. In the center of the web was a single feather. A couple more feathers and twigs hung from the frame, along with what looked like four precious stones.

"Is that a dream catcher?" Dream catchers were pretty little tokens that tweens made into earrings and edgy teens turned into tattoos. It was cultural appropriation packed into trinkets created in bulk for cheap southwestern-themed motels. Laurent couldn't mean that this was his secret weapon against a monster.

"*Asabikeshiinh.*" He said the word with respect.

"Is that French?"

"*Non.* Surely, you know? It is Native American. Of the Ojibwe tribe." His look of surprise faded into disappointment. It was a judgmental look. Or that was how I chose to perceive it.

"You said the Sarramauca was from Occitan. I *know* that's not American." I took his look as a personal attack, and I was defensive. I didn't want him to think I was completely uncultured. I got enough of that from Drew.

"The Sarramauca might have come from Occitan, but it has no borders. It needs no passport to travel into dreams."

Obviously. He didn't say that, but I heard it anyway. I didn't think it was possible for me to feel even lamer, but there it was. I didn't respond.

"No one knows for certain, but everyone tries. They say we must use fennel and hawthorn. So, *oui.* I do also." He gestured to the window. On the narrow ledge, there were green and brown plants drying in the sun.

I stepped closer to investigate. I wasn't familiar with the plants and couldn't tell one from the other. One looked like dill but smelled faintly like licorice. The other didn't look as fresh. It seemed to be just a collection of twigs. I didn't want to touch either.

He threw his hands up. "But I do not know if it works. I hope to delay it until I leave. That is the only way for sure. To leave."

"It can't find you when you leave?" For a monster that didn't need a boarding pass, it didn't seem that distance would dissuade it.

"Sometimes it follows. Sometimes it does not. Sometimes it is years." He looked so resigned.

"Where did you get the … um … the …" I looked at him pleadingly.

He smiled. If anything, at least I made him smile. "The asabikeshiinh?"

How did he say that so easily? How did he make everything sound so nice? I stumbled over it but repeated it until he nodded.

"Where did you get the asabikeshiinh?" I asked when I was finally able to string together the sentence.

"It was a gift to my parents when I was born."

"So … not Amazon, huh?"

My sarcasm kept the smile on his face. "*Non*. My asabikeshiinh was made with layers of apotropaic magic. Asabikeshiinh does not actually mean dream catcher as you understand. It means *araignée*. Spider."

I grinned. "So you're telling me that the Sarramauca is afraid of spiders?"

There was a twinkle in his eye. The first time I saw something other than the heaviness that carried through the fear and anger. "Are not most people? Spiders are frightening." He staged an exaggerated shudder for effect.

He had a great smile. It was a peek into what kind of man Laurent must have been like before the Sarramauca changed him. He sat on the edge of the bed. With his feet on the floor, he lay on his back, staring up at the asabikeshiinh. He folded his arms behind his head. "Legend says that *Asibikaashi*, the Spider Woman, kept the Woolgatherers of the tribe safe. Like a mother would. But as the tribe grew larger and spread around the world, she could not watch over everyone. It became the responsibility of the Woolgatherer daughters to weave the web of protection."

He turned his head to look at me but otherwise didn't move from his position. "The Sarramauca is responsible for all nightmares. Nightmares are weapons." He looked back up at the asabikeshiinh. "The web captures the nightmares. It filters the dreams. When there is no nightmare, there is no attack."

He stared a little longer at his talisman of safety, a small defense for such a formidable foe. I didn't interrupt. Outside his windows, I could hear the faint sounds of a city beginning a day, unaware of the monsters of the night that threatened us.

"But if the nightmares are many," he said in a strangled voice, "this cannot stop it."

Wuv Yu

Mondays were my least favorite day of the week. Friday the thirteenth had nothing on Mondays. Mondays were a magnet for everything to go wrong. Out of toothpaste? Monday. Snag a sweater on the smallest nail in the world? Monday. Can't find your keys? Monday. Pop quiz? Monday.

I probably should not have taken my bike to school. I may as well have dared the universe. I looked out the window of the noisy cafeteria at the gloomy sky. There wasn't any rain yet. Just the looming threat of it.

Rain? Monday.

"You probably shouldn't have taken your bike," Drew said, finishing the last of his cafeteria cheeseburger. Students carrying standard issue commissary plastic trays, some were piled with prepackaged snacks, others had unidentifiable splodge posing as consumable substances, walked the aisle behind him. The noise that teenagers make among friends is always magnified when you add carbs, sugary soda, and a room that reverberates high-pitched laughter.

Fortunately, as a teenager myself, I was uniquely suited to filter the unnecessary hubbub and could easily understand Drew in spite of all the pubescent bedlam. "I like the idea of being able to bike in the winter," I argued, even if I completely agreed with him. Mondays were for pointless arguing too.

"Well, if it rains, I can give you a ride home," he offered. "I don't have anything going on after school."

I brightened up. "I'm so glad you said that. Remember all those bins of Christmas stuff you helped me pull into the house? I need help putting them back in storage …"

He groaned. "I said I'd take you home. I didn't say I'd stay." But I already knew he would. I extended a silent invitation to Brieann, who was sitting next to him. Just as I knew Drew would help despite his complaints, Brieann knew what I was asking without me having to say anything.

"I'd help, but I've got a couple of club meetings after school." Brieann was part of almost every important organization or committee in the school. If it wasn't an event, it was planning for one. How I was friends with the most popular girl on campus often mystified me.

Drew snorted. "I'd rather move bins."

"And so you shall. I'm here to grant wishes. You're welcome." I pushed my plate of leftover fries to him. He took it like I knew he would. Teenage boys were receptacles for junk food. Something I'd learned from my brothers.

"I feel like you owe me more than stale fries for this."

"Dinner is on me," I promised.

"I can make it to dinner," Brieann said. "I'll catch up."

"Wait, wait … she gets dinner, and she's not even moving bins?" He acted aghast. "The unfairness of it all!"

"Let's be real," I huffed, unaffected by his display. "Even if she were there, you'd be doing her share anyway."

"I'll make it up to you," she promised. She leaned into him and gave him a kiss on the cheek. He might've gotten that kiss right on his lips had he not been eating greasy fries.

"Ew," I complained. "Gross. I don't need to see that."

"We had to watch you and Ethan make googly eyes at each other for weeks when he was here visiting," Brieann countered. Drew's laugh sounded like a bark. He made kissy faces.

"Oh, Ethan," he said in a shrill voice. "I wuv yu! You're my dream man!" Brieann laughed and made kissy faces back.

"Oh, London," Brieann responded in a low voice and an accent so obnoxious that it should be offensive. "I will fly to the other side of the world to be with you." She made grand gestures with her arms before taking Drew's face in her hands so tightly that it made his kissy face even more ludicrous. "I wuv yu more!"

"No, I wuv yu more!"

"I wuv *yu* more!"

They continued to make ridiculous noises, further amusing themselves. I tried to act upset, but I was laughing at the stupidity of it all.

"First of all, I do *not* sound like that," I protested, pointing at Drew. He responded by batting his eyelashes. I stuck my tongue out at him, then pointed at Brieann. "And that's a *British* accent you're doing! He sounds nothing like that!"

"I only know how to do British and French accents," Brieann

admitted, laughing even harder.

"Well, at least you'll get Laurent's accent right." Not that there was any real doubt. Brieann had been taking French since middle school. She wasn't just in French Honors. She was in AP French. Laurent wouldn't even need to speak English.

"Who, now?" Drew abandoned his kissy faces in favor of squeezing ketchup over the fries. Brieann opened a tube of lip gloss, still smiling.

"Oh, right." I hadn't yet told them about Laurent. "Remember the dead guy in my nightmare?"

"You know his name?" Brieann frowned. Her hand was frozen halfway into retouching her makeup.

I nodded. "Turns out he's not so much dead after all."

Brieann and Drew exchanged a look. I didn't elaborate. Drew slowly raised his hand. "I have questions …"

The school speakers came alive with a musical reminder that the period was over. I stood up to collect trays. Neither of them moved.

"Wait, wait. I said I have questions!"

"I have questions too," Brieann agreed.

"Maybe you'll just have to ditch all those club meetings you have lined up and come over, then." I waited, but neither of them moved. I shrugged. Since they decided to stay, they inherited responsibility for the trays. I tucked my phone into my jeans and grabbed my pack. "Up to you …"

Brieann's eyes narrowed as she watched me leave. She pouted. "Not fair!" she yelled when I was a few steps away.

I spun on my heel to face them, winked, and threw them both kisses. "I wuv yu guys!"

Look It Up

The bins stayed where they were.

Brieann was sitting cross-legged on the couch next to Drew. Both looked at me expectantly. There were more important things to discuss than home organization.

"I'm probably going to regret missing those meetings, so this better be worth it, London." Brieann tried to sound threatening, but I waved her off.

"I make no promises."

"You were saying the French dude survived the dream killing?" Drew prompted, impatiently rolling his hands at me. "Elaborate, please?"

I told them how I had skipped a couple more times since we had last talked, where I had skipped and what I had learned from Laurent. I recounted the first conversation with him.

"He said I'm a Woolgatherer." I made quotation marks in the air. "And that it's an ability I inherited from my mother. Like a birthmark."

"Paris," Brieann said with a bit of wonder. Knowing that no one had actually died made the nightmare a little less alarming. She seemed to be more concerned about the idea I had been in Europe than anything else. "I wonder why Paris. Have you always wanted to go to Paris?"

I shrugged. "Not really? To be honest, I'd much rather visit London …"

They both laughed. "The selfie possibilities are endless for you in London," Brieann agreed. "But Paris is just so romantic, isn't it?"

"I didn't actually leave Laurent's place, so I wouldn't know."

"Ooooh … spending the evening with an older French dude in the most romantic city in the world," Drew teased. "Does Captain Kiwi know you're hanging out with Laurent?" He said Laurent's name with a fake French accent and a raised eyebrow.

I rolled my eyes. "Ethan is aware. I mean, he did show up that first time we spoke, and they alpha-maled each other until I woke up."

Drew howled. "I feel like I need popcorn for this."

Brieann bumped him with her shoulder. "Oh, stop being such a juvenile," she chided. He threw his hands up in mock surrender but kept the mischievous expression on his face. "We kinda knew you were just like your mom," she said to me. "Isn't that how your parents met? Your mom skipped to him."

I nodded. This was something I had only learned myself recently. "That's what Dad said. I guess Laurent just confirmed it? But the whole Woolgathering thing is new to me. And according to Laurent, it's sort of a girl thing. My brothers are technically Woolgatherers, but they don't have the ability to dream skip."

"Empowerment," Drew said and raised a fist in the air. "I hear you."

"So what about the whole demon thing? What was that about? Was it real or just some weird Woolgathering vision?" Brieann asked in a low voice.

"He said it was a Sarramauca." I said the word slowly. "I don't know if I'm saying that right. But he said it's a real thing! It's a monster that hunts Woolgatherers, gives them nightmares, and … just … squeezes the dreams out of them like toothpaste."

"*You're* a Woolgatherer," Brieann pointed out. "Does that mean it's going to come after *you*?"

I shivered. "I don't know? It's possible, I guess? I mean, technically, it can come for my brothers too."

They both looked at me in alarm. Brieann stood up, hands on her mouth. "That's horrible! What can we do about it?" She looked between me and Drew. Drew pulled out his phone.

"What was it called?" he asked.

"A Sarramauca? I don't know how to spell it. It's French."

Drew nodded absentmindedly and started a search on his phone. Brieann sat back down but with her feet on the floor and her elbows on her knees. She leaned forward. "Did he say if there was any way you could protect yourself?"

"He might be the wrong person to ask," Drew said without looking up. "I mean, the dude was attacked, so he hasn't done a very good job keeping it away."

"How did he survive?" Brieann asked before I could defend Laurent.

"He said I saved him." I tried to downplay it, but I was a little proud of that.

Drew didn't look up from his phone, but he lifted a hand to give me a high five. I grinned and slapped the offered hand, realizing that I had already forgiven him for his quick dismissal of Laurent. He went back to scrolling.

"He said there was something different about me."

Brieann raised an eyebrow. "That sounds like a line. Was he hitting on you?"

"No, no, nothing like that. He basically said that guys never skip. My being able to take Ethan with me on a skip is different."

Drew put down his phone and looked up. He hesitated as if there was something he clearly wanted to say. We waited. He started and stopped a couple of times like he didn't know where to begin.

"Oh, just spit it out already," Brieann admonished.

Drew spared her an irritated look. He tried again. "What if," he began haltingly, "he's right. I mean, your mom …" I suddenly understood why he was having difficulty getting the words out. My mother was a very sensitive subject.

I nodded to encourage him to finish his thought.

"She basically sacrificed herself for you." He lifted his shoulders slightly before letting them fall again. "What if that left you with some extra magic?"

"That's beautiful, Drew." Brieann leaned against him. "I can totally see that," she agreed. "Think about it! It makes total sense! You're a Woolgatherer already by birth, but maybe, because of your mom's love and sacrifice, you inherited more?"

She reached over and put one hand over mine. "London," she said, her blue eyes burning with the intensity of total combustion, "what if you're meant to stop it?"

Bangungot

I wasn't prepared for that mic drop.

We sat there in shell-shocked silence for much longer than necessary, pondering the potential pitfalls of this proposal. Until I could no longer stand it.

"I want a milkshake," I declared.

It seemed like a course of action completely unrelated to the topic, yet it was unconditionally fueled by it. Brieann's idea was a bomb, and I wanted to be physically far away from its blast radius.

We piled into Drew's sometimes unreliable car that started after only two tries this time. Milkshakes at Caden's seemed like the appropriate activity at the appropriate destination. The sugar was great, but at this point, it was the brain freeze I was after.

Milkshakes were alcohol for the underaged.

"This nightmare-inducing creature shows up in all sorts of folklore," Drew was saying between bites. He ordered loaded fries to go with his chocolate shake and was using one hand to eat and the other for his phone. "I found the Sarramauca that French dude was talking about."

Brieann and I nursed our drinks. The initial brain freeze from the first deep sip was only just starting to fade.

"Also, a sleep demon called a *Bakhtah*. But there's also the Romanian *Mora*, the Pyrenean *Cauchemar*, and the Brazilian *Pisadeira* …" he continued.

"Do you think it's all the same thing?" Brieann asked.

"Same monster with different names?" Drew tilted his head. "Why not? It's not like people could compare notes back in the day and agree to call it by the same name." He took a generous sip of his shake to wash down a mouthful of fries. "Look at the *Alû*. I think it's Ancient Mesopotamia … Babylonian or Sumerian or Akkadian. I don't know." He waved his hand around. "But then there's also the old German *Alp*. Not only do they have similar names, but it also basically does the same thing."

"Kill you in your sleep?" I asked.

Drew nodded. "It seems to be all about the nightmare. A Babylonian *Alû* can cause nightmares just by being in the room with you," he read off his phone. "And if that's not enough, it'll force you down and suck your breath to *give* you a nightmare."

"Pushy demons, aren't they?" The sarcasm in Brieann's tone was layered with distaste.

"They think it's an evil elf of some kind. It sits on the chest of a sleeper and becomes heavier and heavier until the crushing weight leaves the sleeper terrified and breathless." He looked up. "Sounds like a morbidly obese disgruntled Santa's workshop reject."

I grinned. "Boycotting the dancing sugar plums?"

Brieann got in on the action. She had her phone out, doing her own research. "Even in Asia they have super similar stories. In the Philippines, they have a *Batibat* or a *Bangungot*."

"See?" Drew said, picking up another fry. "They can't even decide on one name in the same country. I wouldn't be surprised if this is all talking about the same monster."

"There are some differences," Brieann observed. "The Bangungot kills the same way. Nightmares and paralysis. But this is supposed to be a tree-dwelling spirit, not an elf."

"Laurent said it's a shape-shifter."

Brieann looked up from her phone, annoyed. "Well, isn't that just convenient?"

I sipped my shake slowly. "Yeah, that's what I said."

"I think people just try to explain things the best they can according to their own culture," Drew suggested. "I still think it's all the same thing. A rose by any other name and all that jazz."

"More like a nightmare by any other scream," Brieann mumbled.

"The nightmare isn't necessarily what kills," I corrected. "I think it's what it uses to hunt. Laurent had a dream catcher over his bed. He said it was created with magic, but it's not enough of a defense if there's a big onslaught of nightmares."

"Dream catchers are French? I thought dream catchers were Native American."

"No, they're definitely Native American in origin. But as Drew said, this one monster shows up in so many different cultures. I guess it makes sense that people deal with them differently."

"What if it's not *one* monster?" Drew asked. "It could be a pack of monsters."

My brain hurt, and it wasn't because of the milkshake.

"A pack?" I asked.

Drew shrugged. "What do you call a group of monsters?"

"A nightmare?" Brieann suggested.

"No, that's what you call a group of crows," Drew countered.

"No," I corrected him. "A group of crows is called a murder."

"I think a nightmare sounds appropriate," Brieann insisted.

"Don't you think it's a little too literal?"

I rubbed my temples. *Are we really talking about this right now?*

"For all we know, it could be an entire race of monsters. I mean, you have all sorts of different kinds of humans; why can't we have all sorts of different kinds of monsters?" Drew polished off the last of his fries. "Vampires are a kind of monster, but they don't have the same weaknesses as werewolves."

"Vampires and werewolves aren't real," Brieann argued, but she lacked conviction. Drew gave her a wry look.

"Really? We're going to debate what's imaginary?" He gestured toward me. "Our best friend is the chosen one who skips to a completely different country in her dreams. Her boyfriend is a bona fide national hero. She's met the spirit of her departed mother, for goodness' sake!" He counted every point he made on his fingers. "And she's about to go head-to-head with a … a …" He glanced quickly at Brieann's phone screen. "A Bangungot."

He leaned back in his chair and made his last point. "Not one thing I said is plausible, and yet here we are."

In a voice so tiny that I almost didn't even hear myself, I asked the inevitable. "Is it just hopeless?"

There was no immediate answer. Brieann let her phone sag limply in her hand. Drew shrugged, unable to put into words the possible futility of our efforts.

Being tasked to handle *one* boogeyman was bad enough. The idea that there could be a myriad of monstrosities was overwhelming. I was barely coordinated enough for gym, how was I supposed to battle supernatural beings?

It turned out that being the heir of dead expectations wasn't even the nuclear bomb of suppositions.

The milkshake wasn't sitting very well in my stomach.

Solid Ground

"We can do this together," Brieann declared abruptly from the passenger seat of Drew's car.

We had made it almost all the way to my house in near complete silence. While we were each digesting all this recent information on our own, the dismal atmosphere gave me the impression that we were riding the same train of thought.

Apparently, Brieann wasn't on the same carriage. She was on an entirely different locomotive. Heading in the opposite direction.

Drew, possibly equally as startled as I was, looked at her sideways without taking his eyes off the road. He made a small noise that could be what a question mark sounded like on its own. No words. Just the punctuation.

She didn't acknowledge him. Brieann was looking straight ahead, shoulders squared. Whatever it was she was seeing, perhaps a more positive outcome than what I was envisioning, encouraged her. "There has to be a way to beat this thing."

She suddenly spun around and strained her seat belt to face me as much as she could. I was slouching so low in the back seat that she didn't find me right away. She waited for us to lock eyes before she continued. "And, yes, it's just *this* thing you have to worry about. Whether or not there are thousands of different monsters out there, it's only *this* one that Laurent is trying to get away from."

I didn't want to agree with her, but this unexpected tenet that fueled her was contagious, and I found myself nodding reluctantly. He had only talked about the one shape-shifting nightmare-inducing angry elf-goblin.

"Drew said they couldn't compare notes before, but we can now." She held up her phone for emphasis. "Generations of myth and legend."

"The internet hive mind," Drew said, getting on board with her.

She smiled at him. Having him agree with her gave her even more confidence. "It's a start. We can cross reference similar stories and sort out what's what." She raised her eyebrows at me, daring me to jump off the transit to hopeless self-pity and join them on the freight of optimism.

I grinned at her.

"Let's stop by the library after school tomorrow," Brieann suggested, knowing she'd convinced me. "Then we can come up with a solid plan of action."

"I didn't know people still did libraries," Drew responded.

"There's actually a whole lot you may not find on the internet." Brieann shrugged. "And I'll already be there for a committee meeting anyway."

Drew laughed. "And *there's* the real reason. Convenience."

"I think it's serendipity," Brieann said with a lofty air of innocence. "I should wrap up around four thirty or five. Does that work for you?"

"Let me check my calendar." I wasn't trying to hide my sarcasm. I didn't have a calendar. I valued my alone time, and they knew it. I waited a beat without moving. "Yup, looks good."

"Hey, hey, hey," Drew protested. "Do I not get a say in this?"

Brieann's eyes widened. "Oh! I'm sorry! I didn't know you had plans."

"I don't," he admitted. "But I don't think I appreciate you assuming that I didn't." He gestured at me. "I have more social obligations than her, and you asked her!"

"You're the boyfriend, remember," I teased him. "All your plans revolve around Brieann now."

Brieann flashed me a look. Her eyes narrowed to slits, and her nostrils flared. She was genuinely angry. She had never looked at me like that before. My stomach fell. I shut up. There was a line that I hadn't realized I'd crossed.

"That's not true at all!" Brieann protested. Drew had one hand lying idle on the gear shift. Brieann laid a gentle hand over his. Her voice changed from the sharp tone she had used on me into one of soft butter. A tone she must reserve solely for Drew. "That's not true," she said again. "I don't think that at all. It was absolutely wrong of me to assume that. I'm sorry."

We rolled to a stop in front of my house. Drew smiled at Brieann and kissed her forehead. "That," he said, "I appreciate."

I had never felt more like the third wheel than I did at that moment.

Drew stepped out of his car to let me out, as usual. I looked at Brieann before I got out, but she had her head turned away, pointedly looking out her own window. She hadn't forgiven me as easily as Drew had forgiven her. In fairness, I hadn't yet apologized. Also in fairness, I didn't know what I was supposed to be apologizing for.

"See you tomorrow," I managed to squeak.

She finally turned to face me right before Drew closed the door. "See you at first period," she replied, and I felt a chill of dread. It felt like a threat. I wasn't sure if she had meant for it to sound that way, but my own guilt amplified the emotion.

They drove away.

My phone rang right as I shut the front door behind me. I sat cross-legged on the couch and answered the video call. It was Ethan.

"What's wrong?" he asked right away. His smile when the image appeared fell into a concerned line before I'd even greeted him.

"How did you know to call?" Until I saw his face and heard his voice, I hadn't realized just how much I needed him.

He looked puzzled. "I always call after our afternoon drills."

I glanced at the clock on the corner of the screen. It was six p.m., which meant that it was three p.m. where he was. "Oh, right. Sorry."

"Are you going to tell me what's wrong?"

"I think I might have pissed Bree off."

I let the sentence hang in the air. I chewed my bottom

lip, trying to find a way to explain what had happened. His eyebrows came together in confusion. He blinked a few times, like he was considering and discarding scenarios in his head. And then he laughed.

"You mean she's angry with you?" he asked.

"Yes." I nodded, still defensive. I didn't find anything funny about this situation.

He smiled, and despite the low resolution of our connection, I could see a glint in his eye. "Lost in translation," he clarified. "When you say 'pissed' you mean angry. Around here, 'pissed' means drunk. So I thought you were upset that you got Bree drunk, and I was trying to figure out how you could accidentally get her drunk. On a Monday!"

In spite of myself, I laughed.

"Was it a prank?" he continued. "Was it a dare? Did they serve it in the cafeteria? Did you think the vodka you were pouring was water? What?"

The more outrageous the situation, the more I laughed. And just like that, the tightness in my chest resolved itself.

"I'm not sure which would be worse," I admitted.

He grinned. "Only one way to find out."

I laughed. I knew he wasn't serious. "I'd rather not, thanks."

"Why is she–" He paused for effect. "Pissed at you, then?"

I didn't want to have to remember Brieann's expression, but at least it was without that heavy feeling of dread. "I think I might have hit a nerve when I made a comment about her and Drew." I chewed my bottom lip again. Such a bad habit. I stopped.

"Were you being mean?"

"I thought I was being funny."

"You're never intentionally funny." There was a mischievous, challenging look in his hazel eyes.

"Hey! What's that supposed to mean?"

He grinned. "I mean, easy to make fun *of* but not necessarily fun*ny*."

I narrowed my eyes. He started laughing. The more indignant I was, the more he laughed.

"That's just proving my point." The paradox that was Ethan was that while it seemed that he was trying to aggravate me with his words, everything else about him was the opposite. His tone. His expression. It was all love.

I stuck my tongue out.

"I miss you," I said, feeling the sudden wave of it. The afternoon was an overstimulating carnival ride of emotions that cost too much and made me feel like hurling. I was done. I wanted the ground to stop moving. I wanted to look away from fast-moving objects and just watch the stars. Ethan was my refuge. He was both my solid ground and aspiring sky.

I wanted to feel his arms around me. I wanted to be able to lean on his chest and hear the beating of his heart. I wanted time to stop the way it always did when he hugged me. I wanted the supernovas to explode in my chest the way they always did when he kissed me. I wanted to be lost in an entanglement with him.

"I miss you too."

His longing mirrored mine. And while it was a poor substitute for what I wanted, it was something. I closed my eyes for a second, trying to make the comfort last longer while simultaneously steeling myself to meet the responsibilities of the world. When I opened my eyes again, I felt a little stronger.

"I'll be at the library after school tomorrow," I updated him. "Bree and Drew want to do some heavy research on this whole Sarramauca thing. They have a bunch of theories."

He frowned. "You're not planning on skipping to see Laurent again, are you?" He said Laurent's name with distaste. Ethan was slow to trust.

"I didn't plan on skipping last night either." I thought back on what factors might have affected the unintentional skip. "I didn't think I was super tired when I went to bed."

His frown deepened. "How were you feeling last night?"

I had spent the day cleaning up the house and eating cookies. It had been a busy day, but I wasn't physically exhausted. I hadn't had the appetite for a heavy dinner after the conversation with Dad. Maybe it was emotional fatigue.

"I was feeling a little sick after learning about Nora," I admitted. "Maybe that's what triggered the skip."

He considered that. "Possible. What you're saying is that there's a risk of you skipping now because of how you feel about Brieann?"

I thought about it and compared how I felt now with how I had felt the day before. "I hope not. I mean, it sucks. I know I screwed up. But I also know I can fix it. Yesterday was different. I was more … angry. And helpless. It was a mix of a bunch of things."

He was distracted by something off-screen and then came back to me. "I have to go." I already knew that. We never had a lot of time during these calls squeezed into his tight schedule. I pouted.

"Look," he said, "get something solid to eat. Sleep early. Fill your head with all positive thoughts."

I nodded, resigned. We both knew long distance was going to be difficult. Dad was right. I should have been making an effort to make things easier, not the other way around.

"And remember," he added with emphasis before I could respond, "fill your heart with all my love."

K

The open curtains were a natural alarm clock, letting in the bright morning sun to wake me up. I wrapped my blanket around myself and turned to the side, my back to the window. Turning away from it was my natural snooze button.

I'd slept well.

Ethan had his own kind of magic. I had pulled the covers up to my chin, and the metal on my wrist reflected the sun from the opposite side of the room. I smiled at the ever-present bracelet.

Ethan Robert.

His name was etched into the metal. I hated being apart from him, but it was a comfort knowing that he was a part of my world. It should have been enough to know that he was out there. And that he loved me too.

A few months ago, I hadn't even thought someone like him existed. Then I thought he was just a dream. Then I thought he was part of an alternate universe. Then I thought he was dead.

My chest tightened at the memory of almost losing him. He had been too close to dying. I had been too close to a lifetime without him.

I closed my eyes again, but not with the intention of stealing a few more minutes of sleep. It was an attempt to control my emotions. But in my mind's eye, I saw my mother, flickering between worlds, falling into my father's arms. I watched him live and die all over again on borrowed time. A lifetime in a span of minutes. And now, another lifetime without her.

My phone vibrated. I reached for it, thinking it was the backup alarm I'd set in case the sun didn't convince me.

It was a text from my brother Liam.

> **PSA**
>
> **2day is her anniversary**
>
> **Go easy on him**

He meant it was Mom's death anniversary. I hadn't forgotten. He sent me the same text every year, but this time, particularly after what had happened in Chicago last month, the day might hit a little harder.

> **Noted**

I responded, hearing everything he wasn't saying and hoping he could do the same.

> **Will call l8r**

I held the phone for a little while longer, just staring at the screen. I didn't want to have to deal with the heaviness of the day.

By the time I got dressed and downstairs, Dad had already left for work. In the living room, the photo of Mom and me that I had been looking at two days ago was sitting on the coffee table. I had left it on top of the bins. Dad had moved it.

I sat on the couch, feeling a little defeated. I hadn't anticipated that he would be up earlier than usual. I picked up the photo. Whatever emotions I was experiencing as a daughter that never got to know her mother, it must all be that much worse for him as a husband without his wife. For someone that had known what it was like to have that love and now had to be without it. I hadn't lived long enough to understand that level of loss.

This was evidence that we were right to worry. He was hurting, and he was dealing with it alone.

I texted him.

> **Ur up early**
>
> **Chili dawgs 4 dinner?**

Dad's comfort food was processed junk. I didn't often enable his behavior, but today was different. Maybe if I used good sausage and real beef instead of the artificially pink tube of mystery meat and canned beans, I could improve it a little and alleviate my guilt.

> **Good morning, sweetheart**
>
> **Let's eat out tonight**
>
> **Caden's at 7?**

That was a better response than I was hoping for. I responded with a thumbs-up.

> **Great**
>
> **There's someone I want you to meet.**

Someone I want you to meet? What does that mean?

My hand froze on the phone keyboard. The problem with text is that it was so hard to gauge intent with very limited context. Who was this mysterious someone? A girlfriend?

I don't ever recall Dad talking about another woman. I didn't think it was suspicious of him to stay late at work. There were either faculty meetings or papers that needed grading. I never thought to question it, but then I'd never had cause to before.

I was also very much involved in my own existential crisis. Maybe he wasn't hiding it. I was just very unobservant.

Is he seeing someone?

Mom died seventeen years ago. It wasn't unreasonable for him to move on. He was entitled to.

So why did I feel a little sick at the thought of it?

It was Mom's death anniversary, that was why. It was disrespectful to her for him to introduce this new person in his life to me *on this day*. It wasn't that I didn't think he shouldn't date. I didn't think it was appropriate to talk about it now.

I went from sympathy to righteous anger in the span of a few text messages. The hesitation on my fingers turned into a tight grip on my phone. There were many ways I wanted to respond, but I knew they wouldn't do my sentiments any justice. So I bottled it all into one letter.

K

I stared at the screen much longer than I should have, thinking of all the scenarios that awaited me over dinner. I knew the day was going to suck, but it found a way to be worse.

And it wasn't even a Monday.

Love and Friendship

I caught Brieann by her locker before the first bell. I tended to avoid confrontations, but I also didn't want a large audience when I brought it up. Catching Brieann by herself was a rare occurrence and one I couldn't afford to waste.

"Hey, Bree," I began in the most nonchalant way possible, which wasn't something I pulled off with much success. And when she turned to look at me, I braced myself for the same stonewalled demeanor as the day before.

She smiled.

It threw me off, and I stumbled through my next words. "So, about yesterday …"

She waved a perfectly manicured hand in the air to stop me. I stopped.

"I'm over it."

Brieann wasn't one of the most likable people in our class because she knew how to hold a grudge. It was rare that she stayed angry at anyone. She may not trust you again after a particularly painful betrayal, but she believed that negative energy was just as damaging to her as the one it was directed to. She'd even begun speaking to Tristan, her ex, who had been less than gracious about their breakup.

I wanted to make sure we were OK and that this wasn't something she'd brushed off because she didn't want to deal with it.

"You know," I said, still needing to explain myself, "I was just kidding. I didn't mean it like that."

She shook her head. "I know." She turned her attention back to her locker, replacing the book she was holding with the assigned binder we needed for the first class. She inspected her reflection in the mirror that hung behind the locker door while she spoke. "I overreacted. It wasn't your fault." Satisfied with what she saw, she shut the door and spun the lock.

As tense as I knew I was, I was far more relieved than I expected to be. I leaned against the neighboring locker. "Are you OK?"

Her lips wrinkled in thought. "You know"–she shrugged, stepping away from the lockers to walk down the hall–"I've had a couple of 'boyfriends' over the years." She made quotation marks in the air. "Whatever that really means"–she shifted her binder from one hand to the other–"Drew is different."

"Because he's smart?" I grinned at her. She smiled back.

"Oh, stop! Just because someone enjoys playing football, it doesn't mean they aren't also killing it in their classes." She paused to wave at a couple of football players that yelled out a greeting as if to prove her point. "I've dated guys that were athletes and made the roll. I don't date slackers."

That was true. Brieann had standards.

"Drew isn't a slacker," I agreed.

"Of course he isn't. I'm dating him, aren't I?"

She said it with no semblance of humility, and she knew it. I grinned.

"So why is he different?"

She pulled me into a corner away from the general student traffic. It was her way of creating privacy. The entryway to a closed classroom was papered with announcements such as the upcoming spirit week and after-school activities. There were at least three different notices about the winter formal. They were calling it the Blizzard Ball. As if sunny California had ever experienced a blizzard. I leaned against the poster that was reminding students to buy their tickets.

"He doesn't do things to try and impress me," she reflected, attempting to put into words what she hadn't yet quantified. "I mean, he's impressive without trying anyway, but he also doesn't try to put on a show."

"He's genuine," I volunteered.

"Yes!" Her smile was wide with discovery. It gave her inspiration. "He's totally genuine. He doesn't pretend. He says what he means and doesn't really care if it's unpopular, you know?"

She leaned back against a handwritten sheet of paper that advertised the price of the Blizzard Ball tickets in multicolored magic marker. Her eyes lost focus on me. Instead, she directed her gaze up to the ceiling, presumably at the floating image of Drew in her mind's eye. I grinned. It was amusing to see her like this.

"Who knew that would be such an attractive trait, huh?" I joked.

She looked back at me and pursed her lips. "Actually, now that I really think about it, Drew and I get along because he's so much like you."

I hadn't seen the turn in this conversation going this way. "Wait. What?"

She straightened up and crossed her arms in front of her, confident in what she was saying. "You heard me. Yeah, I think you guys have a lot in common." She let her pointer finger swing between us. "And since you and I are best friends, it makes sense that I get along with him too." Her smile was triumphant. "Drew is, like, the male version of you."

I wasn't sure how to react to that. I just stood there.

"Except taller. With redder hair," she added. "And he smells really, really good."

I didn't realize that my mouth was hanging open until I had to close it.

"I just don't want to treat him like any other guy," she said in a less audacious voice. "I want him to know that I don't just, you know, *like* him … I really care about him."

This was a new side of Brieann. So vulnerable and selfless. She was more worried about how she was treating him than what she was getting out of their relationship. And I already knew that no matter what, Drew would always treat her right.

I didn't have any reservations about them dating, but if I had, they'd be laid to rest. I was proud of them both. The important thing was that they both cared about each other. And as long as they knew that, the rest would sort itself out.

"He's lucky to have you," I assured her. "And you're lucky to have him."

I stepped back into the hallways, and she followed suit.

"More importantly," I finished, "you're both lucky to have me."

She laughed but didn't deny it. The truth was, I was lucky to have them both.

Emotional Landmines

"Can we table our call to arms at the library today?" I said over lunch. "My dad wants to eat out tonight."

"On a Tuesday?" Drew asked. His attention was split between a calzone in one hand and the other on a worksheet that was due next period. "What's the special occasion?"

"You mean other than my mom's death anniversary?"

My slice of pizza had turned cold. Entirely my fault. I didn't have the appetite that I thought I would when I bought it. When I looked up, both of them were just staring at me. Drew had dropped his calzone back on his tray, and his pencil was still in his hand. Brieann blinked at me, wide eyed.

There was an awkward tension in the air. I instantly felt bad for the position I put them in. By acting blasé about it when I was clearly affected, I sent mixed messages. I had made them uncomfortable on purpose just because I was feeling crappy myself. It wasn't an achievement that I was proud of. This must be where the adage *misery loves company* originated from.

"I'm sorry." Drew apologized, making me feel even worse. "I didn't know."

"You didn't say anything," Brieann accused me, a little bit more on the defensive than Drew had been. "Not yesterday. Not even this morning!"

I shook my head. "No, I'm sorry. You're right. I didn't say anything."

Neither of them moved.

"Honestly," I admitted, "it shouldn't have affected anything. I'm more upset at the fact that my dad has decided to introduce me to his new girlfriend today, of all days."

"Your dad has a girlfriend?" Brieann looked sideways at Drew as if to ask for confirmation. He didn't acknowledge her look. "Who? And for how long?"

I shrugged. "I didn't even know he was dating."

I don't know what bothered me more. That he hadn't said anything or that I hadn't noticed. I shouldn't have been this surprised.

"I mean, this is about him, not me." I was trying to be mature. "And it's not like he isn't allowed to date. I'm not saying that. I'm not saying I don't want him to be happy. I want him to be happy. He deserves to be happy. I'm not saying he can't be."

"Of course you aren't," Brieann consoled me. "No one would ever think that."

"That's not why you're mad," Drew agreed.

"Who even said I'm mad?" I snapped at him, clearly proving his point. He raised an eyebrow, not at all put off by my attitude.

"You said you were upset. Isn't that the same thing as being mad?" he asked.

"Of course she's upset!" Brieann jumped to my defense. "She has every right to be upset."

"I didn't say she didn't have any right to be upset!" Drew dropped his pencil and put both hands up in surrender. "No one is saying that!"

I appreciated Brieann's fierce protectiveness, even though it was unwarranted. Poor Drew. That's twice in as many minutes that he'd had to take the brunt of this charged conversation. His eyes darted around, possibly looking for escape routes. You knew it was serious when he was willing to abandon a half-eaten calzone.

"I'm sorry," I said again. I was feeding the stereotype that girls were irrationally emotional. I had to stop. For the sake of feminists everywhere. "I *am* mad," I admitted. "I'm mad at him for dropping this on me. I'm mad at myself for not anticipating it."

I pushed the slice of pizza away from me. What a waste. "And I can't even *be* mad," I complained. "I have to be the supportive daughter. I have to be happy for him."

"No one says you have to be happy about it," Brieann argued.

I sighed. "I know. But he deserves to be happy," I repeated. "Without having to worry about how I feel about it. He's earned it. I've given him his share of stress this past year. It's the right thing to do." I was convincing myself as much as I was my friends. With the same amount of success.

Brieann looked more worried than convinced. Drew was equally concerned. "At least you don't have to pretend around us," he said.

"Yeah," Brieann agreed. "Do all your smiling over dinner. You can call me when you get home, and you can be as angry and shallow and catty as you want!"

I laughed. I felt better already.

"Hopefully, I won't be needing that kind of therapy. Can we do the whole library thing tomorrow instead?"

Brieann shrugged. "I'm actually there every day after school this week. The winter formal is in, like, three weeks. There's still so much to do."

"Ah, yes, the infamous Blizzard Ball," I said with flamboyance laced with sarcasm.

"Where is it going to be held?" Drew asked, back to multitasking his lunch and his homework. "The cafeteria freezer?"

"Dancing between frozen fish sticks and popsicles." I laughed. "The pinnacle of romance!"

Brieann did not look like she appreciated the similarity between Drew and me that she was talking about earlier. The opposite, in fact. Elbows on the table, she pointed one finger from each hand at us. "You laugh, but I'm going to make this the most magical ball ever!"

Brieann had skills. One of them was party planning. She could drop out of high school and still make a career out of it. I had never attended such meticulously arranged parties as I had at any house party she'd hosted thus far. There was no doubt that her mere presence on the committee would elevate the party.

"Of course you will," Drew said, not looking up from his assignment. "Until senior year, when *that's* going to be the most magical ball ever."

He knew her so well.

"That's Future-Brieann's problem." She grinned. "I'm working on *this* dance, so *this* dance is going to be sick."

"Do either of you have a date?" I asked, raising my eyebrows in mock innocence.

Drew spared me a glance before going back to work. He was grinning. "Working on it," he said mysteriously.

"I'm waiting for the right guy to ask," Brieann said, nudging Drew with her elbow. He almost dropped the last of his calzone.

"Good things come to those who wait," Drew quoted without looking at her. He finished his calzone.

"Great things come to those who take action," Brieann concluded, shaking her hair out casually.

That made Drew stop completely to give her his full attention. He grinned. "Then I'd better get moving," he said in a low voice. He leaned toward her. A challenge.

"Yes," she agreed, lowering her chin and bringing her face closer to his. "Otherwise, you may never know what you're missing."

"Aaaaaand we're back to being gross!" I slammed both palms on the table as I got up, intent on breaking the mood. I took satisfaction in watching them both jump. I didn't know if they were surprised by my sudden action, the noise, or the remembering that they weren't alone at the table.

"Don't mind me." I laughed, gathering my things. "I'm just going to take myself out of this three-wheeled circus and head to my next great class."

Drew glanced at his phone. He swore. "I have eight minutes to finish this paper!" His attention was back on his worksheet.

I winked at Brieann. She rolled her eyes, but she was smiling.

"Great things!" I repeated, turning my back and raising a fist in the air.

True Intentions

Dad wanted to meet me at Caden's. That suited me just fine as I'd much rather avoid an awkward ride in the car with his new love interest.

I locked my bike up on the rack but walked around the corner. The mural Drew and the rest of his team had worked on last year took up most of the west wall of the restaurant.

I sat on the curb and leaned back against the painted cement. Close enough to be able to connect to their free Wi-Fi. I was intentionally early so that I could catch Ethan's call before I had to put on the happy daughter mask.

I was scrolling through a search on the mythical Bangungot when Ethan's call came through.

"Talk with Bree didn't go well?" he asked right away when I answered. It took me a second to remember what he was talking about. I was so busy psyching myself up to face Dad's new dating situation that worrying about my friendship with Brieann seemed like a long time ago.

"Actually, it was great. No damage done and all that."

"What's bugging you then?"

I chewed on my bottom lip, wondering where to begin. He waited patiently. His back was to the sun, creating an out worldly glow around him and casting shadows that enhanced his jawline.

"Today is my mom's death anniversary."

He tilted his head slightly to one side in a way that I'd come to learn meant that he would be hugging me if we were physically together. I closed my eyes to better imagine the feel of his arms and the comfort that I would have from them. It only made me miss him more.

"But that's not really what's bothering me," I continued. I moved my phone around to show him where I was sitting. He should have recognized the mural on Caden's wall since he was present at the unveiling. "My dad wanted to have dinner out."

I faced the camera back at me. "So I can meet his new girlfriend," I finished with dramatic effect.

He lifted an eyebrow. "His new girlfriend?" he repeated.

I nodded.

"Today? On your mom's death anniversary?"

I nodded again.

Silence. I didn't feel like elaborating.

"That seems to be in bad taste," he finally said, putting the unspoken rage I was feeling into polite words.

"Yeah, I didn't think his timing was appropriate either."

"I'm sorry."

I sighed. Part of me wanted to hold on to that and slap Dad's new girlfriend in the face with it. Righteous anger. I could probably get away with it. I could play the part of the emotionally charged teenager, scarred by the loss of her mother and unable to control her feelings.

The issue was that as much as I felt this way, my conviction of what he deserved was stronger. And that was why I had to fake it.

"I guess I just thought that with what we went through with Mom last year, the last thing he'd be thinking about was getting back on the dating scene." What I was really admitting was that it was the last thing on *my* mind.

"I suppose he might have considered it a final goodbye?" Ethan suggested gently. "Maybe, in a way, it was the closure he needed to help him move on."

"I didn't think of it that way," I admitted. I frowned at my short-sightedness. Sometimes it was hard to think beyond what I felt like thinking. Dad could have just as easily interpreted their encounter that way.

"I truly don't believe that your father would intentionally disrespect your mother in any way."

He was right. Before I even saw them together, I already knew how devoted Dad was to her. Their brief, out worldly reunion was just additional evidence of that commitment. I had no right to suspect him of anything different.

"How is it that you know my parents better than I do?" I asked, feeling a bit of shame for how I so willingly wanted to misinterpret Dad's intentions. Ethan had a way of opening my eyes to possibilities.

"I don't know them better," he assured me. "But I do understand what it means to love someone that deeply." He smiled, one side of his lips tugging up to a reassuring squint in his eyes.

"I love you," I said, wishing desperately that I could kiss him.

"I love you more."

Then laughing because I suddenly realized how right Brieann and Drew were, I responded, "No, I love you more."

Mystery Date

The comfort I felt when I was with Ethan vanished almost the instant we ended the call.

I sat at the square table set for three, tapping my foot involuntarily to the rhythm of my anxiety. My phone was on the table, screen up but untouched. I wanted to make sure I would see it if Dad tried to reach me, but I also couldn't bring myself to use it as a distraction. Instead, I sipped my second milkshake and stared, unseeing, at the family of four sitting at a booth in front of me. Drowning my thoughts in the murmur of dinner conversation around me and the milky sugar through my straw, I imagined the many ways that the evening could be ruined.

"Sweetheart." Dad's voice came over my shoulder. I closed my eyes for a second to steel my nerves. By the time I turned to face him, a practiced smile was plastered on my face.

"Hi, Dad." I stood up to greet him with the customary kiss on the cheek. He patted me on the shoulder once and then pulled out the chair across from me for the woman that was next to him.

The most striking thing about her was her raven-black hair. It almost looked blue wherever the light hit it. It fell in straight lines past her shoulders like a uniform sheet. It would have made her seem very severe had she not softened the look with minimal makeup and an easy smile.

"I'd like you to meet Mae."

Mae leaned over the table to shake my hand. Her grip was firm, but her hand was soft. Her nails were trimmed short and absent of any polish. At least she didn't seem to be the high-maintenance type.

"Your father hasn't stopped talking about you."

I know nothing about you, was what I almost said, but it wasn't how I wanted to start the conversation. "He thinks embarrassing me is a parental right," I said instead.

I was disappointed in myself, like I was compromising my integrity or something. But it was short-lived because the approving look on Dad's face made it better.

"It's in the constitution," he claimed as he sat down next to me.

How long has this been going on? How did you find him? Are you trying to scam a broken-hearted widower? What do you really want?

Civility was turning out to be more challenging than I'd anticipated. I literally bit my tongue to keep from saying the wrong things. Or at least what Dad was going to perceive as wrong.

Mae pulled up the sleeves of her thin green sweater as she sat down. Not many people looked good in that shade of emerald, but I recognized, with reluctance, that it worked well for her.

In contrast, I tugged down the sleeves of my own blue knit top. I was self-conscious in my clothes. I missed my hoodie. But dinner with company, even if it was just at Caden's, meant I was expected to ramp up my wardrobe.

"Sweetheart," Dad addressed me. His smile was intentionally reserved, suggesting that he was hiding a big reveal of some kind. He did that whenever he was about to give away an elusive answer to an equation that stumped his students. It was every teacher's little sadistic pleasure. "Remember how you were asking about your godmother, Nora, this past weekend?"

Mae's expression matched his. I looked suspiciously at the two of them, wondering where he was going with this. "Yeah?"

"Well, Mae is her cousin." He gestured at the woman. "We actually went to college together."

"I was a year ahead of them," she confirmed. "So I like to think that they followed me."

"Older and wiser." Dad laughed.

"I'm not going to dignify that older comment, but I will admit that I am so much wiser."

I was uncomfortable with their easy camaraderie. At least she wasn't some random sleazy con person off the internet. I smiled politely, but my jaw was already starting to hurt from all the comments I was reining in.

"Nora and Mae were very close," Dad continued.

"We grew up in the same neighborhood, so we were practically sisters," she added. "Went to the same schools and everything."

"Different last names, though," Dad pointed out.

"Yes," she agreed. "Nora's mom was my father's sister." She looked at Dad and flashed him a triumphant grin. "I had the *real* family name."

Dad's grin was slightly more somber when he turned to me. "I realized that I never really looked for Nora after … after everything." Mae put a gentle hand over his. I wasn't sure how I felt about that.

"You had other things to worry about," she assured him gently. "You had your own family to worry about. Nora was not your responsibility."

Was?

"We lost my cousin ten years ago."

I hadn't asked aloud, but she answered. "I'm sorry," I said automatically, devoid of any real emotion.

"By that time, we had moved out of state, and there was just … so much going on." She patted Dad's hand. "We'd lost touch, and there was no real reason to concern you." She withdrew her hand, and I realized that I had been watching it a little too closely. I made an effort to keep my attention on her face.

The shape of her eyes was rounder than most, making them look bigger. There was a touch of brown shadow on her lids but no mascara. She looked friendly. Approachable. Nothing like the vamp I had envisioned.

"Nora and your mother were drawn to each other. Even more like sisters than Nora and me." It sounded like jealousy, but she looked a little sad instead of envious. There was an intensity to her voice that hadn't been there before. "When they were together, they were unstoppable. The things they could accomplish … just incredible."

I felt the little hairs on my arms prickle, and my mouth had gone dry. It was as if I was trying to anticipate what she was going to say, but there was no way to prepare for what she said next.

"They were two of the most powerful Woolgatherers I have ever met."

Destiny

It was exactly at that moment that our server came to take our order.

I sat back in my chair, buried under the weight of all the implications of that single statement.

The two most powerful Woolgatherers …

Mae knew about Woolgatherers. Nora was one too. What did that mean? What did she mean about powerful? How much did Dad know?

I waited for the server to leave, impatience gnawing a hole in my stomach. I felt both energized and completely sick.

"The first place your mother crossed to was Nora's school," she said immediately after our server left the table before I could even get my words together.

Crossed. I had heard that term before. From my own mother before she faded away. Did it mean what I thought it did?

"It was destiny that they'd be friends," she continued, unaware of my musings.

"She may have crossed for Nora," Dad interrupted, "but she chose to spend that first crossing with me."

Mae laughed, but I felt an indescribable dread sink inside of me.

"You said it was Mom's magic." My voice was quiet at first, cracking a little when I spoke. The chuckling stopped when they turned to look at me. I was staring at what was left of my milkshake. I didn't look up. I watched a drop of condensation run down the side of the glass.

"You said that she had the ability to find what her heart was looking for." My voice was getting louder. And when I did look at him, the betrayal must have been clear on my face.

"But that wasn't true. She wasn't there for you. She was there for Nora." I spat out Nora's name in a way that did not mask my disgust.

Dad looked confused. "What does it matter?"

"You said you were meant to be. You said that's how you knew you were supposed to be together. Because she found you." I stood up suddenly, feeling a little wobbly on my feet.

"Sweetheart …"

"But that's not true …"

"Sweetheart, sit down."

I looked at him a few beats and saw through the cloud of my own temper. He was bouncing between emotions himself. I was being disrespectful. In front of a stranger. There are a few things Dad would not tolerate. That was one of them.

I sat down.

I mumbled an apology. Mae shared an uncertain look with Dad. His mouth was a grave line, devoid of the easy laughter present just moments ago. I had totally killed the mood.

"You know about Woolgatherers?" I asked Mae in a much more subdued tone.

"It runs in my father's side of the family," she said. "It usually manifests itself around your age."

"Why don't you know anything about this?" I asked Dad, being careful not to sound accusatory. I had already toed that line.

"It was your mom's thing." He was almost apologetic. "I was never really part of that world."

I wasn't convinced. If he loved her, shouldn't he know all about it as well? Shouldn't he have made an effort to learn? This was a huge part of her life. A huge part of who she was, and he didn't know anything about it? How was that even possible?

He interpreted my expression correctly. "It's like you with your art," he offered by example. "That's your world. I wouldn't know the first thing about it. I don't know why one kind of paper costs three times more than another. Or why you prefer the blue pencils over the yellow ones. I just know that it's important to you, and I respect that."

He glanced at Mae. She smiled encouragingly at him. My eyes narrowed at this exchange, but I'd let it go by the time he looked back at me. I had to make an effort not to antagonize him further.

"Nora knew all about that world, so it made sense to me that they spent so much time together." He shrugged. "It was an easy friendship for them."

"And easy for the rest of us to feel like the third wheel." Mae laughed. I suspected she was trying to lighten the mood and revive the dinner. I couldn't share in it, but it seemed to work well for Dad.

"You too?" he asked her. She nodded. A little too emphatically. "How about those breakfast meetings of theirs?"

"Oh, you mean their bi-weekly *Dreamtime over Donuts*?" It was strange to see an adult like Mae roll her eyes the way that she did. Almost comical. A teenager trapped in an adult body. That must be the effect of nostalgia on old people.

"I think you mean tri-weekly," Dad corrected with a laugh. "I slept in on those days."

"*Dreamtime over Donuts?*" I asked with more incredulity than I had intended.

"Your mother and my cousin would schedule their crossings. What was it? Their second year in college?" She looked at Dad for confirmation.

"Most of it."

"It took them just a year to be able to synchronize their crossings." She leaned back in her chair and bobbed her head in approval. I didn't know what that meant, but she acted as if it was something impressive.

"What did that mean?" I asked. Dad may have dismissed this as her world, but it was very much mine now as well. And I intended to know everything that Mae did.

She leaned forward. "It meant that they could cross in each other's company. That was unheard of before. Woolgatherers always traveled alone. But not Nora and your mom. Their connection was just so much stronger. They could meet up. Wherever one of them went, the other could find them. Like a tether."

"Then they would have breakfast together the next morning and rehash the night's adventures," Dad added.

"Nora was older, so she would usually be the anchor. Your mom would cross to meet her."

"France, Brazil, Germany …"

"The UK, Egypt, Romania, Russia …"

"Don't forget the various countries in Asia …"

"And Australia …"

They were counting off the countries on their fingers, chuckling over shared memories that were before me. My resentment was directly proportional to their combined nostalgia. Significant and increasing.

"They traveled to all those places?" I interrupted when I felt the milkshake threaten to come back up.

Dad's grin was wide. "Why do you think she named you London?"

"Locke says that's where I was adopted from …" I regretted the automatic response even before I completed the sentence. It wasn't what one should say when one wanted to be taken seriously.

"Oh, sweetheart." Dad laughed, the opposite of being serious. "London was the first city that your mom visited on her own."

"It was the first one she anchored," Mae added. "The first one that Nora followed her to."

"Your mom loved the British accent. She was obsessed. When you were born, your name was either going to be London or Queenie."

"I like London better," I said, feeling like I should weigh in on the conversation or else I'd be completely swept to the side in the tide of old memories.

He nodded in acknowledgment but immediately moved on to other things they were more excited to talk about. Like the '80s.

"Remember how they would dress in matching outfits?"

"It only looked like matching outfits to you, but everyone was wearing the same things at that time …"

Our food arrived.

Legacy

I was already feeling full from my back-to-back milkshakes, but it was the conversation that completely killed my appetite. I poked at my eggplant parmesan just so it would look like I was eating.

Mae twirled her pasta around with her fork. Dad dug into his steak and potatoes. He had said he wanted me to meet her, but it looked like they were in their own little bubble, and I was on the outside looking in.

For all the times I felt like the third wheel hanging out with Brieann and Drew, I'd never felt this isolated before.

"How long have you been seeing each other?" I interrupted another round of *Remember When …*

"I found Mae on the Facebook yesterday," Dad responded with a tinge of delighted pride. He was never a big fan of the big, bad internet and especially avoided any social media platforms. He probably thought he had mastered it now that he'd found someone he was looking for.

"It's not *the* Facebook, Edward," she corrected with a laugh. "Just Facebook."

"Whatever." He waved a hand to brush it off as unimportant. "What were the chances that she lived right outside Sacramento? I genuinely didn't think you would ever want to leave Chicagoland," he said to her.

"It's been over a decade since I've been back," she confirmed. Her tone changed from excited reminiscing to reluctant regret. "It was just too difficult."

"Oh." I suddenly realized. "You aren't dating?"

Dad dropped his fork and started coughing. Mae's eyes got very wide. Neither were the reactions I was expecting.

Dad grabbed his glass of water and chugged half of it down. Mae recovered from her surprise much faster. She laughed.

"Oh, no, London," she said before Dad was finished with his drink. "Not at all. We hadn't spoken to each other for years. I'm married," she finished. I hadn't noticed the gold ring on her fourth finger that had suddenly become so obvious now that it had been pointed out. "I have children of my own."

When Dad finally spoke, his voice was strained from coughing. "I looked for her because of our conversation over the weekend. I couldn't find Nora. I didn't even know that she … that she was gone too." He looked at Mae in apology, and she gave him a slight smile. He turned back to look at me. "I found Mae, and I thought if anyone knew anything, it would be her."

I thought he was introducing me to his new girlfriend. I thought he was being thoughtless doing it on Mom's death anniversary. Instead, he was finding ways to introduce me to my mom. A side of her I had never known. It was such a wonderful way to honor her.

I was such an idiot.

"I'm an idiot."

It wasn't much of an apology, but it made Dad laugh. Mae smiled.

"I'm flattered," Mae said graciously. "But we're more like extended family."

"Who haven't spoken to each other in years," Dad said.

"That's why I said *extended* family." The edges of her eyes crinkled a little. I could see the genuine affection now that I wasn't blinded by my distrust.

"Thank you for making the drive," he said to her. She shook her head, still smiling.

"Don't even think twice about it. It was kismet that we could meet up today." She winked at me. "I'm sure it was your mom's doing. If anyone could reach through the spirit world, it would be your mother."

I glanced at Dad, wondering if he had shared events of the last few months with her. He met my eyes and shook his head slightly, clearly understanding what I was silently asking. He hadn't said anything to her.

His phone rang. He glanced at it, probably intending to let it go to voicemail until he saw who it was. "I'm sorry," he said. "It's my son. I have to take this."

"Of course."

He excused himself and left the table. Mae waited until he had gone around the corner before she started speaking again.

"As wonderful as it is to see your father, I came for you." Her demeanor had changed. There was a sense of urgency that wasn't there before. "I'm sure there's much you haven't been told about who you are and what you can do. It's not that your mother didn't want your father to know. It's just that he always respected her space. It was one of the things she loved so much about him."

She looked over her shoulder to where Dad had disappeared, as if she was making sure he wasn't on his way back. She plucked a card from her white leather purse and handed it to me.

"There is so much more I need to tell you. We need to meet again soon. Just us." She searched my eyes, looking for something that I may not have. "You have no idea how powerful you are, London."

Free Will

I played with the business card that Mae had given me. It was glossy white with embossed black text. It didn't actually have her business name on it. Just her contact information.

I was lying in bed, just waiting on Ethan's call before I called it a night. The dinner hadn't gone quite as I expected. Dad wasn't dating. Mae knew more than she had revealed.

By the time Dad had come back to the table, Mae had gone back to being an old college friend. There was a different side to her that Dad knew nothing about. Much like he didn't know about Mom. I pocketed her card, tuning out the discussion of Rubik's Cubes and big hair.

My mind hopped from one thought to another without any real pattern. Mom hadn't crossed for Dad. She was looking for Nora, and Dad just happened to be there. When Dad first told me their real story last year, I didn't realize how much I clung to it. I believed that their great love story was meant to be because she found him the same way I found Ethan. If that wasn't the case, what did that mean for us?

Mom had always been mysterious to me, but this was an entirely new level. Powerful? What did that even mean? What was I capable of?

I was too busy in my own head that the dinner had ended faster than I expected. When we said our goodbyes, Mae held onto my hand a little longer.

"We shouldn't wait too long to get together again soon," she said casually. It sounded like she was talking to Dad, but I knew it was directed at me.

Don't wait too long to call, was what she was really saying.

My phone rang.

Ethan's welcome face filled my screen. It was early enough in the evening that the sun was just starting to get lower. The perfect hour that engulfed the world in golden light, further complementing his eyes.

"How did it go?"

"Not what I expected," I admitted.

"Oh, you liked her?"

The question made me assess how I actually felt about her as a person. I didn't have an answer.

"Turns out Dad wasn't dating her after all. He wanted me to meet her because she knew my mom."

Ethan's eyebrows shot up. They would've been lost in his hair, but since he'd joined the Defence Force, regulations kept it short. His expressions were much easier to read when they weren't as hidden.

"Plot twist, eh?"

I laughed. "Yes." I showed him the card she had handed me. "She wants me to call her. Apparently there's a lot to talk about."

"That's good, right? She might have answers to some of the questions you were asking."

I nodded half-heartedly.

"So what's the problem?"

I sighed. "You remember how my mom and dad got together?"

"Yes, she skipped to him, right?"

"Oh, by the way," I interrupted with a little more enthusiasm, "it's *not* skipped. The correct term is crossed. As in, I crossed to New Zealand and met you." I may have said that with too much triumph.

He laughed. "I like skipped better."

"That's only because you came up with it."

His lips tugged to one side. He raised one eyebrow, puffed his chest up, and spread out a hand as if to say, *'nuff said*. I rolled my eyes, but I was smiling. He grinned at me, and I forgot what I was saying.

"Was your dad lying about it?"

My smile fell. "No, not exactly. I mean, she did cross. He just wasn't the reason she showed up where she did."

"There was another guy?"

"No, another girl, actually."

I didn't realize how that sounded until I saw the look of thoughtful surprise on his face. "OK. Plot twist yet again. Your mom dated another chick for a spell?"

I didn't appreciate the slang, but I chalked it up as a cultural difference. "I think what you meant to say is another *woman*." He didn't seem to understand the difference. I decided to table that conversation for another time. "No, not like that."

"Then I'm confused."

You and me both.

"Something about her fated BFF-to-be anchoring and drawing them together."

"That doesn't help."

"No," I agreed with a heavy sigh. "It really doesn't."

"Help me out here, London. I'm genuinely befuddled."

I sat crossed-legged on the bed. I chewed on my bottom lip a bit before answering. "You and me … what if we weren't meant to be together?"

Wrinkles appeared between his eyebrows. He was instantly very serious. "And how did you arrive at this conclusion?"

"My mom and dad … I thought they were destined to be together because she … she crossed to him. This power of hers brought them together, right?" I was facing my phone but staring beyond it, or at the ceiling, or side to side. I was looking everywhere but at Ethan, because I just couldn't if I was going to be able to voice this out.

"But it turns out that's not the case. She wasn't drawn to him. She was drawn to her BFF-to-be, and he just happened to be there."

"BFF?" he asked, puzzled.

I blinked a couple of times. "Best Friends Forever? How do you not know that?"

He grinned. "Because I'm not a girl?"

"That's sexist."

He laughed. I pouted.

"OK, so she didn't … cross to your father. So what? I would think that the fact that they met was the important thing here."

I stared at him for a moment, not understanding why this didn't bother him. Why it wasn't crushing him. Why it was crushing *me*.

"If *they* weren't meant to be together, what does that mean for *us*?"

I was fighting back tears. That's what was bothering me. That's why Dad's super casual revelation shook me. This wasn't about my parents. This was about Ethan and me. Our long-distance relationship was so difficult. Half the time, the only thing I had to hold on to was that we were destined to be together. If that wasn't true, what was I even fighting for?

Ethan didn't laugh anymore. He was watching me, empathic but not concerned.

"What?" I finally asked.

"I wish I could hug you."

Then I started crying.

"London …" He said my name over and over, gently and reassuringly, until I could get myself under control. I got up to grab a Kleenex, grateful that it was dark in my room other than the lampshade by my bed. I angled my phone away. At least I could hide a little in the shadows without looking like the horrible mess that I felt.

"I miss you," I said when I could speak again. I had gone through three tissues, but I felt that it helped.

"I didn't mean to make you cry."

I smiled, attempting to reassure him. "It's not your fault. I just … I liked the idea that we were meant to be together. It made being apart a little easier."

"We had a similar discussion before, do you remember?"

I didn't. It might have been because my head contained stuffed cotton rather than brains at that moment. So I just shook it.

"I'm not surprised you don't remember. It was a discussion over a sandwich." He smiled at me, prompting me with clues.

Last year, I had crossed to him. He was in the middle of the forest, practicing with his knife. Blindfolded. We talked about self-defense, school, and whether or not there was such a thing as free will. He had used a sandwich as an example to prove that, as humans, we were only the products of our environment. That our decisions were influenced by a current situation and not by free will.

"Something about people reacting differently to a sandwich, depending on when it's presented to them? We're all pawns, right? Forced to live lives dictated by events beyond our control?" I was paraphrasing what he'd said because I couldn't remember it exactly the way he'd said it.

He grinned. "Yes. Heroes aren't heroes because of character. They're only heroes because of the circumstances forcing them to act that way. If everyone has a purpose to fulfill, then there's no such thing as choice. No such thing as free will."

I rolled my eyes. Just as I had done then.

"And what did you say to me?" he prompted.

"I said that you were full of it."

He laughed. I wasn't sure where he was going with this, but I sensed he was about to prove me wrong about something, and I didn't want to give him the satisfaction just yet.

"You said," he began, the sound of victory already in his voice, "that it was a faulty presumption to assume that there exists only one destiny per person. You said that everyone has more than one destiny. That our choices determine our own future. Do you remember that?"

I nodded reluctantly. I felt I had won that argument, but I didn't enjoy it being used against me to prove a point. It felt too much like arguing with myself.

"You should remember. You were very opinionated," he teased.

I stuck my tongue out at him. He reacted with much more maturity.

"I will always choose you, London. You are my best destiny."

Witch Hunt

There were fewer boxes in Laurent's main room when I showed up. It made his place look bigger. Bigger and empty.

I hadn't intended on crossing, but if what I suspected was true, it was probably because I was so unsettled after dinner. Although Ethan had significantly calmed me down, I had lingering concerns. This was evidence of it.

"Merde !" Laurent's voice was accompanied by the crashing of a cup. *"Arrête ça !"*

"You like dropping things." I smiled at him, hoping to divert his irritation. It didn't work.

He didn't just squeeze his eyes shut. His entire face puckered. *"Pourquoi es-tu revenue ?"*

I knew it was a question because of the pitch in his voice, but I couldn't understand exactly what he was saying. Did he forget that this American didn't speak French? I shrugged, a completely useless gesture since his eyes were still closed.

I thought it wasn't possible for him to look more bedraggled, but he'd found a way to accomplish it. Maybe it was the facial hair that wasn't there before. And a good amount of it. The surface area that was free from stubble was sallow. He was having a difficult time.

"I'm sorry," I said, trying to be friendly about my intrusion. "I don't mean to surprise you like that every time."

He opened his eyes, looking more resigned than angry. His shoulders slumped, and he knelt down to pick up the spilled cup. There was little coffee left, so it wasn't as much of a mess as the last time. His hands shook as he reached to clean up.

I moved to help him, but he held a trembling hand up to stop me. I stopped. He took a deep breath and completed the task. Then he turned toward the kitchen. I followed.

"I thought you were leaving."

He made a noncommittal noise and put his cup in the sink. The kitchen was also as bare as the other room had been. He faced me with tired, sunken eyes.

"*Oui, bientôt.*"

I shook my head. He continued to speak French, and though his sentences were short and clipped, I couldn't follow. Other than *oui*, that is.

He looked at me blankly before his eyebrows came together, and he frowned. His one hand, no longer shaking, waved in the air like he was swatting away words. "Eh, that is, yes. I am leaving. Soon."

He dropped his head and used his waving hand to massage the back of his neck. "There were *des choses* that needed to be cared for." He looked up, his hand still resting on the back of his neck. His eyes darted behind me. *"Et bien sûr, il est lá aussi,"* he added in a tired voice.

I followed his gaze and saw that Ethan was standing behind me. He was wearing a plain olive-green shirt, perfectly pressed, and his standard uniform pants. I hadn't noticed when he arrived.

"You're not supposed to be skipping," he reminded me.

"Maybe it is because you kept me up late," I responded, deflecting it right back at him. "Did you just show up?"

He nodded. "This is so weird."

"Pourquoi vous êtes toujours là ?" Laurent's patience was already thin when I arrived. Ethan's appearance must have pushed him over the edge. There was a vein on the side of his forehead that was throbbing.

"Laurent, right?" Ethan asked.

"He's speaking way more French than he usually does," I said under my breath.

"Why are you always here?" Laurent translated. His accent was heavier than usual.

"I don't know," I admitted. "I can't control my … um … crossings."

"Bien sûr que non," he said in a voice heavy with sarcasm. "I am a man that knows more than you." He shook his head at the absurdity of it.

"Woolgathering is not exactly common knowledge," I said defensively. "How am I supposed to know?"

"If all know then there would no longer be any *Rêvasseuses*. They would have all been burned at the stake in the 1700s!" He threw his hands up in the air. He may as well have been talking to children the way he was addressing us. Misbehaving children that didn't know anything. "There is a good reason it remains a family matter. Why has your family not said anything to you? Your recklessness endangers many."

I hadn't thought about that. I was worried about being considered crazy by the modern world of psychiatrists. There would have been more pressing issues back then. Any kind of supernatural ability, especially in women, would classify them as witches. Witches didn't have a very good history.

"My mom died when I was a baby." I might have been more emotional, but I was busy connecting the dots. Every encounter with Laurent taught me more about myself. "My dad doesn't know anything about it."

The surprise on Laurent's face was such a drastic change from his angry impatience that I almost laughed. He looked between Ethan and me. "You are here because she calls you," Laurent said to Ethan. He was more thoughtful now. "She says you are not a *Rêvasseuse*. And even if you are, you cannot dream the same." He looked at me differently, apparently seeing something that he didn't see before. "*Alors, c'est toi*. You make this happen."

"A friend of my mom told me that my mom was one of the most powerful Woolgatherers she has ever met." I tried not to sound too proud, but it wasn't something I could brag about to many people, and he would appreciate what it meant.

Laurent nodded. "Perhaps you are even more powerful." He gestured at Ethan. "His presence here is evidence of that."

Chosen One

Laurent made time for us. I had too many questions, and he seemed to want to learn more about us.

"The Sarramauca has always been the greatest enemy of a *Rêvasseuse*. More so for the daughters, but even for the sons. We are *proie* to the monster. Helpless to the hunter."

Laurent's apartment lacked furniture. We were sitting on the floor. He refreshed his coffee, but neither Ethan nor I accepted any.

"I show you ways to prevent an attack, *oui* ?" he said to me, referring to the measures he had taken in his bedroom. "They are unproven, but it is all we have. Only death follows the Sarramauca." He swallowed more coffee. "But I live because of you. I have never heard of such before."

That was likely why he continued to entertain us despite being as disruptive as we had been. We had saved his life.

"How have you done this?"

Ethan and I exchanged looks. As Laurent should have come to expect, we didn't have answers. I shrugged. Laurent sighed. I think I solidified my reputation as the Idiot *Rêvasseuse*.

"What did you see when the Sarramauca had you?" I asked as respectfully as possible.

Laurent didn't look up. Shadows of memories darkened his face. He stared at his cup as he answered. "In the beginning, it was good. A perfect dream." He paused, swirled the coffee in his cup a little before he continued. "That is how it began. It is said that the Sarramauca can lure you into a perfect world. It knows … what you desire."

There was so much pain in his voice from the memory of a perfect dream that it sounded worse than a nightmare. Was a nightmare the worst you can imagine? Or was the real nightmare having everything you ever wanted taken away from you?

"I cannot recall when it happened. When my … dream was twisted. When the nightmares began." His hand was motionless; the coffee was no longer swirling in his cup. "I could not move. I saw the monster. I was scared and hopeless all at once. I felt the heaviness on my chest."

He looked up at us, and his eyes were red from unshed tears. "The heaviness on my heart."

I felt my own ache for him. Ethan held my hand. I leaned on his shoulder, grateful for his presence.

"But worse still," he continued, "*Je m'en fichais.*" He closed his eyes. "The monster won because I no longer cared whether I lived or died."

He opened his eyes. "You saved my life. I would be dead, but the Sarramauca left me for you. It let go, and I felt the desire to live again."

"It's like mind control," I mumbled. Ethan heard me clearly, and I felt him nod in agreement.

"I cannot allow myself to sleep while I stay." Laurent was beyond exhausted.

"You haven't slept at all?" I asked in surprise. It had been five days since the attack we'd interrupted. Sleep deprivation was a serious thing.

He shook his head. "Sometimes, I cannot help it." He held up his wrist. "I have an alarm. Every fifteen minutes if there is no movement." He let his arm fall. "I can sleep when I leave. I must leave."

"Does everyone leave?" Ethan asked. I had asked Laurent that before but Ethan hadn't been with me then.

"It is the only way that is known. We do not understand how the Sarramauca hunts, but every family that has lost a member to the monster always leaves to stay alive."

"Is that how your parents died?" I asked.

"*Non*. My father … he smoked." He pantomimed a cigarette. "It caused his cancer. My mother had a weak heart. Perhaps a broken one after my father."

"Not from the Sarramauca?"

"*Non*. There has never been an attack on my family. But my cousin's wife whispered of one. The family lived in Marseille. They have not returned."

"Will you ever come back here?" This place seemed to be important to him. It was preserved with care, and even in the rush of his packing, it was clear he was taking measures to shutter it properly. I didn't feel that way when we left Illinois for California, so I couldn't truly understand.

"One cannot know," he said. "Perhaps when I am much older." He smiled at me. It didn't reach his eyes. "Unless you find a way to stop it."

"Me?" I asked, my voice a little louder than I had intended. "Why me?"

"There has been no other like you. None that I have heard of." His eyes burned with a kind of hope suddenly realized. He gestured at Ethan. "You bring him. You interrupt the nightmare. You yourself say you are the daughter of the most powerful *Rêvasseuse*!"

"I didn't say *the* most powerful," I mumbled under my breath. My anxiety was rising, reaching new levels on the back of mounting expectations. I didn't like where this conversation was going. It was one thing to fantasize about it with friends who didn't know any better and a completely different thing when you hear it from someone who should know better.

"If you can stop this," Laurent insisted, half kneeling from his cross-legged position on the floor, "then, London, daughter of the most powerful *Rêvasseuse* …" He was crouched, leaning forward, more alive than I had ever seen him.

"Then you save us all."

Scooby Gang

"Feeling the pressure?"

We finally made it to the library after school the next day. I didn't often visit our public library, even if it was conveniently located just a couple of blocks from our school. Between the many after-school programs held for toddlers and teens, the library was a surprisingly noisy place. I preferred the park for silence. But the park didn't have books.

Brieann and Drew spent their lunch period at different committee meetings for the same big school event. The winter formal was consuming the school body like a virus. In the shadow of all that was happening in my life, a high school dance was insignificant. I felt detached. Not just from high school but from reality.

Had it not been for Brieann and Drew making time for me and my unconventional circumstances, I would have felt like an outsider again. The two of them were my feeble connection to normalcy. To sanity.

Drew's question was designed as an open-ended opportunity for me to elaborate. I took advantage of it.

"That's twice now that it's been suggested that I'm meant to do something about this." I was about a note away from what would qualify as a whine, which demonstrated clearly how I felt about the idea.

"How does Ethan feel about it?" Brieann added another four books to the center of the table. An almost imperceptible small cloud of dust escaped around the pile. Evidence of their neglect. Navigating the library catalog to find the literature we needed was another skill she could add to her growing résumé.

I reached for the book on the top of the stack. It was a hardcover, bound in fake red leather and embossed with fancy gold lettering. And if its appearance was not enough indication, it even smelled old. She must have reached deep into the reference shelves at the back of the building to find these.

"Can you guess?" I responded with a tinge of sarcasm. "He's always against anything that could potentially put me in danger."

She smiled. It was entirely expected of Ethan.

"I think it just added to his mounting dislike of Laurent," I added with a grin.

"I kinda agree with your Frenchie friend, though," Brieann said, sitting next to Drew and opening a book. "I mean, we thought the same thing. The evidence just points to it. Especially after that encounter with your dad's non-date."

I had told them all about Mae, including her ominous request to connect with me privately.

"Do you want us to come with you when you meet her?" Drew asked.

I hadn't contacted Mae right away. I wasn't sure if I was emotionally capable of handling more. But after crossing to Laurent again, I didn't think I should wait. I texted her before I even got out of bed. Her response was immediate, but she wouldn't be able to drive back up for another couple of weeks.

"Ask me again when we nail down the exact time. Right now, I feel like I'll be OK."

On the one hand, Mae would be an excellent source of information. We could potentially know more from her than all the literature piled on the table in front of us. On the other hand, I didn't want all my information to come from her. I didn't know if my feelings were a residual dislike of her when I thought she was dating my dad or if it was something else.

Brieann opened a new spiral notebook to the second page. "Well, we aren't waiting for her. Let's get to it." Brieann was never the type to sit on the sidelines when there was something she could actually do about it. "I think the best thing is to just write down everything relevant to anything resembling the monster. Then we can sort through it to identify weaknesses."

She spread out her set of multicolored highlighters with confidence. "We can do one color for traits, one for potential weapons, and another for things to watch out for."

Suddenly, all the seemingly useless lab work they made us do in school made sense. Brieann handled things like someone who was used to being in charge.

"Some of these are about witches, though," Drew observed. He tilted his head to the side to read the spines. "Not monsters."

"I got those to add to the London column."

"The London column?" I asked, wanting to know but also not wanting to know.

She grinned at my expression. "Frenchie said something about Woolgatherers being thought of as witches back in the witch-burning days, so I figured it wouldn't hurt." Brieann was very thorough.

"Being accused of witchcraft is super broad," I admitted. "They'd burn a woman just because she knew how to read." I shrugged. "I don't know how much helpful information we can collect from all that."

"Honestly," Brieann pointed out, "we're in the process of harvesting anything we can before we can really be choosy about where we look. I think as long as we focus on keywords like, I don't know … dreams? Nightmares? We won't be completely in the dark."

"I'll scour the internet," Drew volunteered. "You guys can handle the books."

"Works for me." I shrugged. I was never successful at navigating search engines.

"I bet we'll learn more from these than you do," Brieann challenged.

"You're on," Drew agreed. He took out his laptop and fired it up, intending to use it along with his phone.

Brieann winked at me. She was very good at motivating the troops. The *Scooby Gang* had nothing on these two.

Bunker

We spent the rest of the week visiting the library any chance we got to build our very own database on monster killing. Specifically, the Sarramauca.

Late Friday night, we were in my living room, collating all the information we'd collected. There were two slices left in the pizza box that we had ordered for dinner. Three open bags of various flavored chips were scattered around the room. Monster research was hard work, and it was important to be properly fueled for it.

I was polishing off a bag of chocolate chip cookies. Drew had an energy drink in one hand. Brieann was sipping a juice cleanse.

Ethan was on the phone.

"You won't believe how many books we went through," I was telling him. "Brieann and I totally won the contest."

"It was two against one," Drew complained.

"You weren't complaining when we started," Brieann pointed out.

"The internet let me down," he said instead, knowing that Brieann was right. "I was well ahead the first couple of days until every new link basically led back to the same blogs I already read."

Ethan smiled, but I could see the worry in his eyes. "What did you find out?"

Brieann held up her colorful notebook with pride. She had used the second half of it to summarize our findings. It was the best way we could make the supernatural more scientific.

"We found commonality between a lot of the stories, actually," she said. "Even in cultures that never had any connection with each other. The Filipino Bangungot seems very different from the German Alp until you realize that it's the cultural equivalent of, well, a kind of elf or faerie."

"I thought we were dealing with a shape-changing monster. Not a tiny insect with wings." Ethan was genuinely confused.

"No, no," Brieann clarified. "Faerie with an 'ae' not 'ai.' "

"There's a difference," I added. "What you're thinking of is a fairy. The one with 'ai.' Pretty, magical creatures with wings that usually live in the woods. A faerie with an 'ae' is more of a malevolent creature. A faerie can be an elf or a goblin."

"Both are immortal and difficult to kill, of course," Drew volunteered. "But there are suggestions. And not just for the *Elf on the Shelf* kind."

"How to kill an *Elf on the Shelf*?" Ethan repeated, amused.

"It was the first thing that popped up when I searched for the demise of elves. I guess it's a very popular subject."

"Were any of the suggestions helpful?"

"Fire was a favorite choice."

"Fire can be cleansing," Ethan agreed.

"I've always wanted a blowtorch."

"No one needs a blowtorch," Brieann jumped back in, setting the conversation back on track. "Cold iron was the predominant deterrent throughout the literature. It's supposed to leave the fae unprotected and without magic. That makes them vulnerable."

"Laurent had a dream catcher over his bed. He said it was infused with layers of magic. Not an easy item to find, though."

"Not to mention," Drew interjected, "more in the protection column, not the weapons column."

Brieann flipped the pages of her notebook and held up a spread that had been subdivided into columns. "I made columns," she said proudly to Ethan, holding up the notebook for him to see.

"What's in the weapons column?" Of course that would be what Ethan was most interested in.

"Other than cold iron?" Brieann brought the notebook down so that she could read it. "Oh, and not necessarily steel. Steel doesn't work as well. It has to be pure iron."

"Why not steel?"

"Well"—Brieann flipped through the pages—"the fae were mostly eradicated during the Iron Age, so maybe that's why iron? But the Iron Age was essentially just industrialization. There was *some* suggestion that any kind of industrialized weapon *should* be able to work."

"The Bangungot is described as a tree-dwelling type of fae, so the whole destroying nature works with that theory," I added.

"Drew is right with the fire," Brieann admitted reluctantly. Drew made a thumbs-up. "But it also came with the warning that it usually causes more damage than good. Like, it's more likely the fae will escape before the house burns down."

"Unless you have a blowtorch," Drew insisted. "Then you can aim it!" He pantomimed wielding such a weapon.

"Sound was a surprising weapon," Brieann continued, ignoring her boyfriend. "Like church bells ringing sort of thing. We can't figure out if it's the sound waves or if it has to do with the metal that the bells are made of …"

"In other words," I summarized, "we don't know if we can replicate it."

"Blowtorch," Drew said again. "Just saying."

"The Brazilian Pisadeira is described as wearing some kind of magical hat," Brieann read from her notes. "Like a red cap. And if you can get it away from it, then you can actually control the monster."

"There was no magical hat on our faerie's head." Ethan was sure of it.

"I don't remember one either," I admitted. "In the absence of a hat, if you know the 'real name' of the fae"–I made one-handed quotations in the air–"then you can control it."

"But that's almost impossible. We're not talking names like, I dunno, Bob. It's more like the Rumpelstiltskin variation." Drew had at least stopped pretending to wield a blowtorch. "Considering that it has a dozen species names in different countries, finding the name mommy monster gave it is highly unlikely."

"I wish it were Bob," I grumbled.

"Maybe you could bring all of us with you when you cross," Drew suggested lightly. "Then we can all read out names from a baby book at the same time, and maybe we'll get lucky. Aaron! Alexander! Agatha!"

I laughed at the visual. I could imagine all of us surrounding this horrible monster and just reading out random names. Brieann rolled her eyes.

"It's probably something we can't even pronounce," I guessed.

"Like Worcestershire?"

"I think controlling it might be a level too high up for us," Brieann reminded us. "We need to focus on stopping it."

I loved that she said *we*. Drew was right; I *was* feeling the pressure. I was never the type of person who wanted the spotlight. I was great in a supporting role. Even better behind the scenes. I never wanted to be the point person on anything. And now, I felt like it was all on me.

What I learned this past week was that no matter how big the burden, it was manageable when distributed among many shoulders. Brieann and Drew readily stepped up to help with the load. And I already knew that Ethan would not let me carry this alone.

Maybe it was the box of cookies I'd recently consumed or the five large cups of coffee I'd had throughout the day, but I was really feeling the emotional moment.

"I think we need to consider another obstacle," Ethan interrupted. "Whether we're talking about an iron knife or a blowtorch … how is London supposed to take that with her in a fight?"

The load was back on my shoulders.

"It should be possible," I said with more uncertainty than I wanted to project. "I mean, I'm never in my jammies when I cross, so it's not tied to what I'm actually wearing at the time."

"Yes," Ethan agreed. "But you don't control that."

"Maybe it's just a matter of practice? I can attempt to cross to you tonight and see if I can take something specific?" I looked around me to find some kind of inspiration. "Maybe my phone?"

"How about something smaller?" Brieann suggested. "Like the bracelet you're wearing?"

I looked at the bracelet that Ethan had given me, securely around my wrist. I hadn't yet crossed wearing it. Maybe because it was so new that my subconscious wasn't accustomed to it yet.

I nodded. "OK. It's smaller, already attached to me, and"–I shook my arm–"it's metal!"

"Not exactly a broadsword of iron …" Ethan observed.

"Or a blowtorch!" Drew piped in.

"But it's a good start." Ethan smiled. "And I do fancy seeing you wear it."

"Since we're tackling obstacles," Brieann interrupted, "another, lesser-known way to kill a fae of this sort is to make sure you attack the physical form and not just the dream form." She looked up from her notes. "That means that it might be unkillable if you encounter it when you cross. I mean, if what you encounter is its dream form and not its physical form."

"London can be hurt even at the place she's crossing to," Ethan said, a severe line replacing the smile.

Brieann shrugged. "Well, London isn't fae."

Ethan's frown deepened.

"Look," Brieann added, "I'm not saying that this is scientific fact. I'm just saying that this came from more than one source, so it's worth paying attention to." She looked apologetic. As if this was a rule she made up by herself. "Just so … you know … we aren't caught totally by surprise or something."

"Not liking the information isn't going to make it any less possible," Drew said, wrapping a protective arm around Brieann. She looked up at him with gratitude. He could always tell what she needed.

I watched this small display of affection with a tint of jealousy. I missed having that with Ethan. I missed that instant sense of asylum when he took me in his arms. How easily he could assuage my fears with a hug. How I felt in his tight embrace. I missed all that every time we had to make do with just a video call. A video call like this one.

Ethan was frowning, not necessarily because he was feeling the same way I was. Likely, it was because he was unhappy with the potential strategic disadvantage Brieann had introduced. "What's our next step?"

This was one of the changes that had happened to him since he joined the military. Pre-cadet Ethan didn't seem to have any long-term plans. He had believed that nothing he did made a difference. He didn't like the few options that were available to him, so he'd told me he didn't want to think too far into the future.

Being a part of something greater than himself gave him a different perspective. The military was teaching him how to think ahead. How to plan. Ethan was better for it.

"I guess it's on me," I said, feeling the weight. "I need to practice."

Drew grinned. "Enter training montage."

La Porte de la Mort

There was no time to train.

It was late morning. Maybe even noon. But the heavy curtains Laurent had kept pulled back during the day were closed, blocking the sunlight. He had completely shuttered his parents' home. He had finally left.

At least that's what I thought.

I was standing at the foot of the stairs. The boxed-up room was free of boxes. Further indication that he was gone. But there were bags by the front door. That was how I knew he hadn't left as I had originally thought. The bags.

Ethan was at the top of the staircase, wearing the same shirt he had on during our video call. He leaned over the banister and saw me, but something else also had his attention. Even with the distance between us, I saw his jaw tighten, and I knew it wasn't good news.

I looked down at my wrist, predictably empty. Brieann and Drew had left near midnight. By the time I got to bed, I didn't have it in me to even attempt. I figured my training montage could start tomorrow. That clearly wasn't the case.

I felt like I was constantly unprepared for the pop quizzes in my life.

Ethan's demeanor warned me to be careful. I zipped up my hoodie to keep it from flapping loose and snagging on something. Then I crept up the stairs, trying to close the distance between us quickly but quietly. My Chucks landed securely on the stairs runner and didn't make a sound. When I got to the top to join him, I immediately saw what had caught his attention.

Laurent's room was glowing again. The light was different this time. Dimmer. Cold. Unnatural.

Ethan looked down at my wrist, checking for the bracelet as I had. I shook my head. I wanted to tell him that I hadn't planned on being here. That I didn't think to attempt to practice yet. But it didn't seem like breaking the silence was a good idea.

Ethan gestured for me to stay behind. I shook my head again. Not because I was feeling particularly brave but because I didn't want to be separated from him. Besides, I was supposed to be the secret weapon against this thing.

He didn't appreciate my stubbornness, but he didn't try to argue. He pulled me behind him as we made our way down the empty hall. Our eyes adjusted to the darkness to the point where I could see the pattern on the hallway carpet.

We both heard the eerie sound of Laurent's moaning. Just as we had before. Possibly weaker. I wanted to exchange a look with Ethan, but his attention was focused ahead, and it wasn't wise to break that. He clenched and unclenched his right fist. Maybe it was because it was still weak, or maybe he wished it wasn't empty. Or both.

The sight that greeted us at the doorway was familiar but no less frightening. The Sarramauca was in the same position, holding Laurent down. But it looked different. No longer the imp it had been and more like a grotesque bull-like body with reddish skin and bumps in all the wrong places. Joints weren't where they should have been. Strands of short hair, like thick wires, grew on random areas of its body. Uneven bumps formed a ridge on its forehead, and pointed ears grew above its head. A demon.

Laurent was halfway off his bed, his left arm reaching vainly to the floor. I could barely make out the shape of his family's dream catcher, just out of reach. Its magic was not enough protection.

Laurent's eyes, red from lack of sleep, were open but unseeing. Sunken like his chest. He was collapsing under the weight of the attack.

The glow we saw was from Laurent himself. It pulsed in rhythm with his weakening breath, emanating from his open mouth like a smoke trail.

Ethan tensed. I saw his eyes dart around the room, looking for something to use as a weapon. Anything made of metal, at least. But Laurent had emptied the room save for the bed he was lying on, stripped of its sheets and the ineffective dream catcher.

I could swear that I didn't make a noise, but the Sarramauca turned our way anyway. Its lips twisted into a vile and sinister smile. A malevolent threat.

Our presence didn't interrupt it like the last time. It moved like it had been expecting us. It didn't immediately leave its perch. Instead, it settled into a deeper squat. It just stared at us, draining Laurent's life away while it smiled.

We weren't prepared. We didn't have a plan. All we could do was watch.

I was crying and didn't know it. Not the hysteria that would probably have been justified. The tears ran whimpering down my face, accompanied by a tremor that I could not control.

I thought I had been afraid before. At that moment, I knew I had been wrong. In the past, what I thought was fear was just anxiety. Anxiety of the unknowable future.

This was fear. The knowledge of a horrible fate and being unable to stop it.

When the last of Laurent's glow faded, the Sarramauca effortlessly stepped off his chest, dismissing the vessel of the life he had just consumed like the refuse it was to him. The bed groaned under the shifting weight, but Laurent was silent.

He was dead.

I stared at Laurent's lifeless body because, as horrible a sight as it was, it was still better than looking into the eyes of the monster. I had made that mistake before, and it had frozen me in place. I could not allow it to happen again.

Ethan squeezed my hand before moving away from me. I hesitated for the briefest moment before reluctantly letting go. This was a tactic to draw attention away from me. But it didn't work. I felt the void of the Sarramauca's eyes targeting me. The heaviness of every step it made as it got closer. Like a promise of the horror to come.

I was next.

I stepped to the other side of Ethan. My gaze went from staring at Laurent to the dream catcher on the floor. It wasn't iron, but it was magic. And it was all we had.

The Sarramauca's moves were deliberate. Slow steps, not unlike a lion closing in on its prey. Playing with its food. I wasn't a threat, and it seemed to be enjoying my helplessness.

I was already as good as dead just standing there. I needed to at least try.

I lunged at the dream catcher, my fingers wrapped around empty air and scraped the bare wood floor a couple of times before closing in around the delicate hoop. I skidded on my side, my shoulder hitting Laurent's cold arm. It didn't even register in my head how awful that sensation was. I didn't have the time.

I scrambled to my feet, backing up as I did. I heard Ethan yell. My sudden movements spurred the monster into action. It turned to face me, the smile growing into an open-mouthed, demonic laugh. It moved faster than before, but I had enough time to hold the magical artifact in front of me.

The Sarramauca looked solid, complete with mass and weight. The bed had sunk under its bulk. I felt every step it took, shaking the old floorboards. But my hand went through it, dream catcher and all, like it was nothing but a cloud. A chilling cloud that burned as it passed through me.

It was a shape-changing demon spirit. Able to project an abnormal force unbound by the laws of nature.

I was the chosen one destined to stop it. And I couldn't even touch it.

I froze for a moment, breathing hard from both the adrenaline and anticipation. The dream catcher hadn't worked, and I was out of possible moves. I scrambled to my feet, almost falling chin-first to the floor. I saw Ethan reaching to grab me when I felt something more than just chills on my neck. A painfully cold, sharp sensation. I spun around to face the demon, accidentally slamming right into Ethan. We both fell back into the doorway.

The Sarramauca was almost on top of us. Ethan rolled me off him, and I tumbled out the door. Before he could step between me and the monster, it was already past him and looming over me.

I scurried backward on my arms, not even feeling the floor scraping through my sleeves. I averted my eyes so I wouldn't look it in the face. And when the back of my head inevitably hit the banister, I closed my eyes tightly. I had a tight grip on Laurent's dream catcher. I held it over my face with one hand, looking for something to grip with the other. But there was nothing.

Ethan yelled my name.

I opened my eyes to look for him. If I was to die, I wanted him to be the last thing I ever saw. I hoped that when it was over for me, it would mean that he would be instantly sent back to safety.

The Sarramauca had its back to Ethan, completely dismissing him. Ethan instinctively reached for it, possibly hoping to distract it. I wanted to tell him to stop. Stop putting himself in any more danger. He was going to get hurt. He couldn't stop it if he couldn't even touch it.

But Ethan *did* touch it. His hand didn't go through it as mine had. He grabbed it by the top of one of its bulging arms.

The Sarramauca, clearly caught by surprise, howled a frightening sound. It turned away from me to face Ethan as if seeing him for the first time. Ethan's hand slipped off. He stepped back, making room between them to maneuver.

It snarled and snapped. Ethan crouched, backing slowly away. He wasn't looking directly at it. He was watching its feet, hoping to be able to anticipate its movements.

The Sarramauca was no longer toying with its prey. It was angry.

It reared back, rising to a height larger than it had ever looked before. And when the tips of its ears threatened to hit the ceiling, it let out a bloodcurdling scream.

It disappeared.

Fallout

"We need to get out of here," I croaked.

Ethan helped me up. "Are you OK?" he asked. He inspected the back of my arms, pulling up the sleeves of my thin hoodie. He frowned at the fabric burns that were tender and had already started to turn a shade of red. I tasted blood from where I had bitten my lip sometime during the altercation. I didn't even remember that happening.

I nodded. I was still holding Laurent's dream catcher tightly in my hand. I eased my grip and saw that it had left an indentation in my palm. One of the sharper precious stones had caused a nick. The leather around the hoop was coming loose. It was losing its shape.

I stepped toward Laurent's body, but Ethan held me back. "Don't touch him," he said.

I'd watched enough procedural shows on TV to know that he was right. Never touch the dead body. Or anything around it. And while I was seemingly compelled to do so, I also really didn't want to.

I sniffled. Unlike every Hollywood actress in every Oscar-nominated scene, I wasn't pretty when I cried. Puffy eyes, red nose, and unsanitary bodily fluids. I wiped my nose on the sleeve of my hoodie. I felt about as banged up as the generations-old artifact in my hand.

Ethan put his arm around me. I leaned on his chest, my eyes on Laurent. It wasn't a graceful demise. His eyes, empty in death, reflected the nightmares he had been subjected to. His body was broken. Already stressed by the events of this past week until, finally, spent. Seeing him like this, one might even think Laurent had never seen a happy day in his life. The scene would confuse the authorities. There would be questions and no answers. In the end, Ethan and I would be the only people in the world that would know exactly how he died.

I met Laurent at the worst point of his life. I didn't know him well at all, but I knew there was so much more to him than this. A lifetime that led to this. How unthinkable. Even after seeing him attacked, it didn't occur to me that he wouldn't be able to escape this. It didn't occur to me that he might actually die.

I wanted to throw up. Nauseated by everything that was not what it should be.

Ethan's expression was hard but stable. Not the bubbling mess that I was. This was gruesome. But just a few months ago, he had seen worse. He had seen friends gunned down. Not just strangers to him. He had watched so many people he allowed himself to care about violently killed.

He had been gutted already then. This was just another trauma to be locked away as he had the others. He'd had more practice coping with it. Or at least hiding it.

"We need to go," I repeated. Ethan didn't point out that I was the one loitering. "It might return."

I was saying it aloud for my sake. Not his.

I took a last look at what was left of Laurent, felt the bile in my throat, then turned away. I held on to Laurent's dream catcher. Ethan and I walked hand in hand to the front door.

"Hang on." I stopped by the bags. A winter coat lay on the top of a duffle. I took the coat and handed it to Ethan. Laurent was leaner but about the same height. It should fit. It was a dead man's coat. He would no longer have use for it.

Winter in France may not be as rough as the Midwestern winters I grew up with, but it was much colder than in California. Ethan was dressed for summer in his military-issued undershirt and green pants. My fault, I'm sure. It was the last thing I saw him wearing. He put Laurent's coat on. It wasn't a perfect fit, but it worked.

I unzipped the duffle and dug into it a little until I found a thick sweater. I held it in my hand, reflecting on who it belonged to, then I pulled it over my thin hoodie. It looked like I was wearing an oversized sweater dress with my jeans. It wasn't the best fashion statement, but at least it would keep me warm.

I lingered in the doorway even after Ethan opened the door. It felt wrong to leave Laurent like that. Ethan squeezed my hand, understanding my hesitation and also silently urging me forward. I looked up at him, taking courage from the strength in his eyes. He smiled. Tight, grim, and controlled.

This silent exchange, where so many things were left unsaid, echoed loud regrets in steeled hearts.

The Paris air was warmer than I expected for January. Cold enough to need a coat but warm enough to leave it open. Ethan shut the door behind us as soon as we were clear of the threshold. We both stood there, just outside Laurent's door, uncertain of what to do next.

It was overcast, but the light was a contrast from how dark Laurent's place had been with all the curtains drawn. While we weren't standing on a busy street, city sounds that had been muted from the inside were all around us. An elevated train, much like I was familiar with in Chicago, rumbled through unseen in the distance. There was music playing from somewhere, punctuated by the noise of traffic and overlapping voices from scattered conversations. Foreign but otherwise indistinct.

It was a world completely detached from the upheaval we had just witnessed.

"How long before you cross again, do you think?" He asked the question without looking at me. He was still absorbing our alternate surroundings.

He knew as well as I did that there was no real way of knowing. He asked anyway. Maybe the universe would listen if we asked it aloud. I fought back tears. My emotions were all over the place, and I didn't have the tools to contend with them properly.

"I've never been to Paris," I said, my voice strangely flat. The complete opposite of the turmoil I was feeling.

"The only time I've ever been out of my country was to be with you." It was his roundabout way of agreeing with me.

Had circumstances been different, I might have wanted to explore. I might have wanted to steal the opportunity to have a croissant. A genuine French macaron. Maybe actually see the famed Eiffel Tower.

We had just watched an unstoppable monster literally drain the life of a human being. A fellow Woolgatherer.

What I wanted to do was hide.

I looked down at the dream catcher I had taken. What useless magic this was. This should have protected him. This should have kept the evil at bay. At least until he got away. This failed him.

I failed him.

I stared at the damaged talisman with an accusation that was fueled by all my anger and fear. My vision blurred from the tears that finally broke free. The perfect lines that made the inner web wavered. The tears came hard and fast, distorting my already unfocused world.

When it cleared, I was home.

Ethan wasn't with me. He presumably returned safely back to New Zealand. A long nightshirt had replaced the layers I was wearing. There were stars outside my window, not the late morning sun. Suburban quiet instead of city noise.

And in my clenched hand, Laurent's enchanted dream catcher. The asabikeshiinh.

Armor

"Maybe that's its magic," Drew suggested. "It can cross with you."

The mood had been bleak all morning. Both Brieann and Drew had come by after breakfast. Ethan, exhausted after last night's interrupted sleep, didn't have time to get on a call for very long before his duties began. I had to share recent events with my friends alone.

We had been flippant after the first nightmare. Laurent was a random stranger then, and we had no idea how serious the situation was. Or even how real.

Our perceptions had since changed. Not just on Laurent but on the danger involved. We had begun this thinking that we had a divine chance of vanquishing a supernatural creature. Victory seemed unreachable now, and my survival was the more immediate goal.

"A lot of good it does," I spat bitterly, still directing my grief to the inanimate object so I didn't have to absorb it myself.

"What if it follows it?" Brieann asked. I had left the dream catcher on the kitchen counter between us. Drew picked it up to study it closer, but Brieann refused to go near it. Laurent had died under its supposed sanctuary. It wasn't a shield. It was a curse.

"What am I supposed to do with it?"

It didn't seem right to discard it. Even less to destroy it. I didn't know how old it was, but it was a family heirloom of some kind. Wasting it seemed like wasting Laurent.

"I don't know," Brieann admitted, hugging her arms around herself. It was a reflection of how uncomfortable she was. "Maybe keep it in another room? Surround it with metal or something."

"If it's any consolation," Drew said more to Brieann than to me, "we didn't see anything in our research suggesting that. It was only really mentioned as protection in all forms of folklore."

The idea that our research meant anything was laughable. We weren't a generously funded foundation run by historians and experts. We hadn't spent an academic career studying the innuendos of culture and language to interpret anything remotely accurately. We were privileged, sheltered high school kids looking through generic, severely underfunded public library material and filtering through rants on the internet. We picked out what we wanted to believe and left out anything that might support otherwise. It wasn't research. It was an elective after-school project.

"The truth is," I admitted, defeated by the facts we didn't want to face, "we don't know anything."

Drew nodded, knowing I was right but hoping to have rallied me otherwise.

"What if she puts it over her bed like he did and it doesn't ward away the … the …" It wasn't that Brieann didn't remember what it was called. It was that she didn't want to say it. "The … thing," she finished, for lack of a better word. "What if it calls it? Like a beacon. What if that's actually the reason he's dead?"

I picked up the asabikeshiinh by the sharper end of the hoop. The leather bindings were coming loose, and the web inside, once taut, was sagging a little. I didn't know if the damage happened before or after I had grabbed it so roughly.

"It doesn't *feel* malevolent." It was a strange thing to say. I didn't really know what I meant by it. How does an inanimate object not feel malevolent? Because it was lacking a fiendish red glow? Because it wasn't smoldering with the fires of hell? It wasn't as if I had any frame of reference.

Brieann twirled a strand of her hair around her finger. She kept her chin down and her eyes lowered. I couldn't tell exactly what she was feeling, but I had an idea. She had been the one to insist that I was special. She had been the one to build on the idea that we could discover a weakness that generations of Woolgatherers in multiple cultures had not discovered. She felt responsible for this defeat. She felt guilty.

I put the asabikeshiinh down and walked around the counter so that I could be next to her. She was one of my best friends, and she didn't deserve this. I leaned my head against her shoulder, and she leaned her head on mine. Our tacit display of solidarity.

"What does Ethan think?" Drew asked.

I sighed. "What you would expect. Leave well enough alone. Stop crossing. Stay safe." I sat on one of the kitchen stools. I was physically tired from lack of sleep, but it wasn't nearly as bad as how weary I was mentally. "Essentially, don't poke the bear."

"He's probably right," Drew agreed. "And maybe consider some extra protection?" He indicated the talisman in question with the tilt of his chin.

"A whole lot of good it did Laurent."

But as Laurent had pointed out before, what else was there to do? Was I supposed to move now too?

"What's under the protection/prevention column, Bree?" Drew leaned on the counter, intent on finding solutions instead of complaining like I was.

Brieann scowled at him. She must have thought that he was teasing her. He lifted his eyebrows and waited, letting her know that he was serious. She grudgingly fished for the notebook in her bag.

"Supposedly, there are protection spells." She didn't sound very convinced.

"We're doing witchcraft now?" I asked. Not that it mattered. I was unwilling to accept any solutions. I was still busy wallowing in the problem.

"You're a Woolgatherer. You're the one that reminded us that being called a witch can mean anything from being a woman that's able to read to being cast in *Hamlet*," Drew pointed out.

"You mean *Macbeth*," Brieann interjected.

"What?" Drew stopped short of what had been the beginnings of what would have been a convincing argument for witches.

"I don't think there are witches in *Hamlet*," she clarified. "I think that involved a ghost. There are three witches in *Macbeth*, though. I think that's what you mean."

He blinked at her, completely off his momentum. "I didn't say *Macbeth*?"

She smiled. I understood. Drew could be cute when he was confused. "You said *Hamlet*. But we know you meant *Macbeth*," she added kindly. "We took *Macbeth* in English Lit last year. We're taking *Hamlet* this semester. That's probably why you said *Hamlet*."

He smiled back at her, apparently momentarily distracted by how she looked at him over what she was actually saying. Then he shook his head slightly as if to reorient himself. "Yeah, *Macbeth*. Anyway, my point was that just because it's a 'spell,' " he said, making quotations in the air, "it doesn't mean that it's witchcraft."

"Drew is right," Brieann added. "In fact, protection spells predate the written word. It's considered one of the most basic types of magic." She gave me a side glance. "And don't you always say that you and Ethan are magic?" She winked.

The speed with which she went from suspicious and sulky to teasing and giddy was enough to give me whiplash. I rolled my eyes, but I preferred Brieann this way.

"Fine," I conceded, convinced more by her change of disposition than anything else. "What would I need?"

She read through the list. We got to work.

By the end of the day, we had moved my bed so that my head pointed south and my feet pointed north. Laurent's battered asabikeshiinh hung over my bed. Brieann had placed a copper mug filled with clean water on the nightstand. The mug was taken from a set of four meant for drinks that Dad never drank. They were stored in the back of one of the higher kitchen cabinets. She covered it with a clean cloth handkerchief with instructions that I was to change out the water every night before I went to sleep.

"And make sure you wash your feet with lukewarm water to clear your dreams," she read from her notebook.

"I have cloves of garlic under my pillow," I complained. "I'm going to be sleeping on it all night. It's going to make me smell like mashed potatoes or something by morning."

"Mmm," Drew teased. "Garlic mashed potatoes. Yummy."

"Not helpful," I growled. "Am I warding off vampires with this?"

"Vampires might be considered elves in some cultures. So …" He shrugged.

"Garlic is universally recognized for its protective power against evil. Vampires or otherwise," Brieann corrected. "From East to West and through the centuries, it was used to guard the home against the intrusion of evil and bad luck. Even bad weather. It's not just against vampires."

"Between the garlic and the random herbs you've left by my window, I feel like I'm being seasoned for the stupid thing." I sat on my bed with much more force than necessary.

"I think live plants would be better than dried," Brieann admitted. "But this is what we have. I'd rather go overboard layering you with protection than … than …" Her eyes were suddenly filled with tears.

That was when I realized just how frightened she was. Not of the monster itself but losing me to it. My stomach sank. They were both doing their best to keep me safe to the best of our limited abilities with bits and pieces of lost folklore, and I was ungratefully throwing a tantrum like a four-year-old that wanted to play in traffic.

Drew got to her before I could even get up. He pulled her into a hug, and she sobbed on his shoulder. He looked over her head at me, his expression blameless but also disappointed. My self-centeredness was making it harder for everyone.

I got up slower than I should have. I put a hand lamely on her shaking shoulder. Feeling how upset she was, in addition to seeing it, made it worse. I was such a bad friend.

"I'm sorry," I mumbled. "You're right, of course. And I appreciate everything. I'm just being stupid."

She wiped her tears. She pulled off the delicate cry. Instead of the soggy mess that I seem to always devolve into, she was vulnerable while maintaining dignity and grace. If I didn't already love her, it would be so easy to hate her.

"I don't like not being prepared," she admitted. Whether it was planning for one of her private parties or a school event, she always covered the bases. There were contingencies in place for everything from the food to the first aid kits. It was bad enough that we were dealing with things beyond our experience, but this was beyond reality as we knew it. Her anxiety must have been off the charts.

"I promise to follow all our newly established routines," I assured her. She nodded, temporarily pacified.

"Keep us in the loop. Every little thing," Drew insisted. "The well checks you will have to endure from us will be obnoxious, but that's the price you pay for being loved." Brieann nodded emphatically, standing by her man.

I rolled my eyes, but I was smiling. My introverted, independent self might feel suffocated by the attention, but I very much appreciated the friendship.

Brieann hugged me. "And I'll say an extra prayer for you before bed," she whispered in my ear.

The Sarramauca might be an all-powerful bogeyman, but I had my friends. And garlic. I thought the odds were on my side.

Routine

Popular belief is that it takes twenty-one days before a new behavior becomes a habit. Psychologists would argue that, on average, it's closer to sixty-six days. I was willing to swear from personal experience that it is less than seven.

It had been a week since Laurent's death. I had followed every one of Brieann's instructions before bed. Including the mandatory half-hour of meditation she made me do to clear my chakra. The recording of waves and soft chimes she wanted me to listen to was exactly thirty minutes long so that I wouldn't cheat. By Thursday, I had the routine down to factory efficiency.

Our combined efforts were successful. So far. And though it also meant I wasn't crossing to see Ethan, he was much happier with this arrangement.

"It's not that I don't want to be able to kiss you," he assured me in almost every conversation. "But this is safer."

"I know, I know." I resolved to be less bratty about everything. It wasn't his fault that there was a soul-eating monster hunting Woolgatherers, and it was unfair to take my frustrations out on him. "This is temporary. Death is more permanent."

It wasn't his fault, but he looked apologetic anyway. And the way his eyebrows scrunched together as he lifted them up made him all the more adorable. It was easy to forgive him for the atrocities of the world. Real or otherwise.

That didn't mean it made it any easier to be apart. Winter formal fever was ramping up like a bad infection. Not only was I immune, but knowing that I couldn't take Ethan with me further inoculated me from the Blizzard Ball bug. Nothing can make someone feel more alone than being in a group of couples.

"Only in California would you find people so excited to get hypothermia," I commented to Drew over lunch.

The cafeteria was peppered with all sorts of hyped-up promotions, as if anyone needed reminding. Beyond the standard hand-drawn posters, streamers of crepe paper in blue and white were strung across the room. Coffee filter snowflakes hung down at irregular intervals. I imagined this is what it would be like to have a meal on the stage of a middle school play. This was just the lead-up to the event, not even the dance itself. That was going to be downright obnoxious.

Drew grinned but didn't comment. Brieann was on the events committee and fully immersed in all the preparations. The ball was her baby, and he wasn't going to risk Mama Bear's wrath. Even if she wasn't physically present at the table.

"Here are your tickets, Drew." Amanda stopped by our table. Never alone, Raven was by her side, playing on her phone. Both had been key players in Brieann's old posse pre-Drew.

I'd maintained a neutral relationship with Raven. We didn't have very much to say to each other nor the desire to change that. There was no reason to make a connection one way or the other. She was just another girl that I went to school with. Neither a friend nor otherwise.

I couldn't say the same for Amanda. My stomach turned as it always did in her presence. Amanda liked to find ways to ruin my day like it was part of her routine. I never knew how I ended up as her favored focus of foulness. Maybe it was fodder for her mean girl mask. It was what kept her makeup perfect every day.

I didn't like the confrontation, so I kept to myself, always hoping to slide under the radar. I was never successful.

"Ah, there you are, London," she said, looking me up and down with more scrutiny than airport security. "It's such a treat to see you. So dependable." She cocked her head very slightly, and the edges of her lips curled up just enough to make it clear that what sounded like a compliment was exactly the opposite. Amanda had mastered the art of backhanded compliments. It wasn't just what she said. It was when she said it. It was how she said it, with just the right amount of sweetness to know it was going to make you sick.

"It must be vintage clothing Friday today." The pause after that statement hadn't settled when she added, "Or was that yesterday?" The smile was almost imperceptibly wider. "Sometimes it's hard to tell when you wear the same thing every day."

There was the punchline. I rolled my eyes but didn't want to add ammunition to her already fully loaded arsenal.

"You must be so excited about the dance," she continued. "It will give you an opportunity to glam yourself up." She tossed her hair back with mock indifference. I thought that would be the end of it when she and Raven started to walk away, but I should have expected more. They took three steps before she looked over her shoulder just to say, "I'm sure you'll be able to find a date in time."

Their exit didn't leave an opportunity to respond, ensuring that she would have the last word. Not that it mattered. I would stay up later in the night thinking about smart comebacks, but at that moment, I had nothing.

I wish it didn't affect me. It was petty, and I knew it. I would have thought that knowing would be enough for me to get over it, but my mind and my emotions didn't always agree on the final destination.

Drew picked up the tickets that Amanda had used as an excuse to saunter by. "Category 5 hurricanes leave less destruction in their wake," he commented. He tried playing down the encounter in an attempt to minimize the sting. I grabbed the safety line as he intended. It helped me save face.

"She's just an effing ray of sunshine," I agreed. "You'd think I would've fallen off her radar now that I'm not taking up real estate at her lunch table anymore."

"Maybe she's not getting enough calories up there." He made wide circular motions around his head. "She's probably just confused."

"Oh, she's something," I mumbled just as Brieann joined us. She placed her tray of fresh fruit in front of her and a stack of colorful papers and folders next to it.

"Who is?" she asked, kissing Drew on the cheek before sitting down.

Drew held up the dance tickets in his hands. No verbalization needed. Brieann grimaced. "Fun," she said sarcastically. "I'm sorry, London. Amanda is in charge of ticket sales, so there's no getting around it." She picked up her plastic spork and began to eat. She had spent half the period in a committee meeting. This was what she considered shoveling food into her mouth, and it was still more refined than me at a formal dinner.

I shrugged. "There's something strangely comforting about being annoyed by her attitude again."

"That's how Stockholm syndrome starts," Drew warned. He had the knack for de-escalating a situation.

"No chance of that." I laughed. "I consider it more like a Devil-You-Know scenario." He understood, but Brieann looked at me expectantly, waiting for further explanation. "A week ago, I watched a fellow Woolgatherer get his life literally squeezed out of him. I couldn't care less what Amanda is up to. If she's what qualifies as a bad day for me these days, then I'm better for it." I shrugged. "Perspective."

Brieann tapped her spork on the side of her plastic bowl. It didn't make a clear noise, but she always did things like that for the repeated motion, not for the sound it made. "I wish you'd talk to someone about the trauma you experienced. These things leave invisible scars on your psyche."

"I'd more likely be misdiagnosed than receive any real help." It didn't sound like it, but I actually agreed with her. I felt the open wounds of trauma. The increased anxiety. The heightened emotions. I wished I knew how to process it properly. I wished I knew if I was actually coping successfully or sliding down the cliff toward a complete mental break.

"What am I supposed to tell a therapist?" I scoffed. "I dream crossed to Paris and watched a mythical creature sit on a guy to death?"

Brieann pursed her lips to the side in a way that I'd come to learn meant she knew I could do better if I tried. She had mastered the art of the disappointed look. She was going to make a great parent someday.

"I just think it'll complicate things," I said in a kinder tone, hoping to pacify her. "I'll have to make do with the two of you."

"And Ethan," she reminded me as if he wasn't already always on my mind.

"And Ethan," I repeated, but I felt a pang in my heart when I said his name. Ethan was always a source of comfort, but his absence was another point on the falling graph of my discontent.

"You should come with us to the dance," Brieann suggested, inspired.

I laughed at the absurdity of the idea. "How romantic," I replied sarcastically. "Is there a third wheel discount available for tickets?"

Brieann first looked at Drew for confirmation. He shrugged, letting her run with the idea. Her excitement ramped up. "For real, though, it will be fun!"

I looked at Drew, surprised that he was on board with this. Brieann was his first serious girlfriend. They had just started dating. This dance would be the first big event that they would attend together as a couple. "You think this is a good idea?"

"Pod people," he replied. He wasn't referencing the Jack Finley novel but rather, his own personal philosophy on instant connections. A notion he had shared with me during the unveiling of his mural last year. It sounded cryptic, but it was efficient. In two words, he reminded me how much he valued all his relationships, romantic or otherwise.

I wasn't convinced. "Going alone seems like providing Amanda with more material for her to use on her continuing anti-London campaign."

"You won't be alone," Brieann insisted. "You're going with us!" She looped one arm through Drew's elbow and leaned on his shoulder. They made such a cute couple.

"That's really not how dates work."

"You should go for us," Drew said wisely. "Not stay home for Amanda."

Well played.

I was even more annoyed that he knew he had won the argument. He grinned while Brieann kissed him again on the cheek, a victor's reward. Insufferable.

"You're both insufferable," I complained.

Drew winked. "Insufferably right."

Blast from the Past

Drew and Brieann had offered to come with me to meet Mae. They said it was for moral support, but I had suspicions that Brieann had questions of her own she wanted answering. She liked to receive her information straight from the source. Drew was probably equally curious but would never admit it.

Either way, I went alone. Mae had requested it that way. It was an easy enough plea to ignore if I wanted company, but I didn't want it. My friends had already invested so much. Their worlds did not revolve around me. I needed to learn to face my fears alone.

I waited for Mae at the same picnic table my friends and I like to occupy when we visit the park. Ethan and I had escaped here for privacy before. It wasn't a particularly secluded spot, and it was surrounded by open space. The accessibility and the fact that it was so public was what made it conversely discreet.

And easy enough to find for someone who wasn't necessarily familiar with the area.

The thick hoodie I had on was enough to keep me warm. It felt more like fall to the Midwesterner in me. Locals sported full-on winter coats and scarves. Winter meant something different to them. It also meant that the park was empty on a Sunday afternoon.

I knew Mae must have grown up in Chicago. It wasn't so much the fitted sweater she had on but the missing coat that meant she wasn't too concerned about the temperature. She carried with her two covered paper cups. Light steam rising from the small openings indicated they were hot. She put one of the covered paper cups in front of me.

"If you're anything like your mother, you take yours with caramel." She sat across from me, unconcerned about how the painted wood bench may dirty the designer jeans she had tucked into tall boots. "Edina loved caramel."

I felt a fierce sense of triumphant defiance in being able to prove her wrong but also a sadness that she wasn't right. "Actually, I like my coffee black."

Her smile faltered, and I instantly felt guilty. "But I like flavored coffee beans, so this should be fine," I amended, taking the offered cup into my hands. Despite the corrugated cardboard meant to protect your hands from burning, I felt the welcome heat. I took a sip from the little opening to prove that I was being sincere.

The strong aroma ribboned under my nose before the hot liquid touched the tip of my tongue. I've learned from painful experience that the first sip should always be a metaphoric toe dip into the shallow end of the pool before full immersion. Not so much to gauge flavor but to assess temperature. I'd burned my tongue on many occasions before this important life lesson was fully imprinted on my brain. I took a deeper drink to fully enjoy the sensation of warmth going down my throat. I liked my desserts sweet, but I liked my coffee bitter. Fortunately, the added caramel was liquid flavoring and not the thick syrup used over ice cream. It made it easier to go down without the sugary aftertaste. "Thank you," I said, putting the cup back down and feeling the heat radiate through the rest of my body.

She looked grateful for my acceptance. She didn't say anything right away, but the way she looked at me said plenty. It wasn't readily clear to me what those things were, but micro changes in her expression meant a rush of memories and all the emotions such memories carried with them.

"I'm glad you decided to reach out to me. Now that you're of age, there's so much you need to know."

That sounded cryptic. "Like what?" I took another sip to help hide my anticipation. I wanted to feign disinterest, but the fact that I had sought her out was already an obvious indication otherwise.

"Like who your mother was."

I held my cup with both hands. Not for warmth. Not to keep it steady. But to hold my arms close to my body. To physically pull myself together in case I fell apart. I straightened my back and squared my shoulders. And with great, deliberate intention, I looked unblinking into her dark eyes.

"Tell me," I demanded.

Where It All Began
November 1982

Edina pulled her shoulder-length chestnut hair up in a high ponytail. She used the scrunchy on her wrist to secure it in place. The purple elastic was the same shade as the pocket T-shirt she wore under her oversized denim overalls. She shook her head, as she did whenever she let go of the elastic. She did that every time. Maybe it was to test if the style would hold. Maybe it was the satisfaction of feeling the ends of her hair swing about. Maybe it was just a compulsion. Edina may have never considered it herself.

Nora watched from the doorway of their shared dorm room. She didn't ask either. It was just something her best friend did, and she accepted that. There were a lot of things that Edina did that surprised her, even after two years of cohabitation.

Nora tucked an errant lock of her own light hair behind her ear to keep it in place. It would defy her again in minutes, but for the moment, it held. She'd had the same hairstyle since her freshman year. She should have been in her third year of college, but she'd switched majors after she met Edina. Not only were they roommates, but they also shared a number of classes together.

It was more than that. Nora was part of a large, tight-knit family. No siblings but plenty of sibling-like cousins. Holidays meant full houses and loud gatherings. Every kid was a cousin, and every adult was either an aunt or an uncle. It didn't matter. She was used to being part of a whole. There was never a time when she would have thought of herself as alone.

Until she met Edina. And suddenly, she realized just how lonely she had been before. The longer they were friends, the stronger their bond. Almost like it reached backward in time, retroactively making them friends since birth. It was no wonder that although they looked nothing alike, people often mistook them for siblings.

"Dr. Michaels is going to lock the door on us if we're late again," Nora reminded her in a deadpanned tone. Edina smiled, unperturbed by the threat.

"Dr. Michaels can bite me." She was confident but was ready to go anyway. She hooked the strap of her brightly colored nylon bag over one shoulder. "We're not even late. He likes to start before he's even supposed to."

She took a tube of cherry-flavored Chapstick and swiped it over her lips, capped the tube and tossed it into her bag. It slid to the very bottom, joining a handful of loose coins, and half a ticket stub, to be lost until she emptied the bag at the end of the semester. "Edward is picking me up after class." Her smile was coy and playful.

Nora rolled her eyes. "Don't act like it's some grand gesture for your boyfriend to walk over and join us like he'll be riding some glorious white horse. His class is down the hall from ours."

Edina wasn't fazed by Nora's cynicism. She licked her lips, enjoying the sweet taste of artificial fruit. "I don't care if he bounces by on a pogo stick. As long as I get to see him."

"You were literally with him all last night." Nora lifted her left hand to indicate the oversized watch wrapped around her wrist. She didn't look at it. She was just making a point. "It's been, what? Five hours? What time did you get back?"

Edina grinned. She didn't answer the question. "Every moment away is a lifetime." She brought her hands to her chest, closed her eyes, and spun around in the exaggerated melodramatic flair that defined her.

Nora was used to this. She shook her head and watched her animated friend saunter by. Cloud Nine was an invisible thing unless you were Edina in love.

Nora locked the door behind them both. The dorm building was a relatively safe place on campus, but Nora was from the city. In the city, doors are always locked. Otherwise, you invited misfortune.

They walked down the hallway of uniformed doors obnoxiously decorated by the occupants of uniformed rooms in an attempt to express a sense of individuality. The administration frowned upon the practice but did nothing to discourage it. If the worst these young adults, drunk with hormones and newly found independence, did was superglue glow-in-the-dark items on their doors, it was an acceptable compromise.

They made it to the main entrance of the building before Mae, one of Nora's older cousins, stopped them. The look on her face suggested that whatever she had to say was worth being locked out of their industrial design analysis class.

She didn't have to say anything. The best friends followed her into the adjacent front room meant to greet guests. There were no guests.

"Betty is dead," Mae blurted as soon as Nora closed the door behind them. She didn't even give Nora time to turn around.

"Betty?" Edina asked. "Betty, your cousin, Betty?"

Mae didn't respond, but she didn't have to. Edina had never met Betty, but both Nora and Mae had spoken about their younger cousin often. She had just turned seventeen. She had just completed her first crossing.

The question was largely rhetorical. Edina knew who she was.

"What? When?" Nora was much more affected by the news. The little color in her face had paled, washing out her features while also emphasizing the green in her eyes.

"Last night," Mae responded mechanically. Anything more might have been too much.

Nora was feeling too much already. She sat down on one of the fancy chairs strategically placed to impress the parents of incoming freshmen. It wasn't a comfortable chair. That wasn't its purpose. It was a statement piece. It was there to assure parents that the thousands that they were spending on their child's housing was a quality investment. Much like their college education. Pretty to look at but not always well suited for the purpose it was intended.

Nora didn't care either way. It was what caught her when her legs no longer kept her upright.

"It's real," Nora said. She hadn't meant to sound so absolute, but it was, nonetheless.

"But that's not possible," she whispered, contradicting herself almost immediately. Her eyes had lost focus, caught somewhere between a dream and reality. "It can't be."

"She died in her sleep," Mae confirmed. "It had to be."

Edina looked between the two of them. Anyone else may have been lost in the conversation, but she knew Nora well enough to hear what was unsaid. And sharp enough to understand.

Mae was watching Nora carefully. Protectively.

Mae was always protective. Her father and Nora's mother were siblings. The cousins grew up together, living on the same block. Mae was at the hospital when Nora was born. She was Nora's favorite cousin. They got into trouble together when they were younger. They got each other out of trouble when they were in high school. They hated the same boys and had crushes on the same boys. They were best friends before Edina arrived.

Edina was Nora's previously undiscovered spiritual half. When Mae found out that the friends crossed together, she understood immediately that their connection was special. Crossing together was unheard of. It was undeniably powerful. There was no competing with that.

Mae stepped aside and watched her younger cousin's bond with her new best friend empower them both. It was something to behold. She might never admit that she was jealous, but she would admit that their friendship was unparalleled. She took consolation in the fact that even though they may grow apart, they would always be family.

Nora's eyes were filled with tears, washing out the color and turning them reflective. The denial had passed, and she was falling just as quickly into anger. Her speech was guttural, coming from the depths of grief and loss. She was looking at Edina when she spoke. "We need to stop it."

It was an impossibility. It was always an impossibility. But caught up in the tragic emotion brought about by devastating news so spartanly delivered, the impossibility was not out of reach. Not only was it suddenly within their grasp, but it was also there to be choked into submission.

Edina met Nora's resolve with her own, seeing her determination reflected in the shine of Nora's tears and letting that strengthen her.

"We will," she assured her grieving friend. "Or die trying."

Obsessions
May 1983

What followed was a slurry of alternating tears, emotion, soul searching, and plenty of late-night screaming. The hours ticked by with unmarked transitions. It could have been one very long day. A day that lasted months. A year.

Mae's and Nora's families had suffered a tragic loss. The kind that was unfathomable … until it wasn't. The kind that always happened to someone else … until it happened to you.

Doctors called it Nocturnal Death Syndrome. Woolgatherers called it a Sarramauca attack. A monster that hunted dreamers.

The Sarramauca was a myth. Stories of a boogeyman that parents would tell their Woolgathering children to curb misbehavior of any kind.

Eat all your veggies or the Sarramauca might come for you.

Clean your room or the Sarramauca will make it its den.

Go to sleep or the Sarramauca will keep you awake.

It wasn't real beyond the imagination of fearful children. Or it shouldn't have been.

But when something happens like what had happened to Betty, then the whispers come alive. The doubt sets in. And there is never any concrete evidence to support any claims. Except there was no other explanation. It was a diagnosis of exclusion.

Betty's family moved almost immediately. It could have been interpreted as a way for her parents to cope after losing their only child, but the families knew better. They moved because it was the only way to prevent another loss. History chronicled stories of entire families lost under mysterious circumstances. The theories ranged from carbon monoxide poisoning to curses. Woolgatherers were superstitious when it came to the Sarramauca. There was no reason to take chances.

Nora had always been fascinated by the legends. Up until she lost Betty, she had approached the idea of the Sarramauca as one might want to prove the existence of Big Foot or the Loch Ness Monster. Ghost hunting for Woolgatherers.

It wasn't supposed to be dangerous. It wasn't supposed to be real.

Betty's death shook their entire family. It fueled Nora's conviction. What had begun as a hobby turned into compulsive fanaticism. She spent more time flipping through books and interviewing relatives than she did studying for her degree. And she took Edina with her.

"This is hopeless," Mae had declared so many times over the past year that she had lost count. Her voice echoed in the empty university library hall. She had joined the friends in their fervent quest. Not so much because she believed in it but because she hoped to save them from the vacuum of obsession.

"You don't have to be here," Nora had responded just as many times. Her hair had grown long, tied in such a low ponytail that it almost looked like it wasn't tied at all. Stray strands fell around her ears. The long nights and restless sleep had darkened her eyes unnaturally. They weren't just tired; they were haunted.

Nora hadn't crossed in a year. The family had cautioned against it. But even when it felt safer, she found that she didn't want to anyway. What had once been a source of joy was now a sharp reminder of the life that was taken because of it. She was forever changed.

Edina laid a hand on Nora's shoulder in quiet admonishment. Edina's carefree spirit had been sobered but enough remained for her to be the constant moderator between embittered Nora and the rest of the world. "Of course she has to be here. Betty was family." As if Nora needed reminding. And maybe she did.

Edina had continued to cross. She had no direct ties to Nora's family, so it was no more dangerous than before. But crossing without Nora wasn't as much fun. The frequency of her crossings dropped dramatically.

Nora didn't apologize, but the slump in her shoulders was her unspoken remorse. Mae did the same.

"Progress is slow," Edina continued. "But remember that we're digging through decades of unverified anecdotes and passed down family knowledge. There's not much to go on."

Nora leaned back in her seat. The university library chair creaked back to receive her, its varnish long since worn out by hundreds of students that had crammed over textbooks throughout the years. She half-heartedly kicked at the table's leg. She wouldn't have risked such a petulant action had she been in the presence of the librarian. As it was, they were the only ones in the room. "We were able to verify the power transfer invocation," she said with a reluctant shrug.

Edina nodded. "We still need to know how to conjure the Sarramauca." The important thing about having a plan was where to go next. Edina was good at staying on track.

"And how to defeat it," Mae pointed out.

"Oh, we'll beat it." Nora seethed between clenched teeth. Her anger was the fuel for this crusade, and it had not dimmed.

"How do you beat something you can't touch?" Edina mused. She was the grounding rod for their polarizing views. The voice of reason.

Mae bit back a retort that would have been unhelpful. More likely, it would have enraged Nora. The whole evening would end in another blowout. They'd all had enough of that. "We found protective spells," she offered instead. She noticed Edina gave her a wry smile. Edina knew exactly what had been almost said and what it took to say something else.

It didn't matter much to Nora. "We're protected fine." She dismissed Mae's contribution. "We spent months on that. That's done. What we need is a weapon."

Mae's jaw tightened. She looked at Edina, taking from her the acceptance that she was looking for. Edina gave her a slight nod. It was enough. Mae was momentarily pacified.

"We're essentially going to war with this thing," Edina summarized. "It took us this long to nail down the armor. Now we need the weapon, and we need to finalize the strategy."

Nora scoffed. She'd heard all this before, and it was getting tiring. Edina wasn't swayed. Repetition was necessary.

"But it won't be tonight," she insisted. "Finals are next week. And while that's nowhere near as important as this," she added in a firm tone before Nora could protest, "it is still important."

Nora might have disagreed, but they'd had this conversation before. She had not been convinced right away, and sometimes she felt that she could use a little more persuading.

Edina had matured in the past year, plotting a life that supported their goals and keeping them both on the right path. Even though Nora didn't care much about the world that failed to mourn the loss of a promising bright young Woolgatherer, finding a solid anchor to it was necessary when crossing into the dream world. And part of living in the waking world meant interacting with it. Edina did that.

"Fine," Nora conceded, partially because she just didn't want to argue. She got up to put the books away. "I'll handle this. You guys go."

Edina hesitated, knowing that it was a tactic of hers to stay longer. But she, too, was too tired to argue. She and Mae walked out silently together.

The silence continued until they were well away from the library building and under the stars. It was Mae who spoke first.

"You didn't tell her." It wasn't an accusation, nor did Edina take it as one.

Edina sighed—a sound that belayed fatigue and heavy burden that went beyond physical exhaustion. She stretched out her left hand in front of her. One of the many sidewalk lamps that lit the way to the dorm buildings bounced off enough light to reflect the shine on her finger. The delicate diamond that sat on a simple gold band represented more than just her engagement to Edward. It was the hope for a happy future. One that Nora was too angry to see.

"She's not ready."

The Next Generation
April 1998

When people remember a life, they do so in general terms. One doesn't tabulate the hours, days, or even months. Years are summarized into mere moments. Flashes of pivotal points in history.

Graduations. Relationships. Weddings. Relocations. Births.

The same could be said for Nora and Edina. The years tumbled by as they do when one is too busy being in it to realize. Both women blended into adulthood without the luxury of carefree dreaming. Responsibilities of the world pushed back Nora's war agenda.

It began with Edina's engagement. It was weeks before Nora finally noticed the ring. And when she did, the guilt that slapped her in the face was only slightly more painful than Edina's uncertain expression. This should have been a reason to celebrate, but instead of joy, Edina was concerned.

It was at that moment Nora realized she was hurting the one person that meant the most to her in the world.

Nora hugged her more tightly than she had meant to. Unsaid apologies and promises of atonement came in waves. After a slight hesitation, Edina hugged her back. It was a fixed point in their friendship. As unyielding as their first crossing together.

Nora threw herself into all the traditional maid of honor duties of big hair and big dresses. She temporarily shelved the bitterness. She did so because her love for Edina was stronger than her hate for what had taken her cousin. Even if it meant she had to wear the most hideous purple dress at a wedding.

They were adults. There would be no time for dreaming.

Edina moved to the city to be with her new husband. Nora followed, finding a studio apartment in the same building as the newlyweds. Just as they always said they would.

Within two years after the intimate but colorful wedding, Nora witnessed the birth of Edina's firstborn. A son.

Four years later, the family of three became a family of four. A second son. They moved to the suburbs. Nora stayed behind. There were other things to consider now. Like work. Quality of life. And the price of fuel.

The natural, expected ebb and flow of a sheltered life kept them sated. Kept them comfortable. The birth of a third son meant an even busier and more chaotic schedule. Nora was present for every delivery. Every birthday party. Every important milestone.

The fixed points of their friendship were more like floating buoys of contentment that bounced along and shifted. Weekends, holidays, family BBQs. They were predictable and dependable. They were enough to forget the fight.

There are no nightmares when you don't allow yourself to dream.

But the birth of Edina's fourth child changed everything. A daughter.

London Anne Evans.

Cause to Arms
December 1998

The light snow that fell outside the window would have melted when it made contact with the ground had it not been 15°F. As it was, it simply contributed to the perilous driving conditions outdoors. It could be used as an excuse to avoid the roads and stay put.

Nora considered the weather as she held her nine-month-old godchild in her arms. London was a quiet baby. Not as colicky as her older brother Liam had been at this age. And certainly not as demanding as Lincoln. Locke was pushing the terrible twos well into the terrorizing threes. The boys were seemingly as dramatic as their mother from their first breath.

London was different. She must have inherited her father's calm. Nora wondered if the child she was going to have herself would be as easy. Would her baby be a boy? Would she have a daughter of her own? She felt the same rising anxiety that had overwhelmed her the first time she learned of her pregnancy. There was so much to worry about.

London made a tiny sound as if calling her away from future concerns. She wrapped one chubby little hand around her godmother's thumb. Nora conceded.

"This is your life now," Edina teased, watching the two of them. "She's not going to let you leave."

I don't want to leave, Nora thought. Instead, she said, "I will happily leave my job if you can pay my rent."

"I can't offer competitive compensation, but the benefits are unparalleled."

Nora couldn't argue, so she didn't try. She fell into contemplative silence, fully immersing herself in the steady breathing of the tiny human. It was the meditative rhythm she needed.

Edina continued to pick up random toys around the living room. The younger boys were down for a nap. Liam was reading quietly in his room. This gave her a small window to make a dent, however small, in the unending household chores. While the futility of her actions might discourage others in her situation, Edina found that she enjoyed the routine.

She could never have imagined this older version of herself. Boring. Domesticated. Predictable.

A mother.

People assumed that since London was the youngest of four, Edina was already comfortable with parenting. But London, being who she was, made it a completely different experience. Her pride and fear clashed together so often that Edina learned how to mute her feelings through routine. She wasn't prepared to deal with it yet.

"We need to finish this."

Nora had whispered it so quietly that it was almost an unsaid thought hanging in the air. For half a second, Edina wondered if she imagined it.

Edina sighed. It seemed she couldn't put things off any longer. She poured an armful of toys into a half-full bin, closed the lid, and pushed it off to the side. Then she sat on the coffee table instead of the couch so she could face Nora.

London stirred, possibly sensing that her mother was nearby. She tightened her fingers momentarily around Nora's finger, eyes still closed. Her lashes fluttered ever so slightly but didn't interrupt her slumber.

Edina waited until her daughter settled back into a heavier sleep. She watched the baby for a long moment, seeing the many years ahead of her and the many potential dangers that threatened her world.

Edina was an adult.

Her mother.

It was time to dream again.

"What do we need?"

Escape
January 1999

Run.

Edina would have preferred that her baby slept through everything, but that would have been near impossible. It was a marvel that she wasn't wailing. Edina considered that a win. Especially when she wanted to wail herself.

In her haste, she almost didn't buckle all the necessary straps in London's car seat. She looked over her shoulder, fearful of what she might see coming after her. There was nothing but the sound of her heavy breathing and the quiet fall of snow. Just as she was going to give up on the last buckle, it clicked into place. She threw a purple patchwork knit shawl over London for extra warmth.

Edina started the minivan. She glanced in her rearview mirror. It was a futile attempt. The car was completely covered with snow. The wipers could barely function against the heavy snowfall, and there would be no time to clear it.

She skidded out of the parking spot, grazing the back bumper of the car in front. She didn't stop. She overcorrected the turn and felt the van fishtail in protest.

The snow hadn't stopped in days. The city plows couldn't keep up. Worst blizzard Chicago had seen in twenty years. Of course. Edina could barely see past the hood. She was navigating blindly in a perilous world of white.

Everything had gone wrong.

It was Mae that called her earlier that day, not Nora. "She needs you. Bring London. She's a Woolgatherer too."

Worst driving conditions ever. Edina hated to drive to begin with. She never drove in the city. She never drove in bad weather. And here she was, doing both. With her youngest child in the car.

"What's going on?" Edina had asked over the phone while already preparing for her children to head to the neighbor's house. Mrs. Bautista would happily watch the boys. Even on short notice. She was a retired widow without much else to do.

Mae's voice was muffled. "She's about to do something incredibly stupid and irresponsible."

Stupid and irresponsible seemed to be the prevailing themes of the day.

She felt the tires spin even as she hit the brakes. The bulky minivan tilted to the side, slipping on the snow. Had the snow not been so deep, they might have slammed into the parked cars that lined the street. The slush beneath the tires made it impossible to grip the road, but the piled snow around them kept them from spinning completely out of control.

There was very little control.

In her panicked state, she turned right when she should have turned left. It was a one-way road, and she was going the wrong way. Had it been any other day, she would have inadvertently crashed head-on into oncoming traffic. Few people were foolish enough to be driving that evening. She was able to correct herself on the next turn.

But now, she was completely lost. Not just because she wasn't in the right state of mind to make the necessary spatial corrections in her head but also because every physical landmark that could have helped her adjust was covered in cold white.

She concentrated on not going the wrong way down the next street instead. Under any other circumstance, she might have smiled at the idea that she'd made use of the rudimentary compass tacked on her dashboard. She had laughed at its existence, telling Edward aloud that it was a useless feature that she would never use. She was not smiling as she used it now, doing her best to head north.

If she could just see Lake Michigan from where she was, then she would know how to get home. She was in the back alleys of buildings. It was the side of the city that tourists never saw.

London made a sound. Not quite a cry.

"It's OK, sweetheart," Edina promised. She sat up a little straighter in the driver's seat so that she could get a glimpse of her daughter in the rearview mirror. "Mommy has you. We're OK."

A snowplow came down the street in front of them. She should have heard it coming, but the pounding in her chest had been echoing in her ears. By the time the snowplow appeared, she knew that there was not enough room to brake even as she slammed her foot on the pedal.

She felt the vibrations of the ABS kicking in. She turned the wheel sharply into an open alley. The rear of the minivan swung wide, and she felt the momentum pull them backward. She kept her foot on the pedal, feeling it kick back while she tried to regain control.

The world was spinning in that sickening way that reminded her of a carnival ride. The kind that was magically built overnight and torn down in hours. The kind that made you throw up.

The van jolted from impact when the rear hit a snowbank. The sudden stop made the seat belt tighten around her shoulder. Her view of the snow-covered alley was replaced with a rapidly deployed airbag that slapped her hard in the face.

The snowplow continued down the street, ignorant of the disaster it had left in its wake. Everything stopped.

Trapped

January 1999

Are we dead?

Edina didn't realize her eyes were shut until she opened them.
Her knuckles had turned white from their tight grip on the steering
wheel. When she let go, she was shaking.

She swallowed the adrenaline that choked her. She smelled smoke
and immediately thought the engine was on fire, but it was just the
residue from the airbags, making the cabin smell like the evening air
on the Fourth of July. Taking a tentative breath, she braced for pain.
There was none other than a dull ache in her chest and a stinging
on her face. The battered van shuddered. It didn't sound good. She
twisted the key.

London whimpered as the engine died.

"Oh, sweetheart." Edina unbuckled. Pushing back against the
deflated bag, she climbed uncomfortably through the middle
console. She didn't want to attempt to open the door. She unbuckled
her baby and took her in her arms. A comfort to them both.

"Shhhh," Edina coaxed. "Come here." She bounced her baby
on her shoulder. "It'll be OK. I've got you." London responded by
grabbing a handful of her mother's hair to chew on. Under normal
circumstances, Edina would have pulled her hair back, but this time,
she let her daughter have this momentary solace.

"I won't let you die," she whispered and instantly regretted saying
it out loud. "This is not the end," she said with more intention to
counter what she perceived was a moment of weakness.

Her purse had been knocked to the floor. She fished in it for her cell phone with one hand. The momentary feeling of accomplishment disappeared when she realized that the phone she'd found was dead. There would be no calling for help.

"You've been such a good girl, sweetheart," Edina assured her infant. "Thank you for being so good. Hold on a little longer, OK? Mommy has to put you back in your car seat so we can go."

She'd always talked to her children even before they could understand her. Even when they were still in the womb. The sound of her voice seemed to calm them even when, sometimes, she spoke utter nonsense. She started with Liam, speaking to him in a sing-song tone whenever he started to fuss. He would pause and listen to her off-key narrative. Talk about the laundry. The dishes. Why Mommy was losing her mind. She did the same for Lincoln and for Locke. It became a habit that she found as much comfort in as they did.

By the time she got back into the driver's seat, she was relatively calm.

Until she tried the key and the engine wouldn't start.

It turned over weakly the first time and refused to repeat itself after. She wasn't sure what to expect. Do cars still run after the airbag deploys? She didn't know enough about cars to know. Airbags were a new thing. She didn't have them growing up.

Edward was the gearhead. He would have known what to do.

"I wish your daddy was here," she said aloud to London. That wasn't actually true. She didn't wish Edward was there. She wished they were home with him. With the boys. With the rest of the family.

The windows of the van had fogged up already, and she could feel the cold pressing against the glass. She abandoned the front seat and climbed back to her daughter.

She sat there, cooing at the baby and trying to decide what to do. It would be too dangerous to attempt a crossing now. They would be trapped if they were found. Would it help if they waited a few hours? Would it be safe then? Would it ever be safe again?

The snow seemed to have finally stopped, but the temperature continued to drop. She could feel it mingle with her fear.

She rummaged through the van for anything that may have been left behind that could serve as another layer of protection against the cold. She found one of Liam's discarded school PE T-shirts that had found a hiding place under the rear seats. It looked like it had been there since summer break. She sighed, reluctantly adding it over London. She made a makeshift nest in the middle of the vehicle by pushing what she could around them, cocooning them in the center. All the activity had helped keep the cabin warm.

"OK, sweetheart," she said as she wrapped her arms around London, drawing her to her chest. She threw her favorite purple shawl around them both in an attempt to conserve body heat. "Your daddy says that every time I anchor, it gets a little hot around me. Shall we try that?"

She couldn't cross, but maybe she could anchor. And maybe another Woolgatherer would find her.

Earlier
January 1999

Nora and Edina had been holding hands in deep concentration when the portal first appeared. Neither woman had noticed the blur in the air. It was as if the frost on the windows was suspended indoors, a faded barrier between two places. It began small, almost like a passing thing that one might easily dismiss as a trick of the light. But as the four ceremonial candles surrounding the women slowly melted, the trick of the light solidified into something that could no longer be ignored.

The first indication that something was going to shift was the uniform flicker of the candlelight.

No, that wasn't correct.

The first indication that something was going to shift was the sound that London made.

Edina's eyes fluttered open at her daughter's whimper. There was no time for her to do anything but grip Nora's hands tighter. Nora's eyes opened in time to see the Sarramauca upon them. It was certain death.

Except it wasn't.

The monster moved *through* them like a spirit. Nora felt the baby she carried inside her recoil. The sensation was not pleasant. It was like falling from the highest rollercoaster drop but without the wind. In the next second, she felt like every atom in her was being stretched apart to make room for a rushing stream of cold, cold water. Her center was no longer her center. She harnessed her energy from her connection to Edina. From holding her hands. That was her center now.

There was an unnatural ringing in her ears that made her wonder if someone was screaming. Was it Edina? Was she screaming?

When she was finally able to breathe again, she let go of Edina's hand and scrambled backward, toppling two of the candles and dousing the flames in the process.

One glance at her friend, and she knew right away that Edina had felt everything that she had. Apart from the pregnancy. Because Edina's baby was more than an arm's reach away. And there was a monster to contend with.

She pushed Edina toward London.

"Run!"

Left Behind
January 1999

Nora watched Edina pick up the baby and run out the door, leaving it open. She didn't wait to watch the snow blow into the house. There were more immediate things that demanded her attention.

Like the Sarramauca in her living room.

Everything had gone wrong. They weren't supposed to attract it. They were just supposed to locate it.

Well, Nora thought sardonically, *it's been located. Here it is.*

The monster wasn't what she had expected. She thought it would be a goblin-like creature. Instead, it looked more like a grotesquely obese woman that should not have been able to move with the agility that it did. The tips of pointed hairy ears reached high above its head like mountain peaks over a greasy valley of knotted hair. But the lore had described it as a shape-changer, so in a way, it made perfect sense.

She backed away from it slowly, taking care to look for possible alternative exits. It was also taking its time, sizing her up. Perhaps it hadn't intended to pull her molecules apart. Perhaps it was as equally surprised.

Sleep, Woolgatherer.

Who had said that?

She felt a heaviness in her eyelids. The weight of a cursed command. It would have been so effortless to surrender.

But the unborn child inside her rebelled. It was enough.

Enough for Nora to shake the imposition. Enough for her to yell.

"NO!"

Then hoping she had enough distance between them, hoping she had enough time, she scrambled for the back door of the kitchen. Whether or not running out in the snow was a good idea was another matter. But she didn't have the luxury of thinking that far ahead.

She just needed to make it to the door.

Nora felt an unnatural force push her from behind. It wasn't like a kick but more of a large, sweeping current. She lost her footing, tried to break her fall with her arms, and skidded on the kitchen floor. Her back slammed into the table. The books that she had piled unceremoniously on it earlier came tumbling down on her head. It was a strange moment to regret being untidy.

The flames on the remaining candles flickered. Snow was piling up at the entranceway, blown in by the winter gale.

The last things Nora saw before losing consciousness were the candles going out and the Sarramauca being pulled back into the collapsing portal against its will.

In Between

September 2006

"Did you find it?"

Mae stepped into the apartment she shared with her cousin and her cousin's son. The little boy in shorts and a striped shirt was barefoot when he greeted her at the door. Mae held a package in her hand but held it up above his head. He was a tall child, but she was still taller. For now.

"Maybe," she teased. "You won't find out until your seventh birthday, either way."

"But that's not until next week," he whined, more for theatrics than anything.

"Oh, you have *such* a difficult life." She laughed, making sure to place the package up on the shelf above the coats in the entry closet. He watched her intently. "Don't you dare," she warned, knowing that he was already strategizing some kind of acquisition plan.

He shrugged innocently, but the glint in his eyes said something else. Then he bounded up the stairs with the signature reckless abandon of a child whose biggest concern was an upcoming birthday.

"Don't you have homework or something?" she yelled after him. His response was indecipherable, but she could guess. She shook her head in disapproval but chuckled quietly to herself. He was insufferable, but it was easy to love that boy.

"He's got you wrapped around his finger." Nora was just around the corner, sitting on the carpet with a closed bottle of dark rum next to her. She smiled, surrounded by a little over half a dozen open books, but didn't look up from the book she was reading.

Mae often found her this way. She was just as obsessive as she had been when they were in school together, if not more so. The only difference was that her hair was longer. And she had a son now. His existence balanced her.

"He must have learned that from you," Mae responded, clearing an area on the couch for her to use. "What are you working on here?"

Still not looking up, Nora handed her a thin silver chain. Mae turned the bracelet over in her hands. It was beautifully crafted. The chain connected a flat engraved piece together. "Birthday gift?" she asked.

Nora shook her head. "Protection."

The band looked much too pretty to be more than ornamental. "I thought protection artifacts had to be made of iron?" Mae mused.

Nora finally put the book down. She leaned back on her hands, looking proud of herself. "It is."

"It's silver." Mae held up the bracelet by its clasp, letting the chain fall. It caught the setting sun through the window at just the right angle, reflecting in such a way that was not a commonly known characteristic of iron. "This is way too light and way too pretty to be iron."

"It's not about the amount of iron in an object but the purity of it." Nora held out her hand for the bracelet back, and Mae surrendered it. "But pure iron is pretty brittle," she admitted. "So while the inside of this is as pure as I can get it, it's sealed in steel."

"But it's silver," Mae insisted.

"I had it plated," Nora confessed. "Edina loved silver," she added in a little over a whisper.

Nora played with the bracelet in her hands. Although she refused to meet her cousin's eyes, the expression in her own was easy enough to read. Melancholy. She'd kept her heart on her sleeve since Edina's death. In a way, it made her as strong as it did vulnerable.

Mae was the one to find Nora—unconscious in her kitchen—on the night of the attack. She saw the open front door before she could find a place to park. Snow had already piled high enough in the entrance to keep the door firmly ajar. She had feared the worst.

By the time she got inside, the temperature had dropped so low that Nora's skin was cold to the touch. It was only when Mae saw her chest rise and fall that she felt any kind of relief from dread.

In retrospect, she probably should have called an ambulance. But all she wanted to do at that moment was get her cousin far away from there. And she didn't want to answer questions. Especially when she didn't know any of the answers.

She wrapped Nora in a blanket she grabbed from the couch. It was cold, but it was dry. That would have to do. It would serve as some kind of protection. She hoped.

Then with a strength borne of adrenaline and fear, she scooped up the pregnant woman. The fresh snow was deep enough to actually help keep her balance rather than make her slip. It was slow progress but progress. Nora didn't wake up the entire time.

It took Nora almost two weeks to be physically back to normal. That was the easy part.

She had been emotionally destroyed. Especially when she found out that her best friend's body had been recovered and she had been too sick to even attend the funeral.

It was her fault that Edina was dead. Entirely her fault. There was no coming back from that.

The birth of her son gave her hope. He gave her a reason to live. But the guilt was not easy to live with. Nora struggled with it every day, threading that fine line between motivation and hopelessness.

That was why Mae insisted they all move in together. So that she could watch out for her cousin. So that she could make sure the guilt was never too much. They lived together for moments like these.

Nora continued to fidget with the bracelet. Mae put one hand over hers. "It's beautiful," she assured her. "Edina would have loved it."

Nora looked up, grateful for the kind words and all the encouragement that supported them. Her smile was tight, a sign that she was setting aside her grief to make way for a renewed sense of determination. "There's a new moon tonight. I want to add a last layer of protection before I give it to him."

Mae leaned back on the couch with an exaggerated groan. "Great. Candles again." She threw one hand over her forehead to further emphasize her disdain.

"You like candles."

"I like *scented* candles." Mae lifted her arm just slightly, enough that she could make eye contact. "How about some Yankee candles, huh? Or Bath & Body Works? Throw some vanilla in it. Anything other than just burning wax."

Nora grinned. "You know that's not how that works."

Who knows if any of this works, Mae thought but didn't say it aloud. She had pulled Nora out of a lingering depression. Anything negative now would just push her right back. It was a delicate situation. She was always careful with what she said.

"In that case," she said, pulling herself out of the couch, "I'm going out for dinner. Make sure you keep the windows open and air out the witchcraft."

Mae felt a sense of success when she heard Nora laugh.

Hell Breaks Loose

September 2006

It was supposed to be easy.

Nora wasn't worried. Protection spells were simple. She'd done them before. The four candles she had put around them were not new. And their placement was familiar.

So when she was clasping the freshly charmed bracelet around her son's wrist, she wasn't expecting any danger. In fact, she was feeling rather accomplished.

What she didn't know was that the spell changed when two or more powerful Woolgatherers were in physical contact with each other.

What she didn't know was that her son was a powerful Woolgatherer.

The portal that formed in the same way it had seven years ago should have alerted her. But her attention was on her son.

When the candle flames flickered, however, it prompted an emotional response. A traumatic trigger. She was suddenly hyperaware. By that time, the portal was almost complete.

She pulled her son behind her. It was a protective instinct but one she knew meant very little against what was going to come.

She needed alternatives.

She glanced at the open book by her side, wondering what she had done wrong. Wondering how she could change things. Wondering if it was too late.

The Sarramauca waiting on the other side looked different from the one that was responsible for her best friend's death and the destruction of her life. Its lair was dark. Nora couldn't make out the shapes. Globes of faint glowing light outlined the menacing form of the monster.

In contrast to the pounds of flesh and fat she remembered, this one resembled a woman with an athletic body. Bat-like wings stretched out behind it. Nora couldn't tell if the tips on its head were from disproportionately large ears or if they were, in fact, horns.

It looked different, but it was the same monster; she knew it. It was as if she could see through all the possible shifts. It was as if she could see right into its hungry core.

It wasn't particularly malevolent, despite its appearance. Not any more so than any large predator stalking its next meal. The world just looks like an evil, scary place when you're the prey.

"Run!" Nora commanded.

Her son, eyes wide from fear, did not move.

Nora fell to her knees and scrambled through the book on the floor, ripping pages in her haste. She glanced up at the portal when she found what she was looking for, trying to gauge how much time they had. The edges of the mystical doorway were more defined, like the fabric of space was burned between them. Everything was happening much too quickly.

Her hands shook. She grabbed the open bottle of rum on the floor and chugged it, taking three large swallows of the sweet, dark liquid. It was the boost she needed for what she was going to do.

She grabbed her son. It was enough to startle him and get his attention. She let go when he faced her. Her hands flew around him as if compressing a lifetime of motherly touch in one moment. She kissed him on the forehead, a quick and dirty expression of devotion. "If there's anything you should remember from tonight," she insisted, holding on to both wrists, "it's that *you are loved.*" She pressed on the newly placed metal bracelet on his wrist and felt it dig into his skin as if emphasizing her declaration.

She pushed the bottle into his hands. "Drink," she demanded. Staring unblinkingly at her, he put the bottle to his lips and swallowed. He was, as expected, unprepared for the sensation of strong alcohol. He coughed and dropped the bottle. It bounced once before rolling, spilling what was left onto the floor.

It will have to do.

Nora read from the pages of the worn book, damaged by age and her desperation. And when she did, she felt the energy pour out of her like an open tap. It was a sensation that she'd never felt before. It scared her but also empowered her. It made her feel like she was doing something instead of allowing them both to be victims. She was giving him a shield, encapsulating him in armor with everything she had.

Even when she'd completed the enchantment, she kept going. Repeating it in the hope of doubling its strength. She only stopped because her son pulled away, yelling for her. She felt a force grab her by the waist. It didn't go through her this time. It didn't rip her molecules apart. She felt the pressure around her, not quite crushing. Paralyzing.

"Run," she repeated, weakened by the enchantment and quickly losing consciousness. "Into the portal." She pleaded instead of commanding. At the very least, the monster had come after her. Not him.

He hesitated, not wanting to leave her. Not wanting to venture alone.

Before the darkness of nightmares completely consumed her, she watched her son, shielded with all her love and power, stumble through the portal. But instead of falling into the forbidding lair of monsters, he was swallowed by the light of a different world.

And she knew that he was safe. She had made certain of that.

Full Circle

"She was alone. There wasn't a mark on her when I found her."

Mae's eyes had lost focus when she spoke, haunted by unseen demons. She was looking into memories, not at me. Unearthing history. Dusting off pieces from long ago. Fully immersed in the task.

I knew her story was coming to an end not because we had come to Nora's fate but because she finally actually looked at me.

"They said it was carbon monoxide poisoning. They said there wasn't enough ventilation and the candles caused it." She shook her head, clearly not believing it. I couldn't say that I would have believed it either. "I don't know exactly what happened, but I know that wasn't it."

"What did you do?" I prompted.

"I left." Her body surrendered to the failure. She sighed and took a sip of her coffee, already cold. "Not right away," she confessed. "But I had to. It was too dangerous to stay."

She put down her cup, seemingly as full as it was when she first started talking. She spun it twice in place. Her lips twitched. There was something else she wanted to say.

No, something she *didn't* want to say but something she knew she *had* to. I waited for her to continue.

"There was an Amber Alert for her boy." I didn't think she could look any more defeated. "I searched for years."

It was obvious that he was never found.

My coffee was too sweet. I had stopped drinking halfway through her story. I had stopped drinking when she told me how my mother had died.

I hated Nora even more.

"It was her fault," I blurted out. Blaming a dead woman for my dead mother. "This wasn't her fight."

Mae didn't react. Maybe she felt the same.

"Your family," I accused her. "This is all because of *your* family. Your stupid, selfish cousin and her obsession!" I felt the tears in my eyes. The cold air stung, but it felt good. I needed that small, inconvenient pain to further my righteous anger. "My mother is *dead* because of her!"

She reached out a hand to me. Maybe it was in comfort, but I took it as an assault. An insult.

"Don't *touch* me!" I jerked my hand away, spilling cold coffee on my other sleeve. I swore. Loudly.

I suddenly felt very confined in this open space. The tears had blurred my vision. The coffee was bleeding through my hoodie, feeling sticky and gross. I felt like all my emotions were stuck in my throat. The rage, disbelief, fear, and uncertainty. It was a ball too big and too tight to swallow.

I stood up, scrambling off the bench. I started to pull my hoodie off my head as I did. I was clumsy. And maybe taking off a hoodie in the middle of winter wasn't the smartest thing to do. Even if it *was* California.

I was wearing a regular T-shirt underneath. I felt the cold on my bare arms even before I was able to clear the offending garment off my head. I threw it on the ground. The cold made me feel better. I was able to breathe again.

Mae stood up when I did but otherwise hadn't moved. When I put my hands on the table between us, she reached across and grabbed my arm. I struggled to get away from her, but she held on tightly. I almost stumbled back over the bench.

"Let *go*!" I yelled. She didn't.

I leaned forward, prepared to scream right in her face, when I was stopped short by her expression.

She had paled unnaturally. The look of sympathy she had earlier was gone. Not replaced by sadness or regret. Her jaw slackened. Her lips were open in an unflattering open gape. It was shock. The look of someone who had seen the unexplainable. The look of someone who had seen a ghost.

I followed her gaze down the arm she was holding. To the bracelet around my wrist.

"Ethan," she whispered.

Turmoil

For the first time, I was grateful that Ethan was on the other side of the world. Where the misfortunes of his family couldn't reach him. Mae had become near unreasonable and manic. Demanding to know everything there was to know about him. Attacking me as if I was the one who took him away. She didn't see that I was the one who had lost here. It was *my* mother that was taken away. By an obsession that wasn't even her own.

I know I should have probably been more sympathetic to this woman who had lost so much in her family, but I was too consumed with my personal tragedy and desperately wanting to protect what I had left. I didn't want to tell her anything. She had finally relented when I promised to call her after speaking with him.

"Tell him I looked for him," she pleaded, edging close to hysteria. "Tell him I never stopped thinking of him. Tell him he has family."

I didn't want to do that. I felt I didn't owe her anything. I didn't want to ever have any contact with her ever again. It would be just fine with me to act like I'd never met her.

I threw my soiled hoodie to the ground when I got home and kicked it across the floor. I was screaming before it slid to a stop by the foot of the stairs. It was that or I would start throwing objects. I wanted to break things. I wanted to see the immediate world around me shatter in the same way I felt shattered. I was furious, appalled, terrified, and confused. All of that and none of that. I didn't have the words to articulate what I was feeling.

The scream started out piercing, like the barbs of loss that sliced into me. But by the end, I was howling sobs of defeated casualty. I don't remember how I ended up on the living room floor. I sat there, my back to the couch, staring into the empty space where a fake plastic tree used to be, thinking very little but feeling so much. Feeling too much.

I always thought of my parents as wiser human beings. They were born that way. Parents from the start. They knew all the answers and dispensed their knowledge strategically to their children. I didn't think what they would've been like at my age. I never thought of them as being younger. Younger and irresponsible.

I never expected my mother to be so stupid.

Reckless. Blind to the danger her best friend had dragged her into. Just. So. Stupid.

I was angry again, but what was I supposed to do? Pretend the afternoon never happened? Pretend that the past didn't just reach out and punch me in the stomach?

If only.

I shut my eyes and let my head fall back. My throat hurt from all the screaming. My fury had drained. I was exhausted. The reality of my situation was this was just as much my fault. I had wanted to know my mother. I had wanted to know what happened. I had so many questions, but the more I learned, the more I wished I didn't know. The more I understood the burden of knowing.

So stupid.

I played with the bracelet on my wrist like I often find myself doing when I miss Ethan. I had never been anything but genuine with him, but I didn't want to tell him about this. That family didn't deserve him. They abandoned him. They left him alone to deal with all the trauma. He had suffered through a system of abuse because of it. Because they couldn't leave well enough alone.

He deserved better.

Proof that I once had someone love me, he had said before he had put it around my wrist two months ago. I sighed, running my thumb over the engraving on the metal. This talisman, a token of love and protection, meant more than either of us realized. The fact that it had somehow found its way to me made it that much more magical and true.

Mae didn't deserve my cooperation. That entire clan could take their cursed blood and fade into history for all I cared.

But that wasn't fair to Ethan.

So I would tell him. But for his sake, not theirs.

Family

"You found my family?"

I didn't realize that I had been expecting him to react a certain way until he didn't react that way at all. His calm was almost the complete opposite of my internal debacles.

"How are you not freaking out about this?" I was lying in bed, feeling depleted by the experience. Feeling like I had just lived multiple lives in one afternoon. Ethan had just been released from the day's maneuvers.

"Are *we* related?"

I bolted upright. "Ew. No." For whatever reason, that added to my strange panic. "No," I repeated. "Your mom and my mom were best friends, not cousins."

He ducked behind a prefabricated building. The setting sun fell behind the rooftop, casting him in shadow. The camera on his phone adjusted. "Choice. One less thing to worry about."

"You were worried that we were related?" I grinned in spite of myself.

"Stranger things have happened, yeah?"

I laid back down again. "Like me showing up in New Zealand?"

"More like *me* showing up in New Zealand. How the devil did I end up here?"

"You're weird?" I giggled.

He grinned. "Well, I *am* American."

I laughed. "Hey! Are you trying to be offensive?"

"I'm allowed to say anything I want now. I'm American."

The weight that was lifted came slamming back down. I tried not to let it show. "Now what? Like, will you talk to her?"

He shrugged. "Shouldn't I? There are DNA tests now to verify the truth." He leaned back against the corrugated wall behind him. "I don't remember anything, but it would actually explain a lot, yeah? Why I have no family here. Why I've been alone all this time."

I couldn't disagree, but it didn't mean I had to like it.

"Why I'm weird," he finished with a self-deprecating smile. I recognized it as his attempt to lift my spirits. It alleviated a bit of the dread, and it made me feel better for telling him. We were always better together, and being level about this was the right decision.

"You shouldn't have been able to do anything," I mused. "You're a boy."

"Oh, you noticed that, did you?"

I stuck my tongue out at him. "I mean, as a boy, you're not supposed to have any Woolgatherer abilities."

"According to Laurent."

"According to your aunt Mae too," I pointed out. "*She* doesn't even have any abilities. Just because she's connected to the bloodline through her father."

"I don't think she's my aunt."

I blinked. "I thought you believed her."

"I mean, I don't think that makes her my aunt. She's supposedly my mother's cousin, right? Not sister? If they were *sisters*, then she'd be my aunt."

I shrugged. "If they were sisters, Mae would be a Woolgatherer that crossed too. They're not. They're cousins."

"So, I think that makes her"—he paused, thinking—"my first cousin once removed?"

"*This* is what you're concerned about? Titles?"

"It's tantalizing. I went from being a total outsider to suddenly being a part of a family that has cousins that are … *removed*."

I laughed. The Ethan I first met the year before was sullen, disillusioned, and angry. This Ethan was confident and self-assured. And a little silly.

"I feel like I'm part of a reality TV show." He waved a hand in the air. "The possibilities are endless. *The American Family*. Featuring a black sheep prodigal son."

"Featuring a black sheep prodigal first cousin once removed," I corrected. "You sound like Drew."

"Maybe I'm related to the bloke too."

I laughed. I might see the similarities between Mae and Ethan, however slight. But there was no way that Drew and Ethan shared any DNA.

"Look," he said, "just give me her info. I'll send her an email before I think about giving her a ring." He looked past the camera at something or someone, and I knew it meant he would have to go.

"Get some rest," he commanded. "Do all that chakra centering meditation thing that Brieann has you doing. Be safe. I will ring you in the morning."

"I love you," I said right before he ended the call.

I stared at the screen a moment after the call concluded, and it reverted to my home page. I sighed. Our conversations always ended too soon. It reminded me of how far away he was.

My screen lit up.

I luv u 2

Infinite Hope

*"We must accept finite disappointment
but never lose infinite hope …"
—Martin Luther King Jr.*

"He's American?"

I was spending Martin Luther King Day with Drew and Brieann. Specifically in Drew's garage. The Blizzard Ball was Saturday. There were backdrops and decorations to be completed. Guess who got voluntold into getting them done?

Neither Drew nor I were at all surprised. Sometimes, it was simpler to concede than to argue.

"That's your takeaway here?" I was creating a long chain with strips of blue and white construction paper. Brieann said we would be more efficient working in an assembly line but that only intensified the back-alley sweatshop vibes.

Drew didn't look up from painting. The backdrop was almost complete. He had used acrylic paint instead of his preferred oil medium. I thought he'd protest when Brieann handed him the materials, but he didn't. Despite the beautiful blend of winter colors that most artists would be hard-pressed to duplicate, Drew didn't consider this art. To him, he may as well have been painting a house.

"It's funny." He shrugged.

"Because he has an accent?" I was being sarcastic.

Drew sat on his haunches and pointed the brush he was holding at me. "You said it, not me." He grinned. "No, I mean because he's in the New Zealand Army, and he's not even *from* New Zealand."

"How did he even *get* to New Zealand," Brieann asked. "It's not like a seven-year-old can hitchhike to get there."

"I think he was six," I corrected.

"*That's* your takeaway here?" Drew inserted before Brieann could react.

I laughed. "Touché."

"It's hard enough to believe that *you* manifest some kind of doppelgänger dream variant of yourself when you sleep. What if there's a copy of him in a coma somewhere in this country?" Brieann's eyes widened at her own theory.

"Well, according to all our new sources, guys don't cross." I shrugged. But the idea of it bothered me too.

"That's sexist," Drew commented without looking up.

"I don't make the rules."

"So maybe guys do other things."

"We do plenty," Drew said, winking. Brieann ignored him. I did too.

"Mae doesn't seem to know what happened, either. And Laurent thought I was the chosen one or something. That clearly isn't the case." I shrugged. "I think our guesses are just as good as theirs."

"Maybe he teleported."

Any other time, I might have dismissed the idea as a comment meant more to be funny than constructive. But at this point, it was all up for grabs.

"Mae said that Ethan's mom was planning on doing some kind of protection spell on this." I raised my arm and shook the bracelet on my wrist. "There were a bunch of candles all over the place and stuff. Maybe she did more than just a protection spell?"

"Teleportation spell?" Brieann wondered aloud, mentally going through the material she had collated during our big research phase. "Is that really a thing?"

"As much of a thing as crossing in one's sleep to meet the man of one's dreams, I would think." Drew winked at me. I stuck my tongue out at him because I knew he was trying to be cheeky even though I agreed with him.

"I think it's sort of sweet that your parents were actually best friends," Brieann said.

I felt the resentment I'd tried to lock into a room, turn the doorknob. I was among friends, so I allowed it to rear its head a little. "If they hadn't been friends, then maybe my mom would still be alive."

Drew put down his brush, his expression grave. He looked from me to Brieann but didn't say anything. Brieann bit her bottom lip. The atmosphere in the room sagged with the weight of my bitterness. I felt guilty but not enough to regret saying it.

"London," Brieann began.

I waved a hand in the air to cut her off. "Whatever."

I didn't want to give her an opportunity to talk. I didn't want her to make me feel better. I was angry. I owed it to my mother. More so, I owed it to my father.

The silence in the room stretched a little longer. It fed my emotions.

"I was grounded," Drew said, seemingly out of context. He sat cross-legged on the garage floor next to the completed mural. Brieann moved to sit next to him. She put an arm through one of his and leaned against his shoulder.

I blinked.

"When you ran off to Chicago last year," he clarified. "My parents found out that I took you to the airport."

I had planned on catching an Uber, but Drew had insisted on taking Ethan and me to the airport himself. He said it would be one less thing to worry about.

"Why would you get into trouble for that?" I asked, genuinely perplexed. This was the first I'd heard of it.

He shrugged. "Because I cut class? Because they found out that I helped you 'run away'?" He made quotation marks in the air with paint-stained fingers. "Because that's technically 'Contributing to the Delinquency of a Minor'?" More quotation marks. "Because it was irresponsible and illegal?"

"I didn't run away," I protested. "It was just for the weekend! It was to find my mother!"

He put his hands up in surrender. "You don't have to convince *me*. I was there. I get it. They just didn't see it that way."

I felt sick.

My actions had consequences that I was too self-absorbed to notice. I was selfish. I was no better than Nora. The only difference was that no one had died.

Yet.

"I'm sorry," I said more quietly than he deserved. "I didn't know you got into trouble. Why didn't you say anything?"

"I'm not telling you now to make you feel bad. I didn't tell you *because* I didn't want you to feel bad." His shoulders lifted and fell, accepting my apology while also casually dismissing it. "We all do things for each other because we *want* to. Even when we don't want to. That's sort of part of being in the same pod."

Brieann nodded emphatically when she saw that I was unconvinced. "You do it too," she pointed out.

"Case in point," Drew added, spreading his hands in my direction, presenting me as an example to myself. "Don't you just *love* putting paper décor together?"

I snorted.

"And yet," he pointed out, "here you are."

"Why are you here?" Brieann asked. I was beginning to feel like I was a sitting target when I looked between the two of them. I could feel them circling me, and they weren't even moving.

"Because you asked me!"

"So what?"

"What?" I didn't understand.

"So what if I asked you? You could say no."

Saying no to Brieann was laughable. She had ways of getting what she wanted and making you feel good about it. I narrowed my eyes. Her smile was an indication that she knew what I was thinking.

"You're here," Drew summarized when it was clear that I refused to say it aloud, "because we're friends. And you're a good person. Because you want to see good things happen to your friends. Because you want to help your friends reach their goals." I knew where he was going with this.

"It's not the same," I argued.

"So no one is hurt," he agreed. *No one is dead*, is what he should have said, but he probably thought it wasn't prudent. "That doesn't change the fact that you're doing something you wouldn't normally do. You're giving up your free day to work on something you have zero interest in."

"What you're saying is that I succumb way too easily to peer pressure."

"What I'm saying is that your mom wouldn't want you to hate her best friend."

I was uncomfortable. It wasn't what I wanted to hear, but maybe, if I were to be honest, I knew it already. I didn't want to accept it. It was easier to be angry. It would also have been easier to yell at Drew. To yell at them both. To tell them that they couldn't possibly understand me because their families were intact and they hadn't lost anything. It would have been unfair.

"Choose love," Brieann advised.

My mother had died protecting me. My mother had died attempting to help a friend. All her decisions were made with love. Even Dad knew it. I've never seen him harbor any hate. And he had lost the most. Who was I? What did I think I was doing for her?

I thought I was being righteous with my anger, but I was defacing her memory and cheapening her sacrifice. The hate I was feeling was for my benefit, not hers. Because it was easier. I was the one being selfish. Again.

I felt the conflict manifest itself in tears, surrendering to the painful truth. I was finally accepting that what they were saying was true.

"I hate you both," I said. It was clear I meant the complete opposite.

Brieann left Drew's side to hug me. Drew stayed where he was, watching me with something that looked a little like pride.

"There's magic in you, London," Brieann reminded me.

"And maybe there's magic in our accented American too," Drew joked.

"Love and sacrifice are power spells," Brieann agreed.

I smiled, feeling a little less like the target. I sighed. "Maybe he can teleport to the damn dance and be my date." I was only partially kidding.

"What color is your dress?"

"What dress?"

Brieann dropped her jaw. The execution was too dramatic to be taken seriously. She looked at Drew as if to say, *This is what I have to deal with*. Drew laughed. I rolled my eyes. If she was going to make a production out of it, I would too. Even if I wasn't exactly sure what she was talking about.

"For. The. Dance."

Oh.

"You need a dress," she declared in case it wasn't already clear.

"Or a suit!" Drew added.

"Or a suit," she conceded. "But you cannot wear jeans."

"I hadn't planned on wearing jeans," I retorted defensively. I hadn't planned at all, to be honest. "I think I own a dress."

"Like, a summer dress or an actual evening gown dress?"

I didn't respond right away, and that only infuriated her more. "I'm not sure I know the difference?"

Brieann's groan was just as loud as Drew's laughter.

"The dance is on Saturday!" Brieann whined.

"Yes, I know. That's why we're spending our free day painting." Now, I was just having fun with her frustration. She frowned at me, hands expectedly on her hips for additional effect.

"We're cutting it close to finding you something in five days," she complained.

"Or, I could just not go?"

"Nice try." Then to Drew, she said, "You've got this, right? This is an emergency."

Drew saluted with a paintbrush. "Oh, I would much rather stay here. I think I'm allergic to anything resembling a mall."

"I am too," I grumbled. "It's on my medical chart."

Brieann was unsympathetic. She grabbed her purse and motioned me to follow her out. "You'll survive."

I might have disagreed, but I followed anyway. "This is one of those things I do against my better judgment because I'm a good friend, right?"

"See?" Drew grinned, immune to my fate. "I knew you'd get it."

"Have I told you how much I hate you?" I repeated, pouting.

"Constantly."

Mature Colors

The ride to the center of our town, where the nearest boutiques were, wasn't long. But with Brieann driving, it always felt perilous. In fairness, I didn't know if she'd actually ever been in a collision. There were just too many near misses.

She prattled on about what cuts would look flattering on me and what I should and shouldn't want in a dress while I braced myself with both hands for vehicular accidents that never came to pass. I exhaled a little too loudly when we arrived safely.

If she ever noticed my opinions regarding her skills, she didn't let on. I imagined that there was some side of her that enjoyed teasing me that way. She seemed extra peppy when she got out of her silver Volkswagen. It may have been because we were about to begin one of her favorite pastimes, or it may have been because I was right about her not-so-hidden masochistic tendencies. I was suspicious either way.

"I think you'd look killer in a green dress," she said, linking one arm through mine. It was a sign of affection. Or else insurance against an escape attempt on my part. "Not kelly green, but maybe a nice sage."

"I like blue."

"You *think* you like blue," she said. "But you like green."

"Are you trying to say that I don't know what my favorite color is?"

"If your favorite color is blue, why is your room *not* blue? *You* painted it. You could have chosen blue, but you didn't."

I painted my room to match the color of Ethan's eyes. I opened my mouth to respond, but nothing came out. What was I supposed to say? That I had believed the artist in me was inspired by an elusive dream? That it turned out I wasn't more evolved than just a hormone-driven teenager obsessed with some boy's eyes? Was I supposed to admit how lame that was?

"See?" She accepted my silence as triumph. "Blue is *not* your favorite color."

"My bathroom is blue," I mumbled lamely. I couldn't even pretend it was a valid point.

She scoffed. "It's the color of toilet water."

It sounded offensive, but she was entirely correct. That was exactly what I patterned it after. Inspired by toilet water. I couldn't argue. How did she know me so well? *When* did she know me so well?

"Maybe," she offered in consolation, "you liked blue at one point, but you evolved and didn't know it."

"That doesn't make sense. It's a favorite color. That stays the same no matter how old you get."

"Of course it makes sense!" She unlinked her arm from mine so she could talk more animatedly with her hands. "And, of course, that changes! Your favorite things aren't, like, perpetual monuments. They're more like fashion. It develops as you grow."

"Whatever is popular?"

"No," she responded automatically but contradicted herself immediately to clarify. "I mean, it can be, but not always. Like, just because you had a favorite onesie when you were a baby, it doesn't mean it's your favorite outfit when you're twenty-one!"

I laughed at the visual, just as she intended. It did sound ridiculous. "But it feels, I don't know, sort of flakey to change opinions like that? Like today my favorite color is blue, but tomorrow, not so much?"

"It's not always like that!"

"It sounds like that!"

"You're evolving. Like, you're experiencing the world that your younger self didn't know about. Our experiences change us, whether or not we believe it or even notice it." I was skeptical. She could sense it.

"It's OK to be OK with that," she insisted. "You're not being disloyal to your younger self. Or flakey. You're embracing who you are now." She grabbed me in a tight hug. "It's self-care. You're loving yourself!"

"Did you just equate shopping with self-care?"

She let go of the hug when she laughed. "No! I'm equating recognizing personal growth as self-care." She studied her perfectly manicured nails. "But, I mean, hey, if that involves a little retail therapy, I'm not arguing."

Brieann was very easy to underestimate. She was stereotypically beautiful in a way that should mean she couldn't possibly be an honor student. Because that would be unfair.

Except that she was. I felt like she often hid her intelligence to make less secure people more comfortable. She never had to do that with me.

I shook my head, amused. She knew that she had made her point successfully.

"Sometimes," she added with a grin, "you just need to trust your friends."

Pressures and Pinafores

Just when I thought my feelings of dread about this little field trip of ours had finally settled, Amanda and Raven walked into the same store we were shopping in. The disadvantage of living in a small town was the likelihood you might bump into people you disliked was high.

Their presence kicked up all sorts of anxiety that had been comfortable in the dust at my feet. It swirled, disturbing other things like insecurity and angst. By the time Amanda started to speak, there was an invisible tornado of unease spiraling around me.

"London!" she squealed. Her voice, dripping with insincerity, was artificially high-pitched so that it attracted the attention of random people around her. They followed her progress with their eyes. Additional bystanders to witness my humiliation. She glossed over Brieann's presence with such flourish that by just saying my name, she successfully insulted us both.

That must be some kind of bullying skill set.

I didn't respond. I felt that would just give her more ammunition. She sauntered up to us, wearing a perfect smile and a look in her eyes that every victim was familiar with. A look that was positively gleaming with such negative intent.

"Did you find someone willing to go with you to the dance?" She and Raven shared a sly look as she spoke.

"You know her boyfriend is out of the country, Amanda," Brieann said on my behalf.

Amanda didn't even look at her. "So, no?" Her perfectly made-up face contorted into mock sympathy. "Don't you worry," she added over her shoulder as she turned to walk out the door they had come in. "I'm sure you'll find some*body* before Saturday." Bystanders might have considered these words encouraging, but we knew better. She giggled loudly with Raven for no apparent reason as they made their exit, making sure that they maintained their audience wherever they went.

"She has such a punchable face," I mumbled when they were safely out of earshot.

Brieann laughed—a little harder than I thought my comment deserved. Her reaction startled me. She waved a hand to me between her laughter. "It's just funny because Drew said those exact same words to me before."

I smiled. "It's a universal feeling."

"I just want to remind you that before you moved here, *that* was what passed as friendship to me."

"Yikes."

"Exactly."

She dismissed all talk of Amanda and company by turning her full attention to the rack of dresses beside us. "Are you thinking long or short?"

"I genuinely don't care."

Brieann clicked her tongue in mild disapproval. "Fine. I'll choose then."

Maybe it was a bad idea not to have an opinion.

She handed me two dresses, both in shades of sage. "These are more spring than winter," she admitted, "but I think they'll look great on you. Plus, they're on sale. Bonus! Go try them on, and I'll scour some more."

I took the dresses to the dressing room, which wasn't more than three walls and a heavy curtain that hooked to the side. That was the lock. The fact that the curtain was drawn shut meant that it was in use. I had to trust that strangers understood that and wouldn't tug it open while I stood there in my underwear. I knew the little hook on the end would provide some kind of resistance and serve as a reminder to anyone that tried, but there was a nagging feeling inside me that was not convinced.

My first instinct was to turn my back to the curtain so that if it did get accidentally pulled open, eye contact could be avoided. But the full-length mirror directly across from it would just provide a full view anyway. I decided to face the curtain. That might, at least, give me a chance to hold the curtain closed in case the reinforcement was necessary. I didn't turn to face the mirror until I was fully dressed.

I hated shopping for clothes. It was always an ordeal.

The first dress I tried on was on the longer side. Just enough to sweep the floor and intended for heels. That alone was enough reason for me to reject it, but I had to hand it to Brieann; the dress made me look good. It hugged just the right places and flowed effortlessly over areas that made me insecure, though I would never admit it aloud.

And the color was perfect.

I fished for my phone so I could take a picture of my reflection. I never thought I would be one of those people that did that. I used to make fun of people who took selfies. It seemed vain to me. Self-absorbed. And yet, there I was, capturing the moment.

It's self-care, I thought to myself. *I'm loving myself.*

I grinned at my reflection, sharing this quiet conspiracy. If all else failed, Brieann could still be blamed. My reflection agreed.

I tried on eight dresses in total. It may have been all the dresses in the store that would remotely fit me. Every time I thought I was done, Brieann handed me another one. I didn't even get a chance to leave the dressing room.

"Do we have a winner?" Brieann asked when I let her see the last one. The dress left one shoulder bare. It hugged my waist but flared over my hips. The front edge fell just below my knees but dipped lower in the back.

"It has pockets." In itself, this was enough reason for me to approve it. I stuck my hands in and spread my elbows out.

"You look like a chicken." She snorted.

"A chicken with pockets," I corrected her.

"Whatever. It looks good on you, so I approve …"

"Not that I need your approval or anything!"

"… so I think that's the one to beat."

My shoulders fell. "What do you mean, 'the one to beat'? We're not done?"

She laughed. "This is our *first* store, London. There are other options."

"Nope. No. Nay. Negative. We are done." She opened her mouth to argue, but I stopped her. "I am standing my ground, Bree. I like this dress. It fits fine. It's not dragging on the floor. It has pockets. I'm getting this one. I'm not looking at others. This is it. This is the dress. I'm buying it."

I was proud of myself for making a solid decision. It wasn't until I glimpsed that crafty, satisfied look on her face that I realized this was her plan all along. She had somehow played me into wanting this dress. Into *arguing* for it. For a dress that I didn't want to shop for to begin with.

"Wait a minute," I began. "You did this."

And the look was gone, replaced so efficiently by one of convincing innocence. "I don't know what you mean."

I stared at her with narrowed eyes. Her air of innocence deepened. There was no winning this one.

I sighed. "Fine. You win. Whatever. I don't know how you did this, but this is entirely your doing."

"I'm confused," she said in a tone that made it obvious she wasn't confused at all. "You want the dress, right?"

I *did* want the dress. I nodded, still scowling because I didn't want to admit anything.

To her credit, the most gloating she did was to smile, tilt her head, and wink. I closed the curtain so I didn't have to see her face. I heard her laugh. She was so infuriating.

I took one last look at myself in the mirror before removing the dress. I smiled. In the privacy of a dressing room cluttered with seven discarded dresses, I was willing to admit that this made me happy.

And it would look great with that new pair of Chucks Ethan bought for me.

Interlude

The days leading up to the dance were just a countdown. Teachers gave up introducing any new lessons, understanding that the likelihood of retention would be low. Getting a trigonometry quiz rescheduled was the best thing out of this whole affair.

The school did put its foot down regarding potential attendance issues on Friday. Absences would not be tolerated. Anyone who missed school on Friday wasn't going to be allowed to the dance. The dance wasn't until Saturday, so I couldn't understand why such a large number of Juniors were planning on it.

"It doesn't take a whole twenty-four hours to get ready for a dance. What's the big deal about being required to go to class tomorrow?" I waited until I was at the table with Brieann before verbalizing my opinions over the conversations I overheard in line.

Brieann set her tray down next to mine. She didn't share my outrage. "Salon appointments are completely full for Saturday. Maybe the only available times left are tomorrow."

"You can't get your hair styled the day before," I argued. "It'll be useless by the time you're actually getting ready for the dance!" I thought about how unkempt I looked every morning and could not possibly imagine that any careful styling would survive.

"Depends on what you're getting done. If it's, like, a treatment instead of a style. Or like coloring or straightening. Those are fine the day before." She shrugged. "It doesn't have to be hair. They might be wanting to get their nails done too."

I looked down at my nails. I kept them short, clean, and unpolished. Not as a protest or statement but out of convenience. I'd never thought twice about them before, but they felt suddenly naked. "Are you calling me out?"

"We don't need a salon," she assured me. "I've got it covered."

"That sounds ominous." It sounded like a threat.

"I'll be at your place bright and early. We'll have all day to prep and pamper." It was most definitely a threat.

"Don't you have to be setting up or something?" I asked, looking for a way out.

"Everything will be ready by tomorrow night. I've got a pass on all my classes to set up. Then on Saturday, school officials handle the rest."

"Wait. You're excused from *all* your classes?"

She nodded. "Perks of being on the planning committee."

"I'm beginning to see the advantages."

"More fun than sitting in Government. Snorefest."

Drew joined us, sliding onto the bench with his tray. "Backdrops and decor have been safely delivered," he reported. "Balloons are en route tomorrow morning."

Brieann's smile was more because of his presence than it was for the news he brought with him. I could tell because that was how I imagined I smiled whenever Ethan was around.

I liked to complain and pretend that all this production associated with something as pedestrian as a high school dance was beneath me, but I found myself pulled into the excitement. Not nearly at the same level as most everyone around me, but significantly more than I was letting on.

It also made me miss Ethan more.

"I'm picking you up at London's, right?" Drew took an inhumanly large bite of his calzone. And yet, not a single drop of hot tomato sauce was wasted. It was a skill set he could put on a résumé.

"I can just come to you," I offered to Brieann. "I might not have all the necessary tools you're accustomed to having at your disposal." I waved my hands in the air to pantomime hair curling and product spray.

"No, it's cool. I can bring everything we need."

"She wants to keep you in her sights at all times in case you make excuses and back out," Drew clarified. The look she gave him confirmed it.

"I won't back out," I promised. "That ticket was too expensive to waste."

"I'm not picking you guys up in a limo," Drew warned. "Don't expect a limo."

"The only thing I expect is flowers," Brieann demanded.

"Lavender to match your outfit," Drew intoned in a sing-song voice, indicating that he'd heard this more than once before.

She nodded. "That's right."

"So does that mean you've been officially asked to the dance?" I teased Brieann. "Was it worth the wait?"

She smiled and shared a shy look with Drew. "Yes." But that was all she offered.

I didn't press. They were my best friends, but they were also a couple. There were things they shared that remained between the two of them. I respected that. There were many things between Ethan and me that I kept selfishly close.

It was as if Drew could tell whenever my thoughts wandered. "You sure Captain Kiwi can't just teleport this way?" Brieann had coined that nickname, but it seemed that Drew had picked it up as fair use. His tone was jovial. He kept it light so that I knew not to take it seriously.

"I wish!" I said with more yearning than I had intended to convey. "But I bet he wouldn't, even if he could. You know how Ethan is about all this."

"He's right," Brieann reminded me. "It's safer. And you've been doing a really good job. It's been, like, two weeks since Laurent and you haven't crossed."

"No crossing. No monster." It was almost a mantra I repeated to myself every night. The waking world kept me busy. Between school, the dance, and the information dump that was my mom's legacy, I was sufficiently distracted. But the danger that waited in my sleep was always front and center before I closed my eyes.

I played with the metal band around my wrist. A hopeful talisman to help keep me safe, and I wondered, not for the first time, if it would be enough.

First Look

Drew pulled up in his candy-red classic 3 series, freshly waxed for the occasion. I watched Brieann watch him from the window. Soft curls fell around her face, some strands strategically held in place with little sparkling clips that resembled diamonds. She had done her own hair, expertly manipulating it into perfect submission so that it looked effortless and yet fully intentional. I'd seen bridal magazine covers with less finesse. She was perfect but uncharacteristically flustered.

There were no less than three clutch bags overflowing with makeup scattered around the room. That wasn't even counting the hair curler, hair straightener, hair dryer and all the other hair paraphernalia that Brieann had unloaded on my unmade bed. I pushed her backpack out of the way with my foot so that I could get to my bedroom door. "You look great," I assured her, somewhat surprised that this was even a concern. She always looked great. It was a given. There was never a need for insecurity.

She lightly tugged at the soft material of her dress, straightening the thin straps that held it in place. It fell to her ankles, shimmering in such a way that it seemed to be iridescent. It was lavender, but when it hit the light just right, it was silver. "Do you think he'll like it?"

I searched her eyes for a hint of sarcasm. All I saw was genuine worry. "Are you serious?" I asked.

"I don't know why I'm so nervous. It's not like we've never been on a date before. It's not like he's not already my boyfriend." She clenched her hands together, being careful not to damage her freshly dried nail polish. "But I am. I'm just so nervous."

I studied her for a moment, wondering what to do about this side of Brieann that I'd never seen before. "It's actually cute to see you this way." I leaned against my closet door to demonstrate my total disregard for her distress. "It's almost like you aren't perfect."

She put her hands on her hips and regarded me with the sour look of someone who might have just discovered a bad smell. "I'm so glad that my suffering can make you happy." Her words were sautéed to sarcastic perfection.

"No, no"—I pretended to protest—"this is good. So much more human and approachable."

She rolled her eyes. The momentary insecurity was gone, and she was back to being the confident powerhouse I recognized. Mission accomplished. I felt that I could literally pat myself on the back for my expert handling of that situation, but the doorbell rang before I could execute any self-congratulatory maneuvers.

"Look at that," Drew said when I greeted him at the door, "you clean up well!"

"I have pockets." I straightened one leg to lift it slightly off the floor. "And it goes well with my Chucks!" Brieann was not happy that I'd balked at wearing heels for the evening, but it wasn't the hill she was willing to die on, so she let me be.

Drew's shoes were much more appropriate for his outfit. He was in a slim gray three-piece suit. He'd left his coat in the car, but the vest he had on matched his pants. He wore a bow tie in the exact shade of Brieann's dress. That was clearly her doing. In one hand, he carried a clear box that contained a delicate wrist corsage. He held a single lavender-colored rose in the other.

Neither one was for me.

I opened the door wide and stepped out of the way. Brieann waited by the stairs. If there was such a thing as shy confidence, she wore it better than any dress. It was like she knew she'd nailed the look but was apologizing for it. Sorry but not sorry.

Drew's teasing smile froze when he saw her. It slowly fell away, leaving his lips slightly parted, the beginnings of a word that refused to come out. I couldn't identify the emotions that filtered through his eyes faster than he could blink. He took one step forward but stopped breathing.

Brieann looked as proud of his reaction as she was coy. She did a slow turn in place. "What do you think?" It was almost cruel how she was teasing him.

"Wow," he whispered. A declaration more to himself than anyone else. Then he took a deep breath and said more loudly, "I think you are incredible."

Her smile was triumphant.

He handed her the lavender rose first. "As promised," he said, sounding more like himself again.

She accepted the rose and brought it to her nose, but I wondered if she actually smelled it or if she was distracted by the box in his hand. "Thank you. What's that?"

"This," he said with a flourish, "is so you can have your flowers and still eat cake." He removed the corsage from the box. "Hands-free flowers."

She giggled demurely while he tied it to her wrist. Ordinarily, I'd have made puking noises, but I was too busy taking pictures of the sickeningly sweet scene with my phone.

"Where's your dad?" Drew asked after he'd secured the flora.

"He's chairing some committee or another tonight. I wasn't really listening." I thought that being a teacher meant that you had weekends and summer off, but that wasn't true. Especially not when the teacher in question was a college professor. "He was home earlier, though, so Bree and I already got our photos in."

"With a *real* camera," Brieann added, referring to the Nikon that Dad pulled out for the occasion. While he took our photos, he talked about all the features of his Digital Single-Lens Reflex that he claimed made it better than the low-quality sorry excuse for cameras that we had on our phones.

"You kids and your fancy phones." He sounded like an old-timer sitting on the porch rocker and talking about the good old days. I'd rolled my eyes, but Brieann just smiled.

"Those aren't cameras. They're barely even phones anymore. And the battery life is dismal," he lectured. "Maybe they're good for those selfie shots you like to take, but for real occasions, you should use real cameras." I wanted him to stop, but Brieann indulged him.

In the end, it made him happy. And I suspect likely less guilty that he had to miss seeing me off to the party.

"Shall we?" Drew offered Brieann a crooked arm, which she took with a smile. Then, rose in hand, she linked her other arm with mine.

"We shall!"

And so we did.

Solo

Ethan tried calling when we were already on our way. I was sitting in the back seat of Drew's car, cradling my phone with both hands. I hunched back, creating a little space pocket that ultimately made no difference but made me feel like we were in our own little world. Brieann and Drew were in quiet conversation, allowing me a semblance of privacy.

"We're on the move, so my connection sucks," I warned him. As if to prove my point, the video froze. It was annoying, but it allowed me a quiet moment in time to study his image.

His hair used to be long enough to shade his eyes but was now cut back to expose his face to the New Zealand summer sun. He had tanned nicely in the past few weeks, bringing out the gold in his hazel eyes. He looked so different from the boy I'd met in my dream almost six months before. Not so much because of the haircut and tan but because the look in his eyes had shifted. While they still harbored the pain and trauma he'd experienced in his life, they were less distrustful now. Less angry. It made all the difference.

I blinked when the video played again, but the audio was choppy. "… can't … maybe … tonight …"

I waited to see if the call would stabilize, but it froze again. My thumb hovered over the end call button, hesitant to quit. After a few more seconds, I ended the call.

Old school? I texted instead.

He sent me a thumbs-up emoji.

Cnt stay n chat nywy

Wntd 2 c u

I responded in kind and sent him one of the pictures that Brieann had taken of me earlier.

Beautiful

I sent him a heart emoji. I wasn't eloquent enough to do much more. I clashed between waves of missing him terribly to being grateful he was in my life to miss.

Wish I culd b wid u

Will call u l8r

Hve a gr8 tym

Luv u

I held the phone to my chest and felt like crying. I closed my eyes to control myself. Not only was I unprepared to deal with this, but I also didn't want to ruin the makeup that Brieann had so painstakingly applied.

"Are you OK?" Brieann asked from the front passenger seat.

"Yeah," I said unconvincingly before I opened my eyes. "This is just one of those times that I miss him so hard."

Her smile was understanding, which almost made things worse. She studied me for a moment while I pretended I wasn't looking. I cringed in anticipation of what she would say next.

"Long distance blows."

I exhaled. I was glad she said that. Glad that she didn't project some kind of fake optimism. It was what I needed to hear. It made it possible for *me* to project a fake optimism.

I put my phone in my pocket and leaned forward, draping one arm on each of their shoulders. "It's cool. I've got friends. There will be food. We shall have fun." And to further rally the troops, I let out a hoot.

Brieann grinned at my resolve. She followed suit, raising a fist in the air as she hooted. It was such a contrast to see her in her elegant dress, sparkly heels, and updo, acting like she was sitting in the bleachers of a football game. Come to think of it, I don't think she was ever in the bleachers of a football game. Cheerleaders had their own space. And they hooted with so much more finesse than whatever it was she was doing at that moment.

I laughed. Drew did too. Encouraged, she repeated herself, adding a bounce to her repertoire. It was an invitation to do the same. Drew contributed to the hooting. He honked the horn. I lifted both hands and yelled. The ridiculousness of it all induced more laughter.

By the time we got to school, I had stopped feeling sorry for myself. I felt like I could take on the world.

Blizzard Ball

"Hey! I made those paper chains!"

I felt a surprisingly strange sense of pride at seeing them hanging from the rafters. They were dots of color on an otherwise black ceiling. Long strands of silver tinsel were strung low. Hundreds of paper snowflake cutouts hung on invisible wire. An arc of winter-blue and white balloons greeted guests at the entrance. Even more balloons, some transparent and filled with confetti, covered the dance floor. I knew it was the dance floor because it was the only opening among the big round dinner tables.

A light fog crawled on the floor. It helped obscure the basketball court to give the impression that we were somewhere other than the school gym.

"We have a fog machine?" I looked at Brieann in awe.

She appeared entirely pleased with how everything looked. She had orchestrated the whole thing, bringing together the best elements to make it happen. "The theater department has two, actually."

"Memories of *A Midsummer Night's Dream*," Drew added knowingly. I didn't know what that meant, but Brieann nodded.

The main lights were off, but the DJ had slow spinning balls that threw the entire room into a dreamlike glow of cool colors. One of the backdrops that Drew had worked on hung behind the low stage where the DJ had set up. Floor lights faced up, creating a grand effect.

"Are we expecting a snow machine?" I asked, only half kidding. The faint disappointment in Brieann's eyes meant it was something she had actually considered.

"No," Drew answered for her. "But she equipped the DJ with confetti poppers."

"Come on, let's get our pictures done!" Brieann pulled Drew along before I could add to the commentary. I followed.

We walked along one wall, past the long tables of food. The tables were covered in disposable party cloths for easy cleanup. There were paper plates and plastic utensils on one end, followed by generic chips, chopped salad from the cafeteria, pizza still in boxes, two trays of artificially red pasta, and hotdogs wrapped in foil. A large punch bowl marked the end of the buffet. Two adult chaperones hovered around it, presumably to intervene in the event of questionable behavior. All in all, the food was less appetizing than the typical everyday lunch menu.

"Did you empty out the food budget so you could kill it with the decorations?" I teased Brieann.

"The food committee was not my department," she said with a casual wave of her hand. The smile meant she appreciated the implied compliment.

There was already a line on the other side of the gym where the other backdrop Drew had painted was flanked with more balloons. A folding table next to it was set up with various accessories one could don if one wanted. Feather boas, hats, masks, humorously large glasses, and even signs. A couple of volunteer students were manning the area with a faculty member, who looked like he was there only because he'd lost a bet.

We were almost at the front when I heard Amanda's stage voice behind us. My good mood ran and hid. "London!" she called as if we were childhood friends that hadn't seen each other in decades. The crowd parted for her.

"And just when I thought I was having a good time," I mumbled to Brieann. She gave me a sympathetic look.

I grudgingly turned around. Amanda, in a stunning silver gown, looked like the high school iteration of an evil winter witch queen. Complete with the understated tiara in her hair. She had a freshly manicured hand in the crook of an older boy's arm. I didn't recognize him, but his facial hair and sharp features meant he was one of the seniors. Or possibly a college freshman. He was her contrast, in a dark suit that matched his dark hair. He was the perfect accessory to her. Nothing more.

Acutely aware that people were watching, she acted like we were alone in the room. "You are so brave," she said in a stage whisper as if she and I were part of a grand conspiracy. She put one hand over the deep neckline of her dress for effect. "For coming alone like this. Just so brave."

"She's not alone, Amanda." As usual, Brieann wasn't afraid to step in.

Amanda made a point to look around the room, attempting to spot someone she knew would not be there. "I don't see that boy you claim is your boyfriend. Is he parking the car?"

"He's not here," I said without thinking, adding to the fire that was already making my insides blister.

"Oh dear," she said in mock sympathy. I watched her gaze travel from my face to my feet. She ditched the sympathy and went full mocking. "I see you couldn't find a date or appropriate shoes."

That was her big miscalculation. There were many things that I was insecure about, but my Chucks was not one of them. Ethan had given me these shoes. I was not going to allow anyone, especially not Amanda, ruin that for me.

Her insult fired me up in a different way. I propped my heel to show her that my choice of footwear was not something I was ashamed of. "Fashion is all about how you pull it off," I said with a confidence I didn't know I had.

She snorted her distaste. I didn't give her an opportunity to continue. I straightened up and stepped closer to her. It was an act of defiance.

"I thought you knew that." I dared look *her* up and down as if *I* were the one that was sizing her up. "But I guess when you're too busy trying to be a trend, you forget what it takes to be a classic." My voice was loud enough to carry over the music that three people down the line turned to watch.

"A classic loser." She laughed, but I'd caught her by surprise by actually responding. She lost her edge, and it sounded a little uncomfortable.

"Loser? Really? That's your big comeback?" I put my hands

on my waist in a pose I had never done before but had seen others do. "Oh, honey," I continued, my voice swimming in the gravy of contempt, "the only thing lost here is my ability to care about what comes out of your mouth."

I didn't wait for a response. Her reaction was all I needed. I turned around, effectively dismissing her. Brieann and Drew strategically nudged me forward so they could be a human barrier between Amanda and me. Their backs were like a door I just slammed in her face.

It was satisfying.

Bullies prey on weakness. She'd picked the wrong target. I was done being a victim.

I suspected that she knew she'd lost face and would lose even more if she tried to physically push her way to get close enough to speak to me. So she gave up. "Whatever," I heard her say, and I knew she had left.

"Where did that come from?" Brieann asked under her breath, just in case Amanda was within earshot. I looked over my shoulder to see Amanda and her date getting a seat at one of the round tables.

The adrenaline that had made me brave faded with her exit. I tried to cover up my nervous energy with laughter. "I don't know," I admitted, "but at least I got out of it without pig blood on my dress."

"The night is still young," Drew warned.

But despite his premonition, no scenes from Stephen King's *Carrie* were reenacted that night. On the contrary, it turned out to be more fun than I had anticipated.

I had been so caught up in missing what I didn't have, *who* I didn't have, that I didn't appreciate what I *did* have. The altercation with Amanda was a defibrillator jolt to a behavior pattern that had become unhealthy. There were so many things beyond my control, but my happiness wasn't one of them. That was completely up to me.

Armed with that insight, I decided I would enjoy the evening. And so I did.

Copious amounts of overly sweet punch were consumed. I used it to wash down all the pizza and chips I kept going back for. I also blamed the sugar rush for all the dancing I did. Because, unlike Brieann, I didn't know how to dance. Dancing meant rhythm, of which I had none. But what made it so great was that it didn't even matter.

Near the end of the evening, they brought out the cupcakes. I loved the cupcakes. It was the best thing out of the entire dance. It didn't matter what the flavors were; they were all decorated with white buttercream frosting and winter-themed sprinkles. Drew and I made it a game to commandeer as many as we could possibly get away with while Brieann shook her head and pretended not to know who we were.

I hadn't laughed so hard since Ethan left.

By the time Drew had dropped me off at home, I was coming down from the sugar rush like a bat without wings.

That was the first mistake.

Other mistakes followed. Such as not following the routine that I had ascribed to for the past two weeks. I didn't meditate. Or even glance at the prayer of protection Brieann had taped to my dressing mirror. I didn't affix Laurent's asabikeshiinh over my bed. I left the copper pot in the bathroom—unfilled. Save for the bracelet around my wrist, there was nothing in place to protect me.

Instead, I crashed into bed after a quick shower. I didn't wake up when Brieann texted me that she was home. I didn't wake up when Ethan tried to initiate a video call. I didn't even wake up when Dad looked in on me and pulled my comforter over me.

I didn't wake up because I was dreaming.

I didn't wake up because I was crossing.

Radioactive

It was a place I had never been to before. I was so tired that it took me longer than it should have for me to realize that I had crossed. And before I even wondered where I was, I already felt that overwhelming sense of fear.

I looked down at my wrist and saw that, as usual, it was bare. Wherever I had crossed to, I had not taken Ethan's bracelet with me. Nor Laurent's asabikeshiinh that was, no doubt, laying limply by my side table where I had left it. I should have let it hang as I had before, but I had taken it down because Brieann insisted that my dress had to be steamed before I dressed for the dance, and that was the only place I could think to hang it. Then I forgot to return it to its place. Not that it mattered. It had already proved to be useless in an actual fight.

Was that what was waiting for me? A fight?

Sure enough, I was in my favorite jeans, tank top, hoodie, and an old pair of Chucks. The same outfit I had on when I first met Ethan. The same outfit I had on when I first crossed.

Except I wasn't in the woodlands of New Zealand. I was in a wasteland. It wasn't like the kind of desert that had always been a desert. It was what used to be a once fertile area that had fallen into centuries of decay until it was no longer habitable. Any life and color had been long drained away. I was walking in a black-and-white dystopian painting. The broken shapes of abandoned structures were hard to identify. Were they stone? Burnt metal?

Did they used to be people?

A fog that could have been straight from the Blizzard Ball might not have been so eerie had it not also been black and putrid. It smelled of decay. I was grateful that it didn't go past my ankles.

This place echoed death.

Convinced that nothing here could be alive, I desperately hoped not to see Ethan while simultaneously hoping to see him. I did not want to be alone.

I had crossed to Ethan. I had crossed to watch him get shot. I had crossed to a vestige of my dead mother. I had crossed to witness the death of another Woolgatherer. Why was death always involved? Where had I crossed to now?

I turned in a slow circle, trying to find recognizable landmarks or a hint of which direction to walk. While the fog remained low, a strange haze in the air made it difficult to see very far. Almost every direction looked eerily the same. Nothingness.

I caught a silhouette of something larger, but it was just as easily engulfed in the haze as if I had imagined it. It was the break in an otherwise invariant landscape. That made it my new destination by default.

Feeling a strange sense of déjà vu gone wrong, I walked toward it.

Petrified

I lost track of how long I was walking in what was possibly radioactive badlands. The landscape changed little, and I wondered, more than once, if I'd made any kind of progress. The longer I stayed in this dream, the more apprehensive I became. It was more than the foreboding nature of the place. The air was thick with misgiving. As if the entire land was on the precipice of a decision, an event that might tip this flatland on its side. The very particles in the fog were watching and waiting.

I also tried meditation, thinking that if it helped me cross, maybe it would help me get out of a dream. But it was impossible. First of all, it was unfeasible for me to meditate standing up. And whenever I tried a position sitting on the disagreeable ground, unidentifiable grit slapped me in the face. I was so desperate that I had even attempted to click the heels of my Chucks and muttered my desire to be home.

It didn't work.

When I finally came to the silhouette that I had glimpsed through the fog earlier, I was so relieved by the change in scenery that I was not initially awed by the size of what appeared to be a crystallized wall. It grew larger as I approached it, as grand structures do.

The surface was irregular; some areas were smooth, and others were sharp and jagged. Every color that was missing from the terrain was represented on the rock that made this wall. It was stunning. Its appearance was in opposition to the barren land that surrounded it.

On my sixteenth birthday, my eldest brother, Liam, gave me a necklace. It was a unique-looking pendant on a leather cord. I rarely wore jewelry, and suspecting it was his girlfriend's idea discouraged me further from putting it on. The gemstone was beautiful, though.

"What is it?" Locke had asked so I didn't have to.

"Petrified wood," Liam had replied with unhidden pride.

"Scared wood?" Locke had been mildly confused but moderately amused. Liam, not so much.

"It's fossilized wood," Liam had explained. "It's a mineralized process. It happens naturally to wood when it's buried in ash or saturated sediment. When the wood decays, it's replaced by minerals. The color is usually from trace metals in the sediment. Every one of them is unique."

Petrified wood. That was what the wall was in front of me. The most extreme example of it. Or the summation of it all. The grandfather of all petrified wood. Something this large wasn't possible in nature, but neither was anything in this place.

What was waiting on the other side of this wall? Was it keeping something out? Was it keeping something in? Was it the edge of the world?

The last time I walked to what seemed like the edge of the world, Ethan appeared. What was at the edge of this one?

I walked along the length of this magical wall of colors and past lives. I thought about all the things that led me here. From my mother's choices, my inherited abilities, and every decision I'd made since that discovery.

My mother's actions had cost her more than she had anticipated. I had only made it this far because I benefited from her sacrifice. And also not without a large helping of dumb luck.

Unless that was what it meant to be the super special chosen one.

I stopped walking. *Chosen for what, exactly?*

A happy ending wasn't guaranteed. So many things can go wrong. Just as it had for my mom. Just as it had for Ethan's mom.

The heft of what was at stake weighed heavily on me. And I was on the fringe of another bad decision.

Forest of Dreams

There didn't seem to be a break in the wall. There were no obvious markings to indicate a doorway or opening. No clue as to its purpose.

I hesitated to touch it, but it was so much more inviting than anything I had seen here so far. I expected it to be cold. There was a warmth to it. Not the kind of heat generated by an external source but the kind generated by something that was alive. Or, at least, had been at one point.

I put both hands on it, wondering if it felt the same at every spot. It did at first. Then the surface became warmer, almost throbbing. Until I didn't feel it anymore.

Because I fell right through it.

I didn't realize how much weight I was putting on my hands until the surface beneath them dissolved. I fell forward. I took a step in an attempt to prevent a face-plant. It made it just that much more spectacular when I *did* fall on my face. My hands that I had splayed in front of me, first to touch the wall and then to stop my fall, fell into thick foliage.

I rolled onto my back and looked back up at the wall. It was still there. Seemingly as solid as it had been before.

I walked through a wall.

The air was different on this side. Like being in a greenhouse filled with thriving plants. Thick with humidity. Certainly, the leaves that had broken my fall were thriving in it. All the vegetation that was missing from the arid terrain was present here. Alive and flourishing.

I sat up in the strange leaves, feeling like I had done this before.

I was surrounded by trees. They were so tightly positioned together that I was gratefully surprised I hadn't fallen into one. They reached up high, hinting at their maturity. Deep colors of brown and green. Their leaves were so thick that they blocked the sky. I couldn't tell if it was the middle of the day or the middle of the night.

The only reason I could see was that there were hundreds—no, thousands—of beautiful glowing orbs of floating light between the thick tree trunks. They were suspended in the air like lanterns hung with invisible thread, swaying in a breeze I could not feel. It was eerie but beautiful. Certainly magical. The soft radiance made the many colors on the fossilized wall shimmer like it was under a spell.

It was breathtaking. This could very well be the Garden of Eden. The wasteland on the other side could be the cursed land that humanity was destined to walk through.

Then why was it I felt my skin prickle? Why did everything feel more dangerous?

Maybe it was the stillness. Other than the glowing orbs, nothing moved. No rustling of leaves. No strange little animals running through the lush undergrowth. An entire forest was watching and waiting.

I stood up, careful not to disturb more than I already had. The growth that cushioned my fall healed in front of my eyes, plumping itself up until it looked untouched. Unnatural. A shiver of dread ran up my spine like invisible multi-legged insects.

I saw something flicker delicately within the orb closest to me. It was just at eye level, making it easy for me to observe it better. I narrowed my eyes, trying to focus on what looked like deliberate movement. I didn't notice that I'd stepped closer and closer until all I could see was the glowing orb and what was within it.

Ghostly images flickered inside like a paranormal silent film. A young Black girl was getting her hair braided by an older woman, who I presumed was her mother. The girl was reading aloud from a board book, though no sound accompanied the images. Her mother was smiling as her hands expertly wove the strands together.

I turned my head to observe another orb. This one was floating a little lower but easy enough to observe. In it, an older girl in a petticoat was riding a pony. The pony was stunningly white, perfectly groomed. A field of pink and white flowers covered the hill that the horse and rider were on. The sky above them was a perfect cloudless blue.

I looked through more orbs. I saw more scenes. Each one was a different girl in a different situation. Some were mundane, like playing on a swing or riding a bike. Others were outlandish, involving unicorns and dragons.

The scenes were all happy, but my unease grew with every one.

Then one of them caught my full attention. It was one of the mundane ones. A young girl, eleven years old, was at an ice cream store with her parents. It was her birthday.

Tears suddenly stung my eyes. I couldn't look away.

Her father juggled the cones as he paid while she went with her mother to find a booth. When her father joined them, he handed the girl her chocolate cone covered in sprinkles. The girl was absolutely delighted. It wasn't so much the ice cream that made the girl smile. It was that she was there with both her parents that made her happy.

I knew that because I recognized that girl.

I was the girl. That was my dream. A dream I had when I was younger and longing for a mother I never knew. A dream I never shared with anyone.

I watched the ghostly scene play out exactly the way I knew it would. My heart was in my throat. Realization rushed at me like a powerful wave, knocking me down and covering me in fear.

These were all dreams. Every one of them had to belong to a Woolgatherer.

I was in a forest of Woolgatherer's dreams.

I was in the Sarramauca's lair.

A Wonderful Life

I staggered, hitting orbs as I blundered backward. They disappeared into a mist as I went through them. I didn't know how many I destroyed or what it meant to do so. I didn't care. I just wanted to get away.

I didn't notice how far I had strayed from the wall when I'd been busy investigating orbs. The extra steps seemed like too large a distance. I pivoted to run back, looking for safety in the expanse outside of what I had thought was a forest paradise.

This was no paradise. It was the trophy room of a voyeur. It was a catacomb of Woolgatherer dreams.

But before I could get to the wall, a figure blocked my way. My mother. Not the ghost of my mother, who was bald, sallow, and faded. But my mother as she looked in old photos. She was young, healthy, and beautiful.

"Mom?" I stopped short, more confused than I was suspicious.

She was taller than I expected. And her smile wasn't quite right. But before I remembered the Sarramauca was a shape-shifter, the forest around us fell away. I blinked, and we were somewhere else.

I was in my kitchen.

I was standing in front of the stove, holding a wide silicone spatula in one hand. It was morning, and the smell of good coffee was strong. Outside the window, I could hear chirping birds.

"Sweetheart, you're going to burn it if you don't flip it."

My mother walked into the kitchen, tying an apron around her waist as she entered. I stepped back away from her, alarmed by the abrupt scene change. She didn't seem to notice my reaction. Or if she did, she didn't let it bother her. She walked around the counter and gestured at the pancakes I was apparently cooking.

The smell of maple syrup blended with the coffee. The sun through the window seemed to shine exactly the way it should and also too bright at the same time. I was disoriented, but I couldn't remember why. It was a mental struggle.

What was I doing before this?

Dad walked in shortly after, carrying an already half-empty cup of coffee. He snapped his fingers playfully in front of my face. "Earth to London. Have we lost contact?"

I blinked. I looked down at the sizzling skillet and flipped the pancakes.

"You shouldn't space out like that when you're that close to a fire," he advised. Mom kissed him on the cheek.

"Oh, leave her alone, Edward. She's completely capable. She made your breakfast, didn't she?" Mom gestured to the table where an appetizing plate of bacon and eggs waited.

I did?

Dad held a hand up in surrender. "Just teasing."

If Dad already had his food and I was still making half a dozen pancakes, it meant that my brothers were home. And as if on cue, Locke walked into the kitchen. "Is there bacon?" he asked, stopping by me only to gauge the doneness of his breakfast before joining Dad at the table. He took a strip of bacon off Dad's plate. Mom swatted his hand playfully but allowed it.

Liam was next. He, too, had his mug of coffee. Chase, the middle brother, followed closely behind, carrying a book instead of a drink. They all found their respective seats at the dinner table. Everyone had a place. The family was complete under one roof. It was like the setup for the title frame of the next family sitcom.

Mom handed me plates. "I think the pancakes should be done."

I looked back at the griddle and saw she was right. The pancakes were impeccable. I began stacking them on the plates as requested. It was a mechanical but expected motion. My body knew what to do, but my eyes didn't know where to look. I was just along for the ride.

I thought I was only making six, but whenever I stacked a plate, more blemishless pancakes showed up on the griddle. Until each plate had five pancakes. All the exact same size. An ideal stack. When I looked back at the griddle, it was empty and clean.

Mom drizzled maple syrup on each one, and it dripped down the sides like I've only seen happen in commercials. Flawless. She smiled at me, and this time, I felt better. A wash of contentment dripped over me like the pancake syrup she was pouring. "Will Ethan be joining us?"

"When has the boyfriend not joined us?" Dad snorted.

"Be nice, Edward," Mom chided. "Ethan is a good boy."

"Ethan is here?" I was surprised but also not surprised. I felt I should be expecting him.

"Right here," a low voice responded. I turned to see Ethan, just as he was the first time I met him. Sans the cut lip. He wore the same dark shirt and jeans that he had that day. A mess of light-colored hair fell over his eyes. The thick band of his watch wrapped around his wrist. No bracelet.

"You're here." It was both a statement of fact and an exclamation of surprise.

"I'm here," he repeated, taking me in his arms. I did not expect that. I dropped the spatula, but he caught it before it hit the floor. Without letting me go. He didn't break eye contact even as he leaned closer to place the spatula gently on the counter. I couldn't breathe.

Then without warning, he kissed me.

In front of my entire family.

I kissed him back.

Then when my brain finally caught up with current events and I felt the full force of my embarrassment, I pushed him away from me. He let go and stepped back, but his expression wasn't one of regret.

I felt the heat on my face, and I knew I was blushing. And not the delicate blush of a storybook princess … more like the flaming head of a snack mascot. I looked away from him because it felt like the only way I could hide my humiliation.

Dad was in some kind of flirty conversation with Mom. Chase was reading his book. Liam and Locke were chatting about the big blockbuster movie that blew their minds. Their conversation should have been louder, but it was strangely muted. Like it was happening in a different room. No one was paying attention to me and my boyfriend.

I had privacy in a room full of people. That had never happened before. I didn't know what to do with that. It was great but also … not right. Ethan grabbed my hand.

"London," he said. I'd always loved the way he said my name, but at that moment, it sent all my internal alarms off. What was so wrong about him that made me feel so uneasy? Was it his hair? When did it get so long?

There was no denying the discomfort. I was in some kind of danger. From what? From whom?

From Ethan?

I hesitated. When I had first crossed to Ethan, logic was telling me to be wary, but I had instantly felt safe with him. This time, logic was telling me it was safe, but my instinct was to run and hide. I was not always the most confident person, but there were some things I trusted about myself. This was one of them.

"I want to show you something." The way he said those words was not particularly alarming. It was delivered in the perfect manner you'd expect from someone who wanted to share a secret with you. Someone who was promising something unexpected but pleasant. I couldn't place where my anxiety was coming from.

I didn't readily go with him. I looked around the room, trying to find a clue. Something that was out of place that caused my apprehension. The kitchen was exactly the way it should be. Maybe not in the disarray it sometimes was when Dad left his folders all over the table or empty coffee mugs in the sink. But everything that was supposed to be there was in its place. The curtains, the jars, the towels. All there. Even the retro kitchen clock Dad loved. Nothing was missing.

Even if something should be. I locked eyes with Mom.

She is not supposed to be here.

But before I could open my mouth to say it aloud, Ethan tugged at my arm. I tried to pull away at first, but when I looked at him, my arm went limp. He was smiling at me. I forgot why I was struggling. I was wavering between my misgivings and accepting the happiness around me. *This makes me happy. It all makes me happy. Why shouldn't I be happy?*

"Come on," he insisted. This time, I followed. My fear and suspicion faded. I was content.

Just as we got to the doorway, I glanced back into the room. Then I realized why I was so distrustful. Why everything seemed out of place.

Because everything is perfect.

No Escape

I tried to pull away from Ethan. I allowed myself to release the unreasonable panic that was crawling under my skin. I didn't know why, but I also knew I shouldn't give myself the chance to think. There was a time for that. This was all instinct and emotion.

Ethan tightened his hold on my wrist, cutting off circulation until it hurt. His expression had turned hard. As if every shadow that fell on his face darkened along with his mood. I had never seen this kind of rage from him. Even when he was angry at me for putting myself in danger. Even when I thought we were breaking up. Never. It was confirmation that my misgivings had merit.

This was not my Ethan.

I curled my arm toward myself and used my other hand to pull his away before he could react. The way my brothers had taught me growing up. A self-defense move that was playfully irrelevant when I learned it. Liam would have been proud to see me make use of it. I felt the familiar burn on the skin of my wrist, which meant I did it properly. It was a small price to pay to be able to twist free.

I tried to kick him, but he stepped back. All the moves I learned from my brothers were useless against Ethan. He had been in more street fights than I knew of and was learning military techniques to add to that. This was one I would never win. But Liam had taught me that the goal was never to win but to get away from it. My feeble offensive attempt gave me an extra second to get away.

If only my mother wasn't blocking my way.

I crashed into her. We would have both fallen to the ground, but she anticipated the impact and absorbed it, stepping back with one foot and engulfing me in a hug. "Be careful, sweetheart," she said, as most mothers say. But her tone was more sinisterly sweet than it was motherly. "You could get really hurt if you continue to act this way," she whispered into my ear.

My eyes went wide, and I felt my throat close up. My escape was short-lived. I stopped struggling. She loosened her hold. When I didn't resist, she completely let go. I wasn't going anywhere. She knew it. I knew it. I was trapped.

This wasn't happening. This could not be happening.

I am in a dream.

"This is a dream," I mumbled. She didn't respond. Her expression didn't even shift. What I said had no bearing on her. "This is a dream," I repeated. "This isn't real." I pointed at them.

"You're not real." My voice grew louder and more resolute with every sentence. I had to yell it out loud. So that I could believe it myself. "This is just a dream!"

I was feeling more confident. I was declaring myself to the universe and inciting my claim to reality. I was not allowing this to beat me. I was going to win. I knew the truth. This was all just a dream.

"Remember," Fake Ethan threatened, "you can still be hurt in a dream."

I glanced involuntarily at the scar on my arm. What had been my personal trophy evidence of my extraordinary abilities as a Woolgatherer was now a harsh reminder of my mortality in a world that was harmless to others. Had I not been my mother's daughter, I would have been safe.

Woolgatherers die in their dreams.

He stepped closer to me, disfiguring his face with an ugly sneer. Even his eyes shifted from light to dark. An unearthly ink of black injected into the color, eating away at the green and gold. It bled into the whites of his eyes, turning them into a single pool of demonic obsidian.

I stared into them, unperturbed by the dream world around me falling apart. I was on the lip of a cliff similar to the one I had been on when I first met Ethan. Except this time, there was no one to coerce me away from the edge. The void was coaxing me into its bowels.

There was a heavy weight on my chest, preventing me from taking a deep breath. Every shallow gasp I could manage only seemed to evaporate before it reached my lungs. There was pressure on my neck, a tightening that came from the inside. I could hear the blood flowing through my veins.

I failed. I failed my mother. I failed Ethan.

I am going to die.

My legs gave way. I closed my eyes in surrender. There were no moves left to play. It was over.

But the arms that caught me were not hostile. They were strong but protective. A sanctuary from what I anticipated would come next.

I could breathe.

Finis

I opened my eyes and saw Real Ethan, his hair cropped short and smelling of summer and soap. The green in his eyes was the same as the army combat uniform he had on. He had one arm around my waist and the other behind my back, holding me close enough to support all my weight. Close enough so I could feel his breath on my face.

"London," he said. And how he said my name made my soul swell with love and hope. The kitchen scene was gone. There was no trace of a cliff. We were back in the Sarramauca's forest.

If all the glowing orbs vanished when contact was made, their absence around our immediate vicinity meant there had been a struggle. The forest was otherwise still. There was no sign of the monster.

"You're here." It was what I had said to Fake Ethan. It felt weird repeating myself. I could have said something else, but I needed to do it this way. I wanted to replace my memories of what had just happened. It was a coping mechanism. A way for me to center myself in a better reality.

"I'm here," he responded, as my dream had anticipated he would. His eyes softened with his words, a relief as palpable as mine.

I was able to stand on my own. He helped me up. When he released his arms around me, he held one of my hands in his. Then he brushed hair away from my face with the other, a gesture so loving and gentle that it was a thousand times more powerful than a kiss.

"What happened?"

"I fell asleep?" His nonchalance was a laughable juxtaposition to our situation. It was a coping mechanism. "I think you did that thing your mother did. Where you broadcast some kind of beacon for me."

"Anchoring."

"You've been doing that a lot lately. Ever since you saw your mother. That's how I end up with you whenever you cross. Our mothers were the only Woolgatherers that could do that." He tipped his head to mine until our foreheads touched. "Until us."

That made Ethan the only male ever in the history of Woolgathering to cross.

He took a breath, then straightened to continue his narrative. Violence burned in his eyes, and how he tightened his jaw hinted at a kind of rampage that he kept tightly under control. "When I got here, the monster was attacking you."

That explained the eerily perfect dream and how quickly it devolved into a nightmare that stole my ability to breathe. "You were able to stop it?" Also unheard of.

He pulled his favored butterfly knife seemingly out of thin air. He flipped it open without effort, letting it dance a little before holding it motionless. He grinned. "Guess what else I got to take with me?" He flipped it closed, then put it away. "Bree said steel isn't as effective, but I guess it was enough."

"I couldn't even cross with a bracelet, and you took a whole weapon with you?" I don't know why I was miffed by that, but I was.

He laughed. "Mae said it's because the bracelet is actually too powerful." I raised my eyebrows, irked to hear Ethan mention her name so casually. It was a petty thing at an inappropriate time.

"Too powerful?" I repeated.

He nodded. "There's pure iron in that bracelet. Not to mention layers of incantations. It's not going anywhere."

"That actually explains a lot," I admitted reluctantly. Of all the items I tried to take with me in a dream, I picked the immovable object to try and move. Typical. "Did you kill it?"

He scowled. "No," he admitted. "I got close enough to nick the bugger, but it disappeared before I could do anything else. It wasn't much, but it was bloody satisfying to hear it scream." It sounded sadistic, but it made me smile.

Then it hit me. We were still in mortal danger, and we were exchanging conversation like it was a coffee date at Caden's. That was how extras were killed in every horror movie ever made. The fear belayed by Ethan's presence was back with reserves, surrounding us with a presence as high as the trees.

"We need to get out of here." My voice trembled a little more than I wanted it to. I looked around, hoping I wouldn't find anything.

He nodded curtly and turned to lead the way, one hand holding his knife at the ready. I followed close behind him, all my senses itching with sensitive anticipation. We had almost made it to the wall when the familiar sickening sensation of a burning cloud went through me. I staggered back. I knew immediately that we were no longer alone.

Ahead of me, Ethan suddenly stopped. He straightened out of the ready crouch he was in. His shoulders relaxed, and he dropped the knife he had been holding so firmly in his grasp. It was immediately swallowed by the dense undergrowth. Thick leaves let it pass before bouncing back into position, undisturbed.

What started as a haze materialized into the shape of a young woman. Not my mother this time. This new likeness had lighter hair. Long enough to be tied in a low ponytail. She was just about Ethan's height. And when she walked around to face him, her eyes were a mirror of his.

I lunged forward to grab him, but I phased right through as if I had tried to reach for nothing but a projected image. My hands splayed forward, and my chin hit the ground. Had it not been for the thick foliage, it might have been more painful than it already was. I flipped on my back, and from my vantage point, I could see Ethan's expressionless face. The shape-shifter had him in a trance. Translucent wisps emanated from Ethan's mouth.

I called his name, to no avail. Then I felt around me for the knife. I remembered where it fell but couldn't find it. Every empty brush of my hand was a failure. I was shaking as I searched. My breathing was ragged and irregular. Not because I was under attack but because adrenaline was mixing with my fear to create an unstable fuel.

I got to my feet instead, frantic to find another way. I circled them both, coming from different angles. Every time I tried to reach out, my hands passed through as they had with the wall. They were ghosts. Or perhaps I was.

The seconds passed like a lifetime. Every breath was borrowed, counting down the limited time Ethan had left. And there was nothing I could do.

Tears streamed freely down my cheeks. I yelled his name over and over, begging for him to hear me. Begging the universe to allow it.

But the universe wasn't listening to me.

There was a strong wind I could not feel. It swirled around Ethan and the shape-shifter. It tugged at their clothes and pulled the shape-shifter's hair loose. The long strands looked gold as they whipped around, caught in an unpredictable cyclone. The monster was shifting. It grew larger as it gained strength, opening its mouth in what looked like a victorious bellow that I could not hear. I was removed from being able to participate in any way but to witness. Witness how it all ended.

"Ethan!" I yelled until my voice broke. Until desperation clawed at the sound and ripped it to shreds. Until I was screaming in silence.

He blinked.

Ever so slowly, moving like he was underwater, he turned his head to me. I couldn't tell if he could see me, so I made large movements and waved my hands while I called out to him, my throat raw with anguish.

Then in the same painfully slow way, he smiled. Not a half smirk. Not a teasing grin. A genuine smile. One that didn't harbor anything but purity of heart. Beautiful.

It was the idea that this could be the very last time I saw that smile that destroyed me. I fell to my knees, sobbing uncontrollably. I had seen him shot, and it had been horrendous. I almost didn't recover. This was so much worse. This was the real nightmare. The one that could kill me, too, even if I woke up.

Ethan turned his head back to the sardonic face of the shape-shifting monster. His smile stayed in place but was tinged with something else. Determination. And the strength of someone with power realized. In one quick move, Ethan engulfed the shifter in a bear hug.

There was a blaze of light so bright it dwarfed all the glowing orbs combined. The shifter, caught in Ethan's embrace, twisted and changed. It went through many forms, pulling images from his very memories. It started with people that Ethan cared for. Friends that had been killed in action. People I had never met. It even, at one point, tried to look like me. Then when none of them worked, it shifted into mythical creatures. Some that we'd seen in the course of our research. It got bigger and bigger, but it could not twist free. The wind around them grew in chaos, fraying at the edges, shredding the leaves in its path. Ethan's hold did not break.

The Sarramauca howled. The sound was deafening, vibrating in my ears. I covered my ears with my hands. When that didn't help, I closed my eyes in an attempt to plug every possible entrance to my head. The howl turned into a scream that made my teeth hurt. I clenched my jaw and crumpled into a ball, trying to physically make myself a smaller target for this assault.

I wanted to keep my eyes closed as much as I wanted to see. I squinted my eyes open. The sound was a force of gravity, keeping them closed. I forced myself to watch. To check on Ethan.

He had not moved. His eyebrows were knitted together in concentration and effort, but otherwise, it did not look as if he was in any danger. He was as tranquil as I was alarmed. My opposite. He was in control.

The light was emanating from the Sarramauca itself. It pulsed with every twist until the sound cut off, and there was a flash of bright, blinding light.

Everything turned white.

You

Silence.

I wondered if I had gone deaf. The Sarramauca was gone. Ethan and I looked at each other, but neither of us moved, momentarily discombobulated by the sudden placidity. The leaves had stopped moving. The glowing orbs stayed in place. The entire world had stopped.

Is it finally over?

Then the ground began to shake, and the loud, rumbling crack of breaking rocks rattled in our ears. Like vines growing from the ground, tiny fissures began to appear on what was a smooth and impenetrable wall. The cracks grew in size as they reached higher, creating wider crevices and causing the crystallized wall to buckle and tumble. Large chunks from the top of the wall fell away. They toppled over each other. The sound of its destruction was like booming thunder.

Ethan, completely released from his trance, was suddenly on me. He instinctively wrapped his arms around me as if he was protecting me from an air raid. We both fell to the ground, huddling together. Dust from the wreckage rose higher than the undergrowth, temporarily obscuring our vision.

When it settled, the ruins exposed the other side, empty and bleak.

Did we do more harm than good?

"Oh no." I coughed as I straightened up and surveyed the devastation. The beautiful wall was no more. Colorful heaps fell into darkness, concealed by the dust and gloom.

"We won," Ethan pointed out. "The Sarramauca is gone. Why 'oh no'?"

"But the wall …" My voice came out in a rough whisper. I had the desire to cry, but I was spent. Used up. "Now this forest is going to be just as bad as the outside." I looked at the lush greenery, wondering how long it would take before it suffered the same fate as the rest of the world.

He took my hand. "Or," he suggested in a surprisingly gentle voice, "the forest can now make the outside just as good as this."

I hadn't thought of it that way. I looked up at him, a little surprised by his uncharacteristic optimism.

"I don't think the wall was keeping the ugliness out," he elaborated. "I think it was hoarding the beauty in. Look." He pointed to one of the larger gaps made by a break near the base. Instead of sand pushing inward, offshoots of ivy had already begun to spill out. The first tiny advancements of life. Progress. "What we really did was release the forest. It has a chance to bring life to a dead world again."

He looked back at me and squeezed my hand. "Sort of like what you did for me."

I didn't understand what he meant, so I didn't respond. He squeezed my hand again, then let go.

I looked around in wonder, seeing things the way he did. The glowing orbs that had looked caught in invisible strings had floated higher above us, away from arm's reach. The undergrowth that had been so tightly packed had already begun to spread out over some of the debris, concealing loss with promise. This forest had been rigidly contained, amassed for the benefit of one. With the gatekeeper removed, the gates came down, and the forest was finally free.

Because of Ethan.

He went looking for his knife in the heavy tangle of leaves, vines, and unidentified vegetation. I watched him with delayed comprehension. All this time, I was worried about what it meant to be the chosen one, but it wasn't even about me.

Ethan is the chosen one.

"It was always you," I said without realizing I had said anything aloud. I was filled with awe, marveling at all he had accomplished.

He glanced at me, smiled, then pulled out his knife, already covered in a mess of ivy. I didn't know how he was able to find it. At the same time, I didn't want to think of what else was being concealed under our feet that we just couldn't see.

"Actually," he countered, flipping his knife closed and putting it away, "it's really all you." He took me in his arms.

I let him, enjoying how good it was to be physically close again. But it didn't mean I agreed with him. I listed all the reasons that led me to my epiphany. "You're the only guy to ever cross. You even brought *weapons* with you when you did. You're the only one who could even touch it." I saved the best argument for last. "And you're the one that destroyed it." I tapped a finger on his chest for extra measure. "Just by *touching* it."

He didn't respond immediately. When he did, it was the beginning of a story. He released me from the hug but held both my hands in his. "When our mothers attempted that ill-fated location spell together, my mother was pregnant with me."

I knew this. Mae had said as much.

"Our mothers were powerful Woolgatherers as individuals. Together, they didn't realize how much their natural energies would affect a regular spell. That's what my mom suspected had gone wrong. It's like plugging too much power into a system that isn't designed to absorb it. It caused everything to go wonky. And when the power didn't know where to travel …" He shrugged. "I guess you could say I was a baby capacitor."

"Listen to you," I interrupted, a little awkwardly, "spell this and spell that. Like it's a thing."

He smiled. "Well, it is. I grew up learning about all of this."

This was new to me. "They taught all this in foster care?" I asked incredulously.

"No, I mean, I learned this before I went into foster care. Before my own mother died." His smile was shy, and I caught a glimpse of what that little boy might have looked like before he was lost in the system. "While spells aren't really much more than what other people may consider wishes or prayer, not everyone has Woolgatherer abilities."

He lifted a shoulder almost apologetically. "My mother raised me to respect the words and the ceremonies. She learned it the hard way. When she lost your mom." I felt his fingers gently caressing mine. "She taught me everything. But most of all, she taught me how dangerous it was."

My head was reeling from all this information. Not so much the information itself but where it was coming from. How did he suddenly know all these things?

"That's probably why I was always opposed to you using your abilities," he continued, seemingly oblivious to my internal turmoil. "Because I was taught not to. It was a deeply rooted lesson. Even when I couldn't remember why."

"How do you remember now?"

He held a breath before he answered. A pause. A slow exhale. "Because of the dream that the Sarramauca had me in." He closed his eyes tightly, then rubbed one hand over them. "What he showed me helped me remember." He opened his eyes. "Every protection spell is a veil over the person it's meant to shield. But the veil will also isolate you from the world. The more layers, the more you forget. A side effect of the magic." He shrugged. "What this monster did was rip the veil away. I remembered everything."

There was pain in his remembering, but he didn't elaborate further.

"What's more important," he said instead, "was that everything changed because of you."

"I tried to pull you away. I was yelling at you. You didn't hear me." There was no difference I could make when the Sarramauca had him.

"London, don't you realize? Before you, I was a very angry person. I was literally and figuratively lost. I didn't have any family. I didn't really have much reason to stay alive. By the time I met you, I had carried so much hate for so long."

He let go of my hands and spread his arms to indicate everything around us. "Everywhere you go, it's like you're tearing down walls." He laughed. "You tore down mine and freed me from myself. I'm so much better now."

This, I could agree with. He *was* better. More certain of himself. More accepting of the world. Just happier.

"You taught me how not to hate anymore," he emphasized. He grabbed my hands again, tilted his head, and regarded me with a look akin to wonder. "You taught me how to love."

He closed his eyes and hugged me tightly. When he spoke, I felt the reverberation of his words. "You taught me how to love *myself.*"

When he let go, there was a luster of unshed tears in his eyes. "That was something the Sarramauca didn't understand. It tried to seduce me with a dream of a life without obstacles. It didn't understand that I needed those obstacles. I needed the whole mess of it."

He shook his head, possibly hearing himself for the first time and realizing that it sounded a tad masochistic. "The heartache. The anger. The pain. All of it led me to you," he explained. "Understand that I would endure it all—a thousand times over if I had to—as long as it brought me back to you."

Mirroring my earlier action, he tapped a finger lightly on my chest. "You make it worth it. You make it make sense."

His eyes shone with renewed conviction. "You are the destiny that I choose. Over and over again. It will always be you. It was always you."

He leaned toward me so his lips brushed against mine. A surge of explosive emotions erupted from my chest. I was flooded with relief, gratitude, and desire. I wrapped my arms around his neck, pulled him close, and kissed him. I only let go because I physically needed to breathe. He leaned his forehead against mine.

"I love you, London."

Written in the Stars

"You defeated the Sarramauca with … *love*?"

It sounded like bad song lyrics. I couldn't keep the absurdity out of my voice. We were sitting side by side on one of the bigger broken pieces of the fallen wall at the edge of the forest, looking outward at the empty land and the promise of something better. I was still trying to internalize everything that had just happened. I needed to go around and around until it made sense.

Ethan laughed. "What better weapon against greed and destruction?"

"It's too cheesy."

"You don't like cheese?"

"I like cheese."

"There you go."

It was a simplistic explanation for what really happened. Ethan didn't need a weapon; he already *was* the weapon. A product of lineage, love, and sacrifice. But without me, he'd not have been able to cross on his own. I was his anchor. He wouldn't have had the chance to confront the Sarramauca in its own lair. And without me, he'd have lost.

"What you're really saying," I tried to summarize, "is that we beat it together."

He leaned over to bump my shoulder with his. His grin should have tipped me off before he got around to even saying the words. "Together … in love."

I groaned. He laughed and bumped me again. I leaned against him.

"Do you think we're safe now?"

"As long as you don't get hit by a truck," he teased, referencing our first meeting. I stuck my tongue out to eloquently depict what I thought about that. He laughed, insufferably proud of himself.

We'd come so far in such a short time. From finding each other to completing what our mothers had started together, we'd both found friends, a sense of belonging, and ourselves. I'd learned more and matured in the past six months than I felt I had over the previous sixteen and a half years.

"Do you think our mothers knew this would happen?" I asked him, but it was a question I was submitting to the universe.

"No." He was thoughtful in his response. "But I think if they could see the product of their sacrifices, they would still think it was worth it."

I thought about the twists in our paths that had led us here. Every circumstance and every decision we'd made, whether it resulted in good or bad, was instrumental in molding us into … us. If anything had been changed in our history, we would not be who we are.

I slid my hand into his, entangling our fingers to further fix me in the moment. If things had been different, maybe it would have been better. But just as easily, it could have been worse. We may have never connected this way. We may never have been the people that could fall in love with each other.

I was here. He was here. We were together.

"You're still here," I said for no reason.

"You're still dreaming."

I squeezed his hand, suddenly anxious. "What happens when I wake up?"

He squeezed mine back reassuringly. "I don't know. But we'll find out together."

At the moment, we were safe. Dreamers were safe. I watched the little leaves that covered the broken barricade at our feet. The wall, as breathtakingly beautiful as it was, was an obstruction that had prevented life from growing. With such boundaries removed, little shoots already stretched out to the unknown desert. Beauty didn't always mean healthy. And sometimes, great things need to collapse so that better things can be built.

Above us, the glowing orbs of Woolgatherer dreams that were also freed rose higher in the sky until they were indistinguishable from the stars. The glimmer lightened the lusterless heavens, highlighting the deep blues and purples with warmer hues. These miniature messengers of hopes and dreams disrupted the night sky and undermined the nightmare. I stared at the tiny lights a little longer. I tried to tell them apart, wondering what it meant. Wondering what the future would hold.

I looked back at Ethan. He was watching me, the gold in his eyes in perfect harmony with the green. I smiled.

Our future wasn't written in the stars. But that was OK. We didn't need our future to be predetermined in order for it to be a dream. A life of dreams isn't stories already told by the cosmos.

The dream is the adventure that happens in the light of every day. Together.

Thank You

BEL LAUREOLA
Claiming to be my sister before my own brothers did.

LORENZ LAUREOLA
Buying another copy of Revenant after losing the first one, even if you didn't admit it right away.

LOGENE LAUREOLA
Never reading my work but telling me you're proud of me anyway.

PEGGY LACSON
Making Revenant your first read after eye surgery.

VICTOR LACSON
Teaching me to be comfortable with attention.

KARI FITZGERALD
Listening to the stories before they made it to print but especially to the ones that will never make it to print.

KARI POHAR
The crowns (tiara) you willing provide others (me) and often straighten.

E.J. NICKSON
Ding-dong-ditch care packages that include wine, chocolates, various stress relievers, and a shoulder to cry on.

H.M. LAWSON
Checking in with me just to make sure I was writing when I said I would be.

NINO & MICHELLE ALEJANDRO
Delivering the irreplaceable grail diary safely back to me.

MICHAELA CABRERA & SIMON NEUQUELMAN
Donner une voix à Laurent.

KATHY WAGHORN
Coaxing a better version of Reveil from across the pond.

THIS OLD BOOK
Hosting every one of The Woolgathering Series book launches.

THE FIRST WOOLGATHERERS
Preordering a book from an untested author.

WOOLGATHERERS AROUND THE WORLD
Making my dream come true.

MOMS WHO WRITE
Amusing mean girl scenario suggestions in a very anti-mean girl platform of social media support.

GAA WRITERS GROUP
Inspiration to continue writing in an environment of local talent and encouragement.

About the Author

ZEE LACSON

Zee Lacson has had practice in different professions. Engineer. Teacher. Photographer. Visual artist. Writer. But throughout her life, she has always been a Dreamer.

The Woolgathering Series is her dream come true.

Born and raised in Manila, Philippines, with her grandparents, father, and twin brothers, she currently lives the dream in the northern suburbs of Chicagoland with her husband and twin sons.

She enjoys good coffee. And sushi. And wine. And ice cream. And cake … though not necessarily together. Or in that order.

Reviews help nourish authors.

Feed me.

Leave a review for

The Woolgathering Series.

Follow Zee Lacson: